Winter Break

ALSO BY KAYLA PERRIN

Spring Break

We'll Never Tell

The Delta Sisters

The Sisters of Theta Phi Kappa

Winter Break

KAYLA PERRIN

St. Martin's Griffin
New York

This is a work of fiction. All of the characters, organizations and events portrayed in this novel are either products of the author's imagination or are used fictitiously.

www.stmartins.com

LIBRARY OF CONGRESS CATALOGING-IN-PUBLICATION DATA

Perrin, Kayla.
Winter break / Kayla Perrin.—1st ed.
p. cm.
ISBN 978-0-312-64458-1
1. College students—Fiction. 2. Couples—Fiction. 3. Missing persons—Fiction. 4. Ocean travel—Fiction. 5. Caribbean Area—Fiction. I. Title.
PR9199.3.P434W56 2011
813'.54—dc22

2010037870

First Edition: January 2011

10 9 8 7 6 5 4 3 2 1

This book is for Jen Enderlin,
my amazing editor.
Thanks for your continued faith in me.
You rock!

Acknowledgments

I WISH TO gratefully acknowledge my friend and fellow author Marcia King Gamble for her cruise expertise while I was writing this book. Having worked for Carnival Cruise Lines for years, Marcia was of great help in answering my cruise-related questions.

Thanks, Marcia! You're a doll!

On another note, I want to point out that the incident involving the kitten in this book is based on a true story my brother relayed to me. While he was attending Kent State years ago, he heard of someone doing there what happens to the kitten in this book. The story horrified me, and I always knew I would incorporate it into a novel one day. Please, people—be kind to animals!

Prologue

IT WAS THE ODD sensation of pressure that had Natalie Laymon's eyelids fluttering open. The sensation of pressure between her thighs, the heat enveloping her, and the musky scent filtering into her nostrils.

She tried—and failed—to force her eyes open. Her eyelids were simply too heavy. And oddly, her brain felt as though it were trapped in a dense fog. But something was registering. The reality of something awful.

A bead of sweat dropped onto her nipple, and all at once it hit her. She understood what was going on.

She was being raped.

The knowledge filled her with terror, and gave her the strength to force her eyes open. She could make out the shape of someone in shadow, someone grunting as he screwed her with relentless thrusts.

"Stop . . ." Her voice sounded hoarse, weak. "Stop!" she repeated, more firmly this time, and she pushed at her rapist's slick chest, trying to get him off of her.

Laughter. From her rapist, or were there other people in the room? People witnessing her rape and laughing about it?

She jerked a foot forward, kicking wildly, hoping to catch her rapist in the chest. When, a moment later, he was off her, she knew that she'd been successful.

And then she scrambled off the bed, pulling at her bra and shirt, which had been pushed up to expose her breasts. She held in the sob that clawed at her throat. She had to get out of there, out of that room, away from the man—or men—who had so vilely taken advantage of her.

Even as she found the door to escape, she wasn't entirely sure where she was. Someone must have given her some kind of date-rape drug that had knocked her out. It was the only thing that explained why she couldn't remember where the hell she was or how she had ended up in some guy's bed.

Natalie opened the door and was nearly blinded by the bright lights in the hallway. A hallway where a handful of people were hanging out. Two women gaped at her for only a moment before they started to giggle. She realized with horror that her skirt was pushed up around her waist, and God only knew where her underwear was. Humiliated, Natalie righted her clothes and rushed forward, nearly tripping over her bare feet in her haste to get down the steps.

When she reached the first floor, it finally clicked where she was.

At Seth Downey's party.

She had come with a new friend, and had been looking forward to attending the party of one of the most popular guys on campus. Her entrance had been guaranteed, as the friend she had arrived with was Rachel Jepson, Seth's current girlfriend.

But Rachel had all but abandoned her once they were inside, leaving Natalie to fend for herself. Rachel had gotten her a beer, then had gone off to suck face with Seth. Natalie remembered that she had been roaming the party like an outcast, unable to strike up a conversation with any of the small groups of people. About thirty minutes into the party, she had gotten herself a second beer in the kitchen. After that, things were fuzzy in her mind. She had a vague memory of feeling like she'd needed to sit down, and someone helping her, but that was it.

No one seemed to notice Natalie as she hustled to the townhouse's front door, and that reality brought tears to her eyes. She had come to this party hoping, for once in her college life, that she would fit in.

But she'd gotten a lot more than she had bargained for.

As she rushed outside she was surprised to hear someone call out to her.

Natalie turned. Saw Rachel.

Rachel was five-foot-eight and stunning, with a full head of black, curly hair that hung halfway down her back. Her sun-kissed brown skin, courtesy of her biracial heritage, meant she never had to spend a dime on those fake tanning sprays or deal with the discomfort of a tanning bed in order to keep her beautiful complexion.

Suddenly, Natalie couldn't help wondering why Rachel had befriended her in the first place. Why she had invited her to this party. Gorgeous girls like Rachel didn't befriend plain ones like her. Sure, Natalie wasn't the ugliest person alive, but her boring brown hair was limp and dull, her pale skin made her look like a walking ghost, and her lack of curves meant her body had the appearance of a teenage boy's.

"My God, Natalie," Rachel said, hurrying down the front steps toward her. "What happened?"

"As if you don't know," Natalie snapped. "You gave me a beer, and the next thing I know, I'm upstairs on someone's bed, passed out and . . . and . . ."

"You think I drugged your beer?" Rachel asked. "For what purpose?"

Her tone was both mortified and sympathetic, and Natalie immediately regretted the accusation. It was the stress of what had happened that had her doubting Rachel. The devastating fact was that she had woken up to find someone on top of her.

Raping her . . .

Maybe no one had given her a date-rape drug. The truth was, Natalie wasn't much of a drinker, and it was entirely possible that two beers had knocked her out.

"No." Natalie spoke softly, shaking her head but not meeting Rachel's eyes. "I know that doesn't make sense." She paused, then hurriedly spoke before she burst into tears. "Look, I need to get out of here."

"Someone hurt you." A statement, not a question. "Oh, Natalie. Tell me what happened."

Maybe it was the fact that someone at this party actually gave a shit. Or maybe it was the fact that hearing Rachel ask the question made what had happened suddenly all too real.

"I . . ." Natalie sniffled, wiped at her eyes. "I was raped."

"No!"

Natalie gestured to her disheveled clothes, and then to her bare—and now freezing—feet. "I didn't imagine it. I woke up and someone was on top of me." Her voice cracked. "Raping me . . ."

"I believe you," Rachel said.

Her voice was gentle, her expression sympathetic, and Natalie immediately felt bad for snapping at the one person who was showing her any concern. "I'm sorry I'm being so bitchy, it's just—"

"No, don't apologize. I know exactly how you feel."

The comment made Natalie narrow her eyes and meet Rachel's gaze dead-on. "You do?"

Rachel nodded, an expression of pain streaking across her face. Even though they stood in near darkness, the only light coming from a nearby streetlamp, Natalie could see the pain, raw and powerful.

Expelling a sigh, Rachel went on. "Drake raped me, too."

"Drake?" The name was like a kick in the gut. Natalie had had a crush on Drake for as long as she could remember. "Drake Shaw?"

"Yes, Drake Shaw. Don't think because he's Lan-U's star basketball player that he's incapable of rape," Rachel said sourly.

"But . . . but he has a girlfriend."

"So what? He's still a creep."

Somehow, the idea that Drake had been her rapist didn't quite fit, but the truth was, Natalie was clueless. She had no idea who had violated her, only that Drake *did* live in the house with Seth and a couple of other guys.

Rachel put an arm around Natalie's shoulders. "You're going

to need someone right now," she said gently. "Someone who understands what you're going through. Someone who'll be there for you when you report the rape to the police."

Natalie gasped. "The police?"

"Yes, the police."

"But . . ." Natalie didn't want to go to the police station. She only wanted to go back to her room, take a shower, and get warmed up.

"You need to be strong right now." Rachel placed her hands on Natalie's shoulders and looked her in the eye. "Report that bastard. Because he can't get away with this. Not again."

Part One

"Aki másnak vermet ás, maga esik bele."

Translation: If you dig a hole for someone else you'll fall into it.

—HUNGARIAN PROVERB

Chapter One

Two weeks later . . .

HER BODY TURNED UP three days after she was last seen. Everyone assumed that Rachel Jepson had gotten into her car and simply taken off. That she'd headed to her sister's place in New York. Or to the airport, where she'd gotten on a plane and headed for home. Or any other place where she could have escaped it all for a while.

People figured that she had wanted to be anywhere but Lancaster University, and who could blame her? Most women who dated Seth Downey didn't escape unscathed. He was simultaneously Lan-U's biggest jerk and most sought after guy. People often overlooked character flaws when an obscene amount of money was involved.

And Seth Downey's parents were obscenely rich. Something Seth flaunted shamelessly, as it bought him a lot of power.

Unfortunately, money couldn't buy class. Nor could it buy decent character. In fact, one could argue that it enhanced one's character deficiencies.

Which was no doubt the case where Seth Downey was concerned.

He dated women for sport—Rachel included. And when he'd had his fill of her, he had humiliated her with some X-rated pictures he'd taken of her—projecting them on his big-screen television at one of his house parties. Rachel, who had been at the party and still officially Seth's girlfriend at the time, had understandably run from the house in tears.

Three days later, Rachel's car was found in a ravine off a rural road heading toward Philadelphia. Maybe she'd been drunk. Maybe she'd simply gotten disoriented on the dark road and had accidentally veered off the paved path. Or maybe she'd swerved to miss hitting a deer. Somehow she had ended up in a ravine obscured by bushes. If not for some kids playing in the area who had spotted her car, her body might not have been found for many months.

News of Rachel's death had spread like wildfire across the campus. Most people speculated that it wasn't really an accident, but a suicide.

I believed the speculation. Given what Seth had done to her, it made sense that Rachel had killed herself.

Her suicide had been the second one since my senior year

started, and it had shaken us all. But after about three days of speculating and feeling sorry for her, we moved on.

Continued with our lives as normal.

I'll admit, I wasn't too torn up over her death. I wasn't Rachel's biggest fan. Not after learning of her *indiscretion* with my boyfriend. She had crossed the line with Drake, and that had been inexcusable.

Inexcusable because we'd all been friends. We came from the same town, and Rachel had gone to high school with my boyfriend before he'd transferred to my high school. With all of us from Oakland, California, we'd had a common bond at Lan-U. But after learning that she'd seduced my man, well, she became one of my least favorite people.

But I did feel sorry that she had been so unhappy that she'd been driven to suicide. I pitied her for dating Seth, and felt her pain at what he had so cruelly done to her.

At the time, I couldn't imagine suffering public humiliation like that.

Little did I know that mere days after Rachel's suicide, I would be the one thrown into the lion's den, publicly humiliated for the entertainment of others.

"Hey, babe." My lips curled into a large smile when I saw Drake, my boyfriend, standing just outside my dorm-room doorway.

He stepped forward, drew me into his arms, and kissed me, the kind of kiss that had me feeling sparks. We had been together for five years, but my passion for him had not faded. Drake was tall, dark, and incredibly handsome. At six-foot-four, with golden brown skin and an athletic build, he was one of the hottest guys on campus.

And he was mine.

"What was that for?" I asked as we pulled apart.

"Can't I kiss the girl I love?"

The sensual timber of his voice had me wanting to get naked, but I knew that my roommate could show up at any minute. "Don't get me all hot and bothered," I whispered. "You know I've got that psych paper to write."

"Actually . . ." Drake slipped an arm around my waist and nuzzled his nose in my neck. "I was thinking we could get away for a couple of days. Head to that hotel we went to last time." He ended the suggestion with a smirk and a raised eyebrow, and my body flooded with heat. We had been to that hotel just before the beginning of our senior year, and we'd had the best time a couple could have.

I was tempted—seriously—but there was no way I could swing it now. "My paper is due on Friday, and I already got an extension."

"Come on, babe," Drake said in his deepest, most sensual voice. "With my basketball this weekend, I won't be able to see you. Which is why I want to get away now."

"Why are you trying to tempt me like this?" I asked, my body flushed.

Before Drake could respond my cell phone rang, loudly interrupting our moment. *Saved by the bell,* I couldn't help thinking, because I knew my resolve had been weakening, and I simply couldn't afford a romantic getaway right now.

"Don't answer that."

I giggled as I turned and headed toward my bed where the phone was, thinking that Drake was seriously trying to turn on the charm. "Gimme a minute, lover boy."

As I reached for the phone on the bed, I saw Roxanne's number flashing on the screen. She was one of my two best friends at Lan-U.

I lifted the phone, then gasped when Drake's fingers curled around my wrist. I looked up at him, expecting to see a playful expression on his face as he continued in his attempt to seduce me. Instead, I saw steely resolve in his eyes.

"Don't answer that."

His tone, coupled with his serious gaze, caused alarm to slither down my spine, as cold as a cube of ice.

"It's only Roxanne," I protested.

Drake wrung the phone from my hands—hard enough that a spike of pain shot through my wrist.

"What the hell's the matter with you?" I asked, an edge to my voice.

"Damn it, I told you to leave the phone."

Fear gripped me from head to toe. Something serious was going on. Something Drake didn't want me to know.

"What is it?" I asked, my heart beating rapidly. Surely he wasn't about to break the kind of news he had when he'd admitted his one-night stand with Rachel.

Drake lowered himself onto my bed and dragged a hand over his face. My cell phone rang again, but I made no move to take it from him.

He groaned. "All I wanted was one night. One night . . . so I could be the one to tell you."

"Tell me what?"

When Drake didn't speak, just sat on my bed looking as if he had the weight of the world on his shoulders, I knew he was about to shake the world as I knew it off its axis.

My iPhone trilled, telling me I had a text message. I waited several seconds for some type of reaction from Drake. Getting none, I took the phone from his fingers. He didn't resist.

The message was from Roxanne, who was clearly anxious to reach me. I pressed the button to open the message and quickly read:

OMG! Didi, go to The Gossip Hour website right now!
Then call me asap!!!

I glanced at Drake, who still wouldn't meet my gaze. Then I hurried to my desk where my netbook sat open.

I quickly brought up the Web site for The Gossip Hour, a campus blog that anonymously dished dirt about Lan-U students for sport. No one was ever named in the oftentimes vicious blog, but enough of a description was given to make it clear who the person was.

My eyes scanned the latest entry to The Gossip Hour site.

And now for the latest bit of Lan-U gossip. And oooh, it's juicy. Rumors abound that a certain Lan-U basketball player—about 6'4" with flawless tanned skin and looks as hot as a movie star's—forced himself onto a certain Plain Jane senior who crawled out of the hole she normally hides in and actually went to a college party. And by "forced himself" I do mean what you think: he raped her.

Allegedly, of course. But this is one of those rumors so bizarre, you can't help wondering if there isn't truth to it. I mean, who would make this up? Hot jock rapes a geeky wallflower? You know what they say: truth is stranger than fiction. And after all, where there's smoke, there's fire.

I sat still, not breathing, staring at the screen. I knew who the girl was. Natalie Laymon, queen of the campus geeks, had shown up at one of Seth's parties just over two weeks ago. Her shocking appearance at the soiree had been the talk of the campus. And just days after Rachel's death, I'd heard some rumors that Natalie was claiming she had been raped.

I was so absorbed in the words on the screen that when Drake's hand touched my shoulder, I nearly jumped out of my skin from fright.

A beat. "Didi, it's not true."

I knew it wasn't true. It *couldn't* be. Drake didn't need to rape anyone, much less a girl who could easily compete for the title of Least Attractive Girl on Campus.

And yet, I couldn't help staring at him, wondering. However fleeting, there was the slightest hint of doubt in my mind—because he had admitted he'd screwed Rachel Jepson. He had hurt me in a way I had believed him incapable of doing.

"Damn it, Didi. Don't look at me like that."

"Why didn't you just tell me?" The fact that Drake had come to my room hoping to lure me away on a supposed romantic getaway made it obvious that he was the star basketball player named in the blog. "You had to know I wouldn't believe it. In fact, I would have laughed at just how ridiculous the idea was. But for you to try to get me to go away in an effort to keep me from finding out—"

"Means I'm guilty?" Drake supplied, anger flashing in his eyes.

I didn't answer right away. "That's not what I said."

Drake's mouth pulled into a tight line. "Yeah, it's real obvious you believe me," he scoffed.

"Don't put this on me," I countered, shooting out of my chair. "You're the one who came in here acting all guilty."

"Guilty?" His eyes grew wide with disbelief. Disbelief that quickly morphed into disgust. "Five years, and this is the best I can expect from you?"

"I didn't say you *were* guilty."

"You may as well have."

And with that, Drake spun on his heel and charged toward the door.

"Drake!" I pleaded, but he didn't stop. He jerked my door open and rushed into the hallway, slamming the door so hard that the framed photo of us—taken at our senior high school prom—fell off the wall.

The photo dropped to the floor, the glass shattering into a million pieces.

Chapter Two

THEY SAY WHAT doesn't kill you makes you stronger. But I'm not sure I agree with that. Sometimes, what doesn't kill you leaves you numb. Leaves you unable to handle the day-to-day activities in your life. Sometimes, it makes you wish you could simply disappear.

Ten days after it happened, my life had undeniably gone to hell. I didn't feel strong. Not one bit. I felt weak and depressed.

And I admit, there were moments when I fantasized about taking the easy way out—like Rachel Jepson did. Moments where I thought that being dead had to be better than living in hell.

I could relate to the overwhelming despair Rachel must have felt. The bitter sting of humiliation. But unlike Rachel, there was fight left in me. The fight to keep going, no matter how hard.

And it was hard. Everywhere I went on campus, I saw the stares. People didn't even try to be surreptitious. They openly gaped at me, their eyes showing condemnation.

From popular to leper in less than twenty-four hours. All because of Natalie Laymon's vicious lie.

Drake and I were talking, but it wasn't the same. It was as if there was a Plexiglas wall between us, keeping us emotionally divided. He was stressed over the accusation, and so was I—so much so that we hadn't even spent one night together since that fight in my dorm room when I'd learned the news.

It felt as if there was nothing good in my life, not anymore.

Perhaps that was why, when the call came, I quickly sprang to action. I needed a distraction. Something other than my life to focus on. An outlet for my anger and frustration.

"A kitten. Are you sure?" I had been lying down, a pillow pulled over my face, wallowing in despair when my cell phone rang. Now, I sat bolt upright.

"That's what Rick told me," Roxanne said.

"Damn it. What's he up to this time?"

"You know Seth. If he's gotten himself a kitten, it's not because he wants something to cuddle with at night."

I did know Seth. Rich. Spoiled. Asshole. "So we're going to rescue the kitten," I said. Not a question.

"You'd better believe it."

I, along with others who had been livid when we learned how Seth had brutalized a puppy, had reported him to his fraternity. As a result, he had been kicked out of the Zeta Kappa Phi fraternity, but if it had bothered him he hadn't shown it. He had continued being as arrogant as always. Walking around on campus as though he ruled the kingdom.

Seth Downey may have had access to the millions his father had made in manufacturing, and sure, he could act like a pompous ass because of it, but being rotten rich did not entitle him to abuse animals.

Which was no doubt what he planned to do to the kitten.

"I'll head to my car now," I said to Roxanne.

"I'm already there."

Ever since Seth had been kicked out of his fraternity—and as a result, the fraternity house—he had been living in a townhouse just off the Lancaster University campus that he had bought. To my dismay, my boyfriend of five years had been one of four guys who moved into the house with him. I tried—for the sake of my relationship—to believe that Drake was simply in denial as to Seth's true nature. The two had become friends because they were both on the Lan-U basketball team; somehow Drake missed all the neon "asshole" signs flashing around Seth's head.

Seth had all-American looks—a thick head of blond hair; a beautiful, boyish face that guaranteed he would age well; and the kind of smile that could charm the pants off of even the most guarded girl. He was gorgeous, wealthy, and had all the toys any boy could ever want. He attracted every guy on campus, and a good portion of the girls. Drake was just as intrigued by Seth as countless others, oblivious to his true nature.

At least Drake hadn't been around when Seth had tasered the puppy. He wouldn't have stood by and watched that kind of cruelty without speaking up. In fact, he told me he didn't believe the story, that an angry ex must have made it up to get back at Seth.

I did believe the story. Which was why a bunch of us had reported Seth to his fraternity. There'd been no proof, only rumor, but Seth had already been on probation for other issues, and the fraternity had decided they didn't want any more trouble from him, so they expelled him.

Taking only a moment to slip into my shoes and a jacket, I raced downstairs to meet Roxanne Miller. She and I had met and bonded in the campus organization SCTA—Stop Cruelty to Animals—that had been formed two years ago when the university had debated culling the numerous deer that grazed the college grounds. I and many others felt that killing innocent deer was cruel and unfair. *We* had encroached on *their* homeland. We protested loudly on campus, at city hall, and in the end, we were heard. The deer were spared.

Reaching the parking lot, I saw Roxanne pacing beside my gold-colored 2004 Ford Focus, a trusty car I had driven all the way from Oakland, California, to Lancaster, Pennsylvania, when I had gotten accepted here. She was fired up, all five feet four inches of her, ready to kick some ass. She didn't look a day over sixteen, and that, coupled with her baby-faced cuteness and radiant smile, often fooled people into thinking she was harmless. But she was feisty as hell when necessary.

I hurried to the car, pressing the remote door opener as I did. Roxanne got into the passenger seat while I quickly got behind the wheel.

"Oh God," Roxanne began. "I just called Rick again, and . . . we might be too late. Didi, what he plans to do to that kitten . . ."

"What?"

"It's the worst thing I've ever heard. The absolute worst . . ."

As Roxanne's voice trailed off on a croak, I stared at her. Saw the tears streaming down her pale brown cheeks. And I knew that something much worse than tasering a helpless animal was going to happen.

"What?" I repeated, but I was already getting a sick feeling. Since the time that Seth had brutalized the puppy, resulting in its death, he had picked up a new pet.

A boa constrictor.

The idea floating through my mind was so horrific, I didn't want to believe it. But I knew that Seth had a dark side. A sick side. "Roxanne, no . . ."

"Just get there as fast as you can."

I floored it, screeching the car to a halt when I got to Seth's townhouse. A number of guys were outside on this chilly early evening, drinking and smoking. Seth's house was known as party central and was always populated. I got that guys were into the eye candy Seth liked to have on hand—sometimes wannabe models who spent the evening in their lingerie to titillate—I just couldn't understand why people were so blind to his true nature.

Money. It all came down to money. Not only did Seth like to show off by wearing designer clothes and driving a top-of-the-line BMW, but he sometimes threw money around on campus like confetti, no doubt taking a perverse thrill in watching the scavengers try to snatch up as much as they could.

Before I even had my car in park, I had the door open. Roxanne flew out of the car, and I quickly charged after her.

"Oh man—that was *sick,*" a guy out in front said.

A swell of nausea rose in my throat. And then came the rage.

If we were too late . . . if Seth had truly murdered a kitten . . .

I rushed into the house. Rap music was blaring on the stereo. Guys and girls were hanging around laughing and drinking, and one couple was making out in a corner of the living room.

"Here comes trouble," a tall guy I recognized from the basketball team said as I marched past him toward the stairs.

I knew my reputation. And I was proud of it.

Before I got to the top of the stairs, Drake appeared from the direction of his bedroom. His eyes widened when he saw me. Guilt? Or simple surprise?

"Didi," he said cautiously.

"Where's the kitten?" I demanded.

He reached for me. "Dee . . ."

I shrugged away from his touch. "Where's the kitten?" But he didn't have to answer. I could see in his eyes that it was too late. "You didn't, Drake. You didn't stand by and let Seth feed a kitten to his snake!"

Drake looked past me, to Roxanne. "I just heard about it when I came in," he admitted, sounding contrite.

"Oh God." I choked back tears. "That scum! I'm gonna—"

"Come here." Drake wrapped an arm around my shoulders and ushered me into his bedroom, which was a few steps away. By the time he closed the door behind me, my breath was coming in ragged spurts. I could hardly take in air.

"How could you let him do it?" I demanded. "How?"

"I didn't let him do it."

"A helpless kitten . . ." My words trailed off on a whimper.

"I came in, saw everyone, and thought it was just a party. Then I heard some guys talking about, well, you know."

"You weren't in the room when it happened?" I had to know.

If Drake had been in there, watched a helpless kitten be sentenced to a horrifying death . . .

"I was *not* in the room."

I eyed him skeptically, looking for any signs of deception.

"I wouldn't have stood by and watched that. Honest."

I believed him. I had to. Because to think that someone I had loved for five years could be as sick as Seth . . .

"That poor kitten." I gasped, picturing an adorable orange tabby. The poor thing had no doubt believed that it had been taken to a loving home when Seth had gotten his hands on it.

"I hear it jumped right out of the aquarium," Drake said grimly. "But Seth grabbed it and put it back in."

"Fucking prick!" My hands were shaking, that's how livid I was. "Seth needs to be arrested. I bet the asshole even had it videotaped, didn't he? A sick memento for a sicko. But at least a video will be proof. If I call the cops and they come now—"

"Didi, let it go."

"Let it go?" My anger flared anew, directed at Drake this time. "A kitten was murdered!"

"Yeah, and there's nothing you can do for it now."

At the dispassionate statement, I stared up at Drake as if seeing him for the first time. Under Seth's influence, he had become a different person.

Just how different? Had he changed so much that he was guilty of what Natalie Laymon had accused him of?

"Why do you even live here?" I asked.

"What kind of question is that?"

"Why didn't you move out after . . ." I paused. Huffed. "Ten days ago, I would have been gone if I were you."

"Someone makes an accusation and I'm supposed to run?"

"Did you do it?" The question tumbled from my lips. It was a question I had wanted to ask for ten days, but until now I hadn't had the guts. Now, Drake's whole indifference to the suffering of a helpless animal was making me question what I thought I knew. "Did you rape Natalie that night at Seth's party?"

Chapter Three

THE LOOK THAT CAME onto Drake's face was one of horror and incredulity. "Are you serious?"

"I don't know what to think anymore." Could Drake have been stoned and done something he didn't remember? He loved his weed, and had claimed that smoking pot helped lead to his lapse in judgment with Rachel the night he'd cheated on me.

"If that's true, then I guess we have nothing more to say."

Fear made my heart begin to pound. I was angry and confused, but I suddenly knew that I couldn't have a life without Drake. Sure, I had entertained that idea over the last ten days, mostly as a way to distance myself from him and the ugly accusation. But instantly, there was no more doubt. I still loved him and wanted the life together we had always talked about.

"I didn't mean that," I quickly backtracked. Stoned or not, Drake would never rape anyone. He couldn't. "I'm just . . . I'm upset. And I'm angry. How could so many people stand by and do nothing to stop Seth's twisted plan?"

"I know. A kitten was killed." Drake's voice held a hint of sarcasm. He gave me a hard look. "You weren't this upset when Rachel died."

"What are you talking about?" Is that what he thought? That I didn't care about what had happened to Rachel? "Of course I was upset, Drake. But that . . . that was . . ."

"Suicide?" he asked. He held my gaze for a moment, then looked away.

"Or an accident." I knew that was easier to accept than the thought that Rachel had killed herself. Especially since she'd been a friend. "No one knows for sure."

"And you don't really care."

"I didn't say that."

"You didn't have to."

I suddenly wondered if Drake was torn up over Rachel's death because he cared for her more than he'd let on. That their one-night stand had meant something to him.

"Looks like you care enough for both of us."

"Jesus," Drake snapped.

"I'm sorry."

"No, you're not." Drake gave me a pointed look before walking toward the window and staring outside. I could hear his heavy breathing from several feet away.

After a long moment, he turned to face me. "And then there's my dad," he went on. "You weren't particularly upset when he died either."

"I *know* you don't mean that."

Drake didn't respond, but the grim set of his mouth told me that he was thinking about that fateful day this past summer when he'd gotten the news that his father had been killed in a tragic hit-and-run as he left a local restaurant. The car hadn't even slowed down after it had plowed him over, leaving him for dead.

"You think I'm not upset about your father?" I asked, incredulous. "I loved him, too." I had known Drake since eleventh grade, and started dating him my senior year of high school. His family had been a huge part of my life. I loved his father probably as much as he had.

Drake said nothing.

"What's really bothering you? Does it have to do with Seth?"

He shook his head, but I couldn't tell if it was an answer to my question or an involuntary gesture.

"Drake, talk to me."

He paced the room, not stopping to face me until a good thirty seconds had passed.

"None of us is perfect," he said, and met my gaze from across the room. Held it. "We all have a past."

I got his meaning immediately. I swallowed hard.

"Sometimes I think you've taken up the cause of animal rights as a way to make amends. As a way to atone." Another pointed look. "That you're running from the memory of what happened."

His words were as painful as a knife plunging into my chest. "I speak up for animals because someone has to."

"Yeah, and because it gives you some warped sense of purpose."

This time I didn't respond. Because he was right.

"So you want me to ignore what Seth did? Let him get away with it so he can do it again?"

"Running to the cops, or to the dean, is not going to help. It's just gonna screw things up for me."

"Screw what up? Your housing arrangements? All the free parties?"

Drake made a face as he looked at me. "I knew you wouldn't understand."

Again, I got the sense there was more going on, something he wasn't sharing with me.

"I can't understand what you don't tell me."

He shook his head. "It's all right."

I walked toward him and placed my hand on his arm. "Tell me."

"I wish you wouldn't think for a second that your boyfriend would ever rape anyone, especially not the school nerd. And isn't she a dyke? If I want to fuck someone, I don't need to take it."

I didn't mean to, but I snorted in derision. I couldn't help myself.

"That's exactly what I'm talking about," he said. "You obviously don't trust me."

"I forgave you," I stressed. I didn't want to remember the affair he'd had, how much it had hurt me.

"And you act like I'm the only one who needs forgiving," he shot back. "What about Chris, huh?"

I wanted to point out that what he was referring to was ancient history, and besides, nothing had ever happened with my high school friend. But I said nothing, because I didn't want to rehash an argument we'd had too many times before. Clearly, no matter the truth, he would believe what he wanted to believe.

The silence that followed was long and strained. I finally broke it. "Have you confronted Natalie?" Maybe that was a part of what was bothering me, the idea that she could get away scott-free after making such a vile allegation. "Asked her why she would tell a lie like this?"

"I don't really care," Drake said. "Maybe she did it for attention. Who knows? The point is, I know it's a lie, and you should, too. She never went to the police. Never had me charged. Because she knew she couldn't."

"I still think you should talk to her. She shouldn't be able to get away with—"

"Leave it alone," Drake snapped. He sounded angry. "For God's sake."

"Why?" I demanded.

"Because talking to her will accomplish nothing," Drake replied. "Actually, it might do more harm. You want me to be seen with her, sitting in Terrell dining hall having a conversation? That's the last thing I want, trust me." He paused for a moment and gave me a hard stare.

I shook my head. I didn't understand his logic.

"Look, I need some time," Drake said. "I thought I was sure about . . . about us. But I'm not sure anymore."

"Drake, don't say that." I reached for him, circling my fingers around his arm, but he yanked it away.

There was a look in his eyes I'd never seen before. And it scared me to death.

"And for God's sake, back off where Seth is concerned. For once in your life just listen to me, okay?"

So that's what this was about? He was pissed about Seth? "Why? What is going on with you two that you haven't told me?"

Drake's lips parted, as if he was going to answer me, but then he looked away.

"Drake, talk to me."

He faced me again. "I need to study, Didi. I've slacked off with economics this semester, and if I don't pass the final in three weeks, I'm screwed."

He was blowing me off, and I wouldn't have it. So I didn't move. I just stared at him, hoping that the look in my eyes would get him to change his mind. But he returned my stare with an unwavering one.

That's when I began to tremble from head to toe. I felt as cold as if I'd been submerged in a tank of ice.

"You're actually dumping me?" I asked. "Why? To save your friendship with Seth?"

"Didi, just—" He stopped abruptly, but I knew there was something else he'd wanted to say.

My eyes narrowed as I regarded him. He seemed on edge. Something was going on. Something bigger than I understood.

"What?" I asked. "What is it?"

A beat passed, and I thought Drake was going to open up to me. Instead he said, "I need time."

"No." I shook my head. "That's not what you were going to say."

"Yes it is," he stressed, sounding annoyed. "This isn't easy for me, and it's not what I want, but I . . . I think it's for the best. You and I . . . we need to take a break. From us."

So his discomfort, his hedging—it was all about him working up the nerve to break up with me?

"We've been having way too many problems," he continued.

"You *are* dumping me." The words escaped on a moan, and I had to spin around, away from him, before he saw the devastation on my face.

Someone pounded on the door. I hoped Drake would ignore the knock and instead wrap his arms around me, but he didn't. Instead, he crossed the room and opened the door.

Roxanne stood there, a grief-stricken look on her face. "I need to get out of here, Didi," she said without preamble.

I looked at Drake. Maybe I was hoping to convey with my eyes that I wanted him to ask me to stay. Surely he didn't really want time away from me.

"We'll talk later," Drake said, not meeting my gaze.

Of course we would, I thought as I went to Roxanne in the hallway. She was weeping openly, and I hugged her, trying to keep my own tears—tears over Drake—under control.

"I saw the snake," she said amid her tears. "It looks like it swallowed a friggin' bowling ball."

Never had I wished anyone bodily harm before, but I wished that Seth's snake would wrap its scaly body around his neck and squeeze the life out of him. I would gladly witness that.

No sooner had the thought formed in my mind than I felt someone watching me. I raised my gaze and saw Seth staring. He grinned at me—cold and menacing.

He was the reason for all of the problems in my life. I hated him. And I wanted him to know it.

Emboldened by my rage, I pulled away from Roxanne and stalked right up to him. I slammed my palms against his chest. His jaw flinched, but he quickly recovered, smiling again to play off my assault.

I was enraged at what he'd done to the kitten, but also

enraged at how my life had changed in the last ten days. It had been at a party at Seth's place that Natalie claimed she'd been sexually assaulted. And though she'd named Drake as her attacker, I blamed Seth for whatever had gone on that night.

"You pull another stunt like this," I said, glaring at him, "and you're going down."

For a moment, Seth's eyes flashed fire. He was pissed, but tried to hide the emotion. In fact, he affected an innocent tone as he asked, "What stunt?"

"You hurt another helpless animal and you're going to know what it feels like to be tortured. I'll personally make sure of that."

"Ooooh," Seth mocked, wiggling his fingers to show his fake fear. "I guess I'd better watch my back."

"Yeah, you'd better."

I turned away from him without another word and charged down the stairs, Roxanne on my heels.

I was steps away from my car when I noticed the deep gash across the entire length of the passenger side.

Quickly making my way to the opposite side of the car, I saw another long and deep scratch there as well.

"Son of a bitch!"

I threw my gaze toward the front door, and there was Seth, staring at me. And then he grinned.

As though he'd just gotten the last laugh.

I had the feeling I'd just made an enemy.

At Seth's place, I'd been acting on adrenaline. My anger had temporarily made me forget my despair. But now that I was back in my room, the weight of my problems came crashing down on me.

Sitting on my bed, I grabbed fistfuls of my short black hair and stared ahead, everything a blur in the small room I shared with my roommate, Jolene Martin. Thankfully, she had gone to spend the weekend with her boyfriend, Scott, and wasn't due to return until Sunday night.

I was crushed and emotionally spent. And it was about more than an innocent kitten or any other animal Seth might want to harm. Ever since that vicious rumor appeared on The Gossip Hour blog, my life had been in a tailspin.

I couldn't help wondering if the person behind the rumor was someone who knew me. Knew me and didn't like me.

A friend of Seth's? Seth himself?

I was thankful that Roxanne wanted to head back to her room and chill. She would probably meet up with her boyfriend, Rick, and spend the evening with him. Which was fine by me. I wanted to spend the evening alone.

I got up and turned off the light, then climbed under the covers with my clothes on and curled into a fetal position. This was the only place I really wanted to be these days. In my bed, not facing the world.

If only being alone in a dark room could help me escape my reality. It was tough knowing that whenever I stepped out of my room, people would stare at me. That people were, right now, likely laughing behind my back or even contributing nasty comments about me to The Gossip Hour.

Until ten days ago, I hadn't given much thought to The Gossip Hour. Sure, I had read it on occasion. And yes, I had snickered at its victims. The Gossip Hour had made targets of plenty of people on campus, exposing dirty little secrets. But it had never affected my life directly before, so I had never really cared about it much one way or the other.

Now, I hated the blog. Hated it because it had caused my life to become a living hell.

Regret settled over me like liquid cement when I remembered how I had asked Drake if the rumor was true. Why, oh why, had I asked him that? Of course it couldn't be true. Drake always had women throwing themselves at him. They willingly offered him sex. He certainly didn't need to rape anybody.

Least of all Natalie Laymon, queen of the campus geeks.

Why had I even asked him the question? I wasn't sure he could ever forgive me. And if he didn't forgive me, what would happen to our big plans for the winter break cruise right after Christmas?

Someone makes an accusation and I'm supposed to run? That was the question Drake had asked me, and oddly, he didn't seem to be the one suffering scorn in public. I didn't see guys treating him like he had the plague. On the other hand, *I* had become the victim of mean-spirited comments on the blog site, and I most definitely noticed the snarky looks when I was out and about. How had I, the girlfriend of the alleged perpetrator, become the bad person?

When I heard the sound of the door opening, I gritted my teeth. Jolene had clearly returned, and earlier than I'd expected. She normally didn't come back from her boyfriend's place until Sunday evening.

After the disastrous meeting with Seth and my unsettled conversation with Drake, I really didn't want to see anyone.

"Didi?" she whispered. "Didi, are you awake?"

I didn't answer, not even when the lights came on. I wanted to lie in bed until sleep finally claimed me.

"Didi?"

I felt the weight of Jolene's body beside me on the bed, but that's not what made me lower the pillow. It was the catch in her voice—one that indicated she'd been crying.

Seeing her face confirmed it. Her shoulder-length black hair was unkempt, her slender, dark brown face wet with tears. Her eyes were swollen from crying.

"What the hell?" I asked. It always took me aback to see Jolene looking vulnerable. At five-foot-eleven, with a lean, almost boyish figure, she exuded strength. That strength had made her a star on Lan-U's women's basketball team.

"It's over," she said. "We're done."

"You and Scott?" I asked, though clearly she couldn't have been talking about anything else.

"Uh huh. He doesn't want to see me anymore."

I stared at Jolene in confusion. She had confided in me that Scott seemed to be pulling away from her, but I never expected them to break up. I just figured they'd been going through a rough patch.

"How can that be possible?" I asked. "He was the one who chased you for, what, four months, begging for a chance to date you?"

Jolene didn't speak, just stared at the ground, a look of utter desolation on her face.

As surprised as I was to hear that Scott had dumped her, I was equally surprised by how crushed Jolene seemed. She had been seeing Scott for two years, their relationship blossoming about six months after we'd become friends. But almost the entire time they'd been dating, Jolene had joked that her true Mr. Right was out there somewhere. I had come to realize that she wasn't really joking. That as much as she was in a relationship with Scott, she was waiting for the next best thing to come along.

"People say it was an accident, but I think . . . I think Rachel killed herself," Jolene said, the sudden change in subject throwing me for a loop.

"Huh?" I narrowed my eyes as I looked at my friend.

"I understand it now," she went on. "I get how a person can have everything going for them one day, and then the next, feel like their world is over."

"Whatever it is, Jo, it can't be that bad."

"It is. I fucked up, Didi. Big time."

Chapter Four

I STARED AT JOLENE, waiting for her to continue.

"I don't think Scott will ever forgive me," she sobbed.

"Forgive you?" I repeated.

Nodding, she wiped at her tears, but her face was still contorted in pain. "I know now how a person can get in her car and drive off into a ditch. I can understand why Rachel felt so hopeless that she killed—"

"Stop talking like that," I said. "You're not going to kill yourself."

"You don't know what I did."

Several beats passed, and Jolene wiped at tears that fell onto her cheeks. "You can't tell anyone about this."

"About what?"

"Not even Roxy," she said, referring to Roxanne. Her eyes held a hint of desperation. "Promise me."

"I promise," I told her, but my brain was already spinning. I was wondering what on earth she could have done that was so horrendous.

"I cheated on Scott."

The bombshell shocked me. Left me speechless.

"I just thought . . . I don't know. I kept thinking that maybe there was something else out there for me. Something better."

"Oh man." As much as Jolene had always said that, I hadn't expected her to actually cheat. Or perhaps what I hadn't expected was for her to meet someone else and not tell me about it.

"I know. I was stupid."

"And you told Scott?" I asked.

"He figured it out."

"Ouch."

"That's not the worst of it." She inhaled a deep, weary breath. "I think . . . I think maybe if it had just been a onetime thing, Scott could have dealt with it."

"You were having a long-term affair?" I gaped at her. How had she not told me about this? We were roommates, had been friends for a good two and a half years, and had, or so I thought, told each other everything.

"Long enough," Jolene admitted.

"I don't get it. Why'd you keep it a secret?"

"Because I did, okay," she retorted, then huffed out an exasperated sigh. "The thing is, I got pregnant."

"You're pregnant!" I shrieked.

Jolene threw a panicked glance over her shoulder, fearful that someone in the hallway had just heard my outcry.

I continued in a lower voice, "You're pregnant?"

"Not anymore."

It took a few seconds for me to process what she had said. "You mean . . ."

"I can't have a baby, Didi. Especially when I don't know who the father is."

My mind scrambled to process this stunning news. I couldn't reconcile what I'd just heard.

"I thought that, by coming clean, Scott would forgive me. I guess . . . I guess I always thought he would be there."

It wasn't the first time Jolene had done something to jeopardize her relationship with Scott. Nothing of this magnitude, of course, but she liked to push him. To test him. She'd stand him up for dates, cancel on him when he'd already bought tickets for a show. That sort of thing.

He wasn't the cutest guy on campus, and she'd always had it in her mind that there was something better out there. Now that she'd sampled something else and lost Scott, she was clearly seeing that he meant more to her than she had believed.

"I thought he was going to forgive me," Jolene said. "He even went with me to the clinic last week so I could have the abortion. But now he says he can never trust me and wants nothing to do with me."

And Jolene was finally figuring out just what Scott meant to her.

"I'm so sorry," I said. I had always liked Scott, and had been impressed by his romantic nature when he had set out to pursue Jolene. After a moment I asked, "Why didn't you tell me?"

"It was my problem. Mine and Scott's. I wanted to deal with it with him. But now . . ."

"Now what?"

Grief streaked across Jolene's face. I had honestly never seen her looking so crestfallen in all the time I'd known her.

"He doesn't understand why I'm so upset," she said.

"Upset because it's over?" I said.

"Because I'm no longer pregnant."

Jolene held my gaze, and I got it. I got what she was trying to say, and was surprised by the revelation.

She, Roxanne, and I had often talked about what we'd do if we ever became pregnant. Given that our whole lives were ahead of us, we'd all agreed that if we ended up pregnant we would go right to a clinic and have an abortion. I always knew I might have some reservations, and if Drake wanted the baby I would likely consider having it, given that we planned to get married one day, but still, abortion would be the option that made the most sense at this stage of our lives.

Yet clearly Jolene was feeling guilty about it.

"I never expected to be this upset," Jolene said. "But I am. I'm feeling *guilty*. I was raised a Catholic, Dee. Having an abortion is a sin. I killed a life that was growing inside of me, and it's eating me up."

"Jolene, you did what you had to do. I know it wasn't an easy decision, but . . . but you've got your whole life ahead of you."

"I keep telling myself that. But I'm not feeling any better."

What could I say to that? I didn't know what she was feeling, what she was going through. I did believe that a baby at this point in her life would have been a huge mistake, but having an abortion had to weigh on a person.

"I'm not sure I'm going on the cruise."

"No!" I retorted at Jolene's announcement. "You can't *not* go! We've been planning this since September."

"Yeah, well, now I'm not in the mood to celebrate."

"You have to go," I said. Everything else in my life had gone to hell. I needed this cruise to look forward to. "Sun. Relaxation. It'll be a good thing."

The cruise wasn't for another five weeks, the last week of our winter break. It was meant to be a time for me, my friends, and our guys to unwind and have a blast after spending Christmas with our families. For more than a year, we had talked about going on a cruise vacation. We had planned for it. Saved for it. We *had* to go.

"I don't know."

"I know how you feel," I said. "Trust me. Right now my life has gone to shit and I don't even want to show my face on campus. But this cruise . . . I think it can help both of us."

"Scott doesn't want to go anymore."

"Then he doesn't have to go. You can room with Roxy. You know she's been looking for a roommate ever since Kyra backed out. And who knows, I might end up in the room with you, too." I paused as a spate of anxiety had me feeling suddenly uneasy. "I'm not really sure what's gonna happen between me and Drake."

One of Jolene's eyebrows raised. "Hmm?"

I waved off the question. I wasn't ready to talk about Drake and the fact that our relationship was heading down the toilet. "We're talking about you right now," I told her. "And I don't want to see you let anyone stop you from going on a cruise you've been looking forward to for so long. Like I said, it might be just what you need to feel better."

Maybe it was what we all needed.

Rachel's death. Natalie's alleged rape. It had been a really shitty term.

Rachel's death . . . Something suddenly occurred to me. A thought that made my heart begin to beat rapidly.

"Dee?" Jolene said, a hint of alarm in her voice as she picked up on the shift in my mood.

I didn't answer her. All I could do was replay in my mind my conversation with Drake.

He had been so adamant when telling me to lay off Seth. Had there been an undertone of fear in his warning?

The thought that materialized was terrifying. What if Rachel's accident hadn't been an accident—or even suicide?

What if Seth had killed her . . . and Drake knew it?

Chapter Five

I CONSIDERED AND DISMISSED the idea of Seth as murderer because it simply didn't make sense. I'd been at the party when Rachel had fled in tears. Seth, laughing at Rachel's misery, had poured himself another beer from the keg and gone on partying. Rachel had driven off to parts unknown, and either accidentally went off the road or did so by design. You could argue that Seth had sent her to her death because of his disgusting stunt, but he didn't directly nor intentionally cause her death.

Asshole, yes. Murderer? I doubted it.

And I had bigger concerns. Like my relationship with Drake.

All through the three weeks at home with my family during winter break, I'd hoped that Drake and I would reconnect. We did talk, but only occasionally and briefly, and I knew he was giving me excuses when he said he had no time to see me. Sure, his older sister was there with the new baby, and yes, I understood that this holiday season was tougher for the family because his father had died five months earlier. But this was the first time in years I hadn't gotten together with Drake on Christmas Day, or at any other point over the holidays.

He still needed time, and I had no choice but to give it.

Inside, I was hurting badly, but I put on a brave face and tried to enjoy the holidays with my parents and older sister, Carla. December 28 seemed to take forever to arrive, but when it did, I felt a sense of relief. Finally, Drake and I would be heading on our cruise—and we would return to Lan-U as the super couple everyone knew us to be.

Though my mother was excited for me regarding my cruise to the Caribbean, she made sure to give me a warning as I gathered my suitcases in the foyer that evening before my red-eye flight. "Be careful, Didi. Always be aware of your surroundings, and don't let anyone you don't know get close to you. Remember what happened to Ashley Hamilton."

Ashley Hamilton was a Lan-U student who disappeared in the Caribbean last year after going there with friends for a spring break vacation. She'd never come home, and her remains had never been found. Everyone suspected that she'd met some guy on the island, had spent a night or two engaging in kinky sex, and then this mystery man had killed her. Others believed in the white slavery rumors that had surfaced, and figured Ashley was living as a sex slave somewhere in the Middle

East. In fact, much of the speculation as to what had happened to Ashley had led to the beginning of The Gossip Hour. Ashley had had a seedy private life, one the national media had exploited for weeks. Sweet girl with a secret life in the porn world? It stood to reason that her story would be exploited on campus for several weeks as well.

"I'm not into anything crazy like Ashley was," I told my mother. "I'll be okay."

"Still, you can't be too careful."

"She'll be fine," my father interjected, waving off my mother's concern. "Don't you worry about a thing, honey. The only thing you have to worry about is all this luggage you've got." His eyes scanned my two fairly large bags. "Are you sure you'll be able to make it back to Lancaster without hired help?"

My father chuckled, and I smiled. We needed something to lighten the mood.

"I'm trying to have a serious conversation," my mother protested, planting her hands on her hips. "Would be just like you to make light of it."

"Carla backpacked across Europe for months with hardly a dollar to her name and she was fine," my father pointed out. He gently framed my cheek. "You're going to have a great time on the cruise. Don't you worry about a thing."

My mother frowned. "I know you're an adult now, but I still worry. And I'll always be your mother, so I'm entitled to give you some advice. Watch out for anything peculiar. If anyone harasses you, make sure you report him."

"Glenda—" my father admonished, rolling his eyes.

"Promise me," my mother said, ignoring my father, and I could hear the worry in her voice. "Promise me you'll stay with your friends at all times. And don't associate with any strangers. Promise me."

"I promise, Mom."

My mother smiled, visibly relieved. "Good." She peered through the door's side window. "Chris should be here any minute."

An hour earlier, my mother had stunned me with the news that she had asked Chris, my old high school friend, to drive me to the airport. She had argued that she and my father didn't like driving at night, that Chris taking me was the perfect solution. I'd wanted to protest, tell her that I knew what she was trying to do, but I didn't. She liked Chris, and apparently had been waiting until Drake and I broke up so that she could try to force him on me. She had always believed that Chris and I would have been a perfect match. And now that she knew Drake and I were having problems, she was ready to play matchmaker.

Maybe, if fate hadn't intervened, Chris and I would have ended up together. But Drake had moved to my neighborhood in Oakland, enrolled at my high school, and had taken an instant liking to me. The rest, as they say, is history.

The doorbell rang. "Oh, there he is now," my mother all but sang as she hurried to open the door.

My mother would suck at poker. Her smile didn't disguise her feelings in the least.

I had spoken to Chris on Christmas Day, briefly, after not talking to him for a good two years. We'd stayed in touch for the first year and a half after we had gone on to college, but then I had cut him out of my life, unable to keep a friendship with him. Every time I thought of him, I thought about the night my life had changed forever.

The night that ended with me behind the wheel of a car, intoxicated, and killing a woman.

Chris had gotten cuter over the last couple of years. As a teenager, he had been lanky. But not anymore. As he gave me a hug, I felt nothing but muscles on his six-foot frame. I knew he'd started playing football, and to see him, and it was obvious.

We pulled apart, and I grinned at him as I took in all the changes in his appearance. A goatee framed lips that seemed suddenly fuller. His dark brown skin was clear now, his forehead no longer speckled with acne. Chris didn't have Drake's height, but at six feet he was tall enough, and had a secret weapon I was sure drove the women crazy: dimples.

After high school, Chris had chosen Berkeley, while I had chosen Lan-U. Our winter breaks weren't at the exact same time, but there was no reason we couldn't have gotten together once or twice over the years. We never had, and I knew why.

Seeing Chris made me remember that night four years ago. Made me remember the ugly argument between him and Drake that had led to me hastily get behind the wheel of my car.

Made me remember that I'd taken a life.

That was my burden to bear, and a secret one at that. Only a few people in the world, Chris among them, knew the truth. I'd been driving drunk, and to protect me from prosecution, Drake had claimed that he was driving the car. Not even my parents knew the real story.

I closed my eyes as I sat in Chris's car, trying to quash the memory. I wished I could turn back the hands of time, change what I had done, but it wasn't possible.

"I broke up with Brenda," Chris announced, pulling me from my thoughts of the past.

Though Chris and I hadn't communicated in two years, I'd known of his relationship with Brenda. They had started dating their first year at Berkeley, and the relationship was serious enough that I figured they would get married.

"Oh no," I said.

"Sometimes things don't work out. You know how that is."

No doubt about it, my mother had filled him in on my split from Drake. I pretended not to get his meaning and simply said, "I'm sorry."

"Don't be. I always knew she wasn't the one."

He glanced at me as he spoke, and I was instantly aware of what he was getting at, as certain as if he had voiced the thought. I looked out the window at the darkness.

"I hear you and Drake have broken up."

"Sheesh, why didn't my mother just take an ad out in the paper?" I asked.

"That's where I saw the announcement," Chris said, deadpan. And then he chuckled.

I laughed, too. "I wouldn't be surprised."

"What happened with you two?" Chris asked. "I thought nothing would ever break you guys up."

"I wouldn't say we've broken up. It's more like we're taking a time-out."

"All isn't perfect in paradise?" The hint of humor in his words softened the blow.

"Just . . . growing pains. You know how it is. You date someone for a while and it's not the same as it was in the beginning. And he's going through a rough time over the death of his dad." I paused briefly. "I'm confident we're going to work things out."

"Damn," Chris said playfully. "And here I was hoping I could finally get my chance."

He may have been speaking in jest, but I couldn't help wondering if he still held a torch for me. After all this time, I figured he would have moved on. In fact, when I'd learned that he was dating Brenda seriously, I figured for sure that he had found the perfect woman for him.

"What about you and Brenda? No chance of reconciliation?"

"Naw." He shook his head.

"That's too bad."

"No, don't feel bad about it. Like I said, I always knew we weren't going to last forever."

"How's she coping?"

"Already dating someone else," Chris explained. "But she's happy, and I'm happy for her."

Sounded to me like he'd never truly loved her, but I didn't want to go there.

The next few minutes of the drive passed in silence. But when I sensed Chris staring at me, I turned to face him. I guessed the direction of his thoughts even before he opened his mouth. "Do you ever wonder—"

"Chris," I interjected, cutting him off.

"I do," he went on. "I think back to that night all the time. And I think that if I'd behaved differently, things could be very different right now."

Was he right? If the whole chain of events that took place hadn't happened, would things be different now? Would I be with Drake?

I didn't want to think about it. Perhaps I had avoided thinking about it. Maybe he was right, but I couldn't tell him what he wanted to hear.

"Things happened the way they did," I told him frankly. "We can't change it. And nothing good will come of remembering it."

"You know—"

"Please," I said. The last thing I wanted to do was remember that night. "I want to leave the past in the past."

There was a flash of disappointment in his eyes, evident even in the dark car. I'd upset him with my answer. I knew that I would. But his lips curled slightly, and he nodded.

Ever the nice guy. There was no doubt as to why my mother adored him.

"Will you promise me something?" Chris said after a moment.

"That depends," I answered honestly.

"Can you promise me that we'll stay in touch?" he asked. "The one thing I regret the most is that we lost touch. I blame myself for that."

I didn't answer right away.

"Sure," I finally said. "We'll stay in touch."

He nodded, satisfied. "Is Drake going on this cruise?"

At the mention of Drake's name, my lungs constricted. So much had changed for me and Drake since we'd booked this trip. Instead of sharing a room with me on the cruise, Drake was now rooming with two of his friends, Kent and Reid. I was rooming with Roxanne and Jolene. Those arrangements couldn't be changed at this point, but that was the least of my concerns. I had hoped that our trip home for the holidays would have led to us getting together again. That hadn't happened. I still loved Drake and wanted him back, and it was my heartfelt desire that once we were on the cruise—away from school and family—we would reconnect.

"Yes, he's going."

"Didi," Chris said softly. "Didi, look at me."

I did.

"If he doesn't appreciate you," Chris went on gently, "don't be afraid to let him go. You don't owe him anything."

"I know that," I quickly said, a little testy. Talking about Drake was only making me anxious. "Look, can we stop talking about Drake?"

"Sorry, I didn't mean to upset you."

"Fine, then let's just drop it, okay?"

"Sure, okay," Chris said. But his voice was strained.

I turned on the radio, found a station playing upbeat hip-hop, then settled back in my seat and closed my eyes, effectively telling Chris I was through talking for the rest of the drive.

"I meant what I said," he said once we arrived at the airport and he pulled up to the curb at departures. "I don't want us to lose touch again."

I was still a little tense over our earlier conversation, I realized. But his warm smile eased my tension, making me realize that I'd lost touch with someone who'd been a good friend.

"Me neither," I agreed, and meant it. "It was really good seeing you again. And for what it's worth, I hope you and Brenda work things out."

He didn't speak for a moment, just stared at me. There was longing in his look. Affection. I knew that Brenda was the last thing on his mind.

"Well"—I reached for the door handle—"I'd better go."

I couldn't have been more mortified to exit the car and see Drake placing his duffel bag on the scale at the curbside check-in counter. As if sensing me, he turned.

Chris followed my line of sight. Saw Drake.

Something passed over Drake's face. Something unreadable. Then he turned his attention back to the counter.

"Shit," I muttered.

"What?" Chris asked.

"Nothing," I said. There was no point in telling him that Drake wouldn't be happy to see me with Chris. He already believed Chris and I had had a thing four years ago.

Finished at the counter, Drake headed inside without even glancing backward. I felt as if someone had physically struck me.

"How long are you going away for?" Chris asked, his tone teasing as he took my large suitcase from his trunk. I knew he was trying to lighten the mood.

"I know it's a lot," I said, "but I'm going straight back to school from the cruise."

Chris rolled my large suitcase to the counter, while I carried my carry-on bag and purse. Minutes later, I was finished with the curbside check-in. I turned to Chris, then hugged him.

"Thanks," I said.

"I'm here for you," he whispered. "If you ever need anything, or need to talk . . ."

"Sure," I said as we pulled apart. "I'll call you after the cruise."

"Have fun."

"I will."

At least, I would try.

Chris went back to his car, and I headed into the departures terminal, knowing I would have to do damage control.

Chapter Six

DRAKE WAS NOWHERE to be seen before we boarded the plane. I had no clue where he was at that hour, but I figured he was avoiding me. I took my seat before he did, and even wondered if he had decided to cancel his trip or catch another flight. But when the plane was about half-boarded, I saw Drake coming down the aisle.

My heart began to race. He was coming right toward me.

But he passed my row and went to the one behind mine, where he settled into the window seat. I, too, was sitting in the window seat. But I, thankfully, had an empty seat beside me, so

I could get more comfortable during the flight. Drake wasn't so lucky.

I glanced back at him, but either he didn't see me or he was pretending he didn't.

Screw him. If that was the way he wanted to play this, I could be just as indifferent.

Once we were airborne, I closed my eyes and went to sleep.

I slept fitfully as the hours passed, but when the sun began to appear on the horizon, I knew I wouldn't sleep anymore. I turned on my iPod and listened to music to pass the time.

I'm not sure how much later it was, but at some point I began to pick up snippets of conversation from the row behind me. The two guys sitting beside Drake had the same shade of dirty-blond hair and matching scruffy beards. They were clearly buddies, if not relatives, and despite the early hour, they were up and having an animated chat. The kind they obviously wanted the entire plane to hear.

"So the stripper was like, is that all? She actually got pissed off. Thought the tip wasn't enough." The man gave an annoying smoker's laugh, which had already gotten on my nerves. He had a southern drawl that screamed redneck. "I told her she was a bitch and grabbed the tip back."

I whipped my head around and peered through the gap between the seat at the guy. *Prick,* I said to myself. Drake still had his eyes closed, but there was no way he could be sleeping with those two loudmouths beside him. I was sure he was now regretting that he had switched seats.

The men kept gabbing, laughing, and pissing off the people around them. I wasn't the only one who threw annoyed glances in their direction.

They talked about a bar fight, and how one of them had avoided getting charged even though he was "drunk as shit." I turned up my iPod and tried to tune them out. But when they started putting down women, I couldn't help listening to what they were saying.

"Can't trust a woman as far as you can throw her," the man went on. "They like to talk about men, but women lie and cheat more than any of us."

Once again, I looked back through the gap in the seats. But maybe I shouldn't have, because the guy who'd been talking caught my eye. "How can I help you, pretty lady?"

I jerked my head around, realizing that the man was talking to me.

"Don't turn away now, honey," the man said and did that annoying cackle again. "Gimme your number. You might get lucky. Hell, I'd let you break my heart."

"Shut the hell up," Drake finally said.

This elicited not only chuckles from those around us, but cheers of support.

"You tellin' me to shut up?" the guy asked, his southern drawl making him sound real dumb-ass.

"We don't need to hear about your adventures in strip clubs and the local jail," Drake went on. I was peering over my shoulder, staring at him now.

"Fuck you, buddy," the jerk said.

"No, fuck you."

I continued to watch Drake and his seatmate, fearing the situation would escalate. But the ignorant moron, though clearly fuming, did as Drake had ordered. He shut the hell up. Most people didn't want to get into an altercation with Drake. Six-foot-four, brawny, *and* black, he wasn't the kind of guy you messed with.

And then I got the strangest sensation. The guy looked familiar. I couldn't place it, but I was sure I had seen him before.

"Thanks," I whispered to Drake once we were both off the plane and standing outside the gate.

"For what?" He didn't look at me. He was scanning the overhead signs.

"For saying what you did to that guy." I shrugged, trying to play nonchalant, but I knew that what Drake had said meant that he still cared. It was almost worth dealing with that annoying pig to learn this truth.

"No big deal," Drake said, also acting casual.

Finding what he'd no doubt been looking for—the direction of baggage claim—Drake started walking. I fell into step beside him. I yawned, my fatigue catching up with me. I was tired from the red-eye, and regretted not getting here yesterday and spending the night in a hotel, getting a good night's sleep before boarding the ship. That's what Roxanne and Jolene had done, but I'd figured the cross-country flight would have left me too exhausted to party the night before the cruise, so I'd opted to arrive early the morning of.

"Well, thanks anyway," I said. I knew Drake didn't want to make a big deal out of the situation. Maybe he wasn't ready to deal with me on a girlfriend-boyfriend level.

And that was fine. A crowded airport wasn't the place for him to show affection. We were heading in the same direction, so I felt I could deal with the pain and uncertainty of this moment if it led to happiness in the end.

He was walking briskly, and I didn't know if he wanted me to walk beside him or not, but I found myself slowing. Miami International Airport was bustling with activity, and Drake and I were quickly separated. I saw the top of his head descending the escalator toward baggage claim.

Damn it! I was trying to be cool, calm, collected. But I was falling apart inside. Couldn't he have waited for me?

Heaving an angst-filled sigh, I turned.

And saw the two guys who'd been sitting beside Drake on the plane. The one who'd made his crude comment saw me instantly. Our eyes locked. I quickly moved ahead down the hallway and rushed toward the escalator. I didn't realize how rapidly my heart was beating until I was safely ahead of the guys, the two of them now out of sight.

Feeling vulnerable, I walked down the left side of the escalator, wanting to get to Drake as quickly as possible. If either of those guys tried to hassle me, he could protect me.

But rather than seeing Drake as I got to the bottom of the escalator, I saw Jolene and Roxanne. Actually, I heard them before I saw them. Jolene called my name, twice, and I volleyed my gaze from right to left, finally spotting them on the far left near one of the exit doors. They were frantically waving at me.

A huge smile spreading on my face, I hurried toward my friends. We all shared a group hug, giggling as we did.

"You made it!" Jolene exclaimed. She was dressed in summer attire—a knee-length white cotton dress and flat, gold sandals. Big, round sunglasses obscured her eyes and her hair was pulled back into a ponytail. Her tall, lean frame made her look like a supermodel. Roxanne was dressed in an almost identical outfit except in pink, but even with dramatic makeup and her black hair softly curled around her wide face, she still looked like a teenager playing dress-up.

We liked to coordinate our outfits, so I would also put on the mini-sundress I'd brought. And because I didn't want to be bothered styling my short, curly hair before we boarded the ship, I would put on my stylish fedora. Problem solved.

"Have you guys been waiting long?" I asked.

"Not too long," Jolene explained. "We got here about fifteen minutes ago."

"I'm impressed," I said. "Did you guys not party all night on South Beach?"

"We did," Roxanne said. "But there was no way we were going to miss picking you up at the airport."

Roxanne's gaze wandered, and I turned to see what she was looking at. In the distance, I saw Drake standing around the fifth baggage claim belt, where our luggage was going to exit.

"How are things with Drake?" she asked me.

I waved off the question, not wanting to talk about it. I feared I might start crying if I did.

"It's okay," Roxanne said, and gave me another hug. "Nothing is going to stop us from having fun, you hear?"

I nodded.

"Now that you're here, I'll go get the car," she went on.

"And I'll help you with your luggage," Jolene announced.

"I'll meet you two at the curb," Roxanne said, and squealed excitedly before heading off.

"Drake's not talking to you?" Jolene asked when Roxanne had run off.

"Barely." I swallowed. "I don't know, Jo. I think it might really be over."

We had been walking toward the baggage claim belt, but Jolene stopped and placed her hands on my shoulders. "You're going on this cruise, you're going to have fun, and you're going to make Drake beg you to take him back." She paused, held my gaze. "Let him see you having a good time, Dee. Then *he'll* wonder if you've stopped caring. Don't give him the upper hand."

It was the mentality Jolene had exercised with Scott, and to her credit, it had served her well for two years.

"How's Scott?" I asked.

Jolene's smile was immediate and radiant. "He's coming around," she said. "He hasn't said he wants me back—not explicitly—but he called me and texted me over the holidays, and I think he's ready to forgive me."

"That's great." I smiled to hide my spate of jealousy.

"If Scott can forgive me, you know Drake will forgive you. Just give him some time."

I shrugged.

"Come on. You're Lan-U's super couple. You know it'll work out. But like I said, you can't act like you're all torn up over him. Make him fear you don't care anymore, and he'll come running back to you."

I hoped Jolene was right.

Drake and I were on opposite sides of the conveyor belt as we waited for our luggage. I did what Jolene had suggested and tried to act carefree, even laughing loudly at something she told me. And in my peripheral vision, I caught Drake looking at me.

I perked up a bit. Maybe Jolene was right after all.

His luggage arrived first, and he gave a nod of acknowledgment in my direction before he walked off. Jolene waved to him, and I nodded back—and then we immediately went back to gabbing. I made sure to throw in another loud laugh that would reach his ears before he exited the airport.

"See?" Jolene said. "He's already wondering if you're ready to move on without him."

I nodded, but I wasn't convinced.

And then I felt the heat of someone's gaze and turned.

The jerks from the plane. Both of them were staring at me.

This time, the feeling that came over me was more than a sense of unease.

It was an intense jolt of fear.

Chapter Seven

THOUGH I HAD NEVER seen a cruise ship in real life, I'd seen plenty of them on TV commercials, as well as tons of pictures in magazines and travel brochures. Excited about this trip, I'd spent a huge amount of time familiarizing myself with the ships of the SunSeekers Cruise Line via the Internet. But knowing what to expect had not prepared me for the reality of seeing this cruise ship in person.

It was massive.

There was no other way to describe it. Looking up at the imposing structure, it was the height of a tall apartment building.

Something Drake said when we were booking this trip suddenly struck me. I'd been interested in a room with a balcony, but he had vetoed that. He said that having a room with a balcony would be tempting fate. In a joking tone, he added that he didn't want to fall off a balcony in the middle of the night after drinking too much.

I had laughed off the comment. People traveled on cruise ships every day, got totally drunk, and no one fell over. Well, not no one, but it was a rare occurrence from what I understood. Yet, I knew what he meant. Every time I was on a high peak, like the time I'd gone to Maine with my family and had stood at the top of a cliff while visiting a lighthouse, there was the fear that somehow you would fall over. That a strong gust of wind might send you plummeting to your death. You knew it wasn't going to happen, but still, the thought was there, in the back of your mind.

Looking up at the ship, however, all I could think about was the irrational. A fall from the upper deck to the water below would be like hitting a brick wall.

Don't even go there, I told myself. There was no point in entertaining something that wouldn't happen.

Instead, I let my gaze wander over the rest of the ship. It was like a floating hotel or condo. The exterior was painted an off-white, while the windows were a bluish green, providing a stunning contrast. On the side of the ship, the word "SunSeekers" was written in large, orange letters that were designed to provoke playfulness. Beneath the name of the cruise line was the name of the ship: *Glorious.*

Before booking this trip, I had checked out photo after photo of the various luxury cruise lines. Every picture had portrayed either relaxation or fun or both. There were photos of people relaxing on the pool deck. Smiling at the formal dining table.

Eyes full of excitement in the casino. Those professional photos had captured the essence of the kind of vacation I wanted to have, and I'd settled on the SunSeekers cruise line—not to mention that their price was better than the competition.

But I'd wanted to have that vacation with my boyfriend.

All day, I had tried to put Drake out of my mind and do what Jolene had said: Concentrate on having a good time. But I couldn't stop the feelings swirling around inside of me. I knew this trip would be do or die for our relationship—things would either be set right, or we'd be saying good-bye for good.

If it ended in a happy reunion, then it would be the trip of a lifetime—the kind of trip we could look back on in years to come and see as a defining moment in our relationship.

I searched the crowd for Drake. It didn't take long to find him. He was about twenty or so feet behind me with two of his buddies, Jamie and Reid. About ten Lan-U students had decided to take this winter break trip.

He looked my way, and I smiled at him.

He turned away.

My shoulders drooped. I felt utterly deflated.

Maybe he hadn't seen me, I rationalized. Maybe he hadn't seen me smile at him.

I turned—and then I saw someone else. And now I felt a different emotion.

An intense sense of fear.

"Oh my God," I said.

"What?" Roxanne asked.

Lowering my sunglasses to have a clear view of him, I checked out the man's face. It was definitely him, right down to the same shirt with the skull and crossbones.

"Remember those guys on the plane," I said. I'd told Roxanne and Jolene about what had transpired. "They're in the crowd right now, getting on the ship."

Roxanne was the first to spin her head around. Then Jolene followed suit. It was out of instinct, as they didn't know what the guys looked like and therefore wouldn't spot them.

"Don't look," I said. "I don't want them to realize I'm talking about them. Damn, talk about shitty luck." The one man had been the true asshole on the plane. A first-class jerk who had singled me out for abuse. And now I would be trapped on a ship with him.

"That sucks," Roxanne agreed. "Let's hope they're not near us in the formal dining room."

"Don't even put that thought out there in the universe," Jolene said. "This ship is huge. Big enough that you might not ever run into him."

"From your lips to God's ears," I said. Once again, I stared up at the towering ship. I couldn't get over how massively huge it was. It was beyond anything I had imagined. It certainly was large enough that a person could easily avoid someone.

Glancing at the crowd once more, I went still. The jerk from the plane was suddenly the least of my problems.

I couldn't believe my eyes. In fact, I blinked several times to make sure my eyes weren't deceiving me.

They were not.

Natalie Laymon was in line to board the ship.

"What the hell is going on?" I muttered.

"What now?" Jolene asked.

"Natalie," I replied, speaking her name with as much contempt as I could muster. "Natalie Laymon."

Jolene's mouth fell open, and then she spun around, following the direction of my gaze. Roxanne did the same.

"Oh no she didn't." Roxanne shook her head. "She did *not* book to come on this cruise!"

But there she was, wearing large sunglasses and dragging a suitcase behind her. I'd looked in her direction and not noticed her before, because she looked so different. She was dressed in a way I had never seen her dress before—stylishly.

In fact, her whole look was different. Her hair was no longer dishwater brown, but platinum blond. And it was pulled back in a sleek ponytail. She was wearing low-heeled black sandals with a crystal flower at the apex of the big toe and the second one. They were expensive shoes. I knew because I had tried on the same pair when I'd been shopping in Oakland on Black Friday. Along with the cute shoes was the simple black dress that I would bet had an expensive label. Completing the look were the silver bangles on her wrist.

"Talk about a makeover," I said.

"I hardly recognize her," Jolene said. "I mean, she actually looks good. At least from afar."

I didn't respond, but I was thinking the same thing. She hardly looked like Lan-U's unpopular nerd.

"But why is she *here*?" Roxanne asked.

The question was disturbing, but an even more disturbing possibility flitted into my mind. The thought that she had gotten herself dolled up and booked this trip because she wanted to get close to Drake. In fact, it suddenly occurred to me that her whole game plan had been to break me and Drake up so she could have a chance with him.

Crazy, perhaps. But people did crazy things in the name of love.

"Do you think she did all of this for Drake?" I couldn't help asking my friends. "I mean, she can't seriously be going on a cruise with people who don't like her unless she has an agenda. Maybe that whole crying rape thing was all about some crazy obsession with Drake."

"You could be right," Jolene said. "The girl's a nutcase. Remember all the talk about how she fixated on that computer geek, Ashton? And when he wanted nothing to do with her, she tried to kill herself?"

"Yeah," I said softly, keeping my eyes on Natalie. Last year, word had spread that she had ended up in the hospital after overdosing on pills because she'd been depressed. I'd taken the news with a grain of salt. Even before the rumor about Drake had spread, I'd doubted the truth of many of the things touted as fact on The Gossip Hour. I understood, as I'm sure others did, that the anonymous blog was akin to a mean girls' club with a license to act without consequence. Mostly, I read the Web site for entertainment. Kind of like reading those supermarket tabloids.

Now I wanted absolutely nothing to do with The Gossip Hour and would never support it in any way again. Rumors that broke couples up and turned people into lepers were not fun.

"She might be delusional enough to be here hoping Drake will fall madly in love with the new her," Roxanne commented.

"Which will *never* happen," Jolene stressed. "Makeover or not, there's nothing she can do that would ever attract Drake."

Roxanne nodded. "Exactly. Don't even sweat it."

"I'm not sweating it," I said, trying to be nonchalant. But the truth was, I was bothered by Natalie's new appearance.

I wanted to be able to ignore her. But the very fact that she was here, about to board the ship with us for five days, had me totally unsettled.

"Or maybe she's here to try and prove a point," I said as another idea came to me. "To make sure that everyone believes her."

Jolene rolled her eyes. "You know what she said was a vicious lie, the same as everyone else does. Just ignore her."

"I'll try," I said. But I knew that I would barely be able to stomach being in her vicinity, much less the same dining hall, or the deck, or the casino. Natalie had made my life hell, and I was certain that she had shown up on this cruise simply to be a thorn in my side.

"I have to say," Roxanne began, "she does clean up well."

I gazed in Natalie's direction again. And as much as I wanted to scoff at what Roxanne had said, it was true. Natalie did clean up well.

She didn't look unsophisticated and frumpy. In fact, she actually looked pretty.

I don't know why that bothered me. Perhaps it was easier to believe that Drake would not have touched her if she were naturally unattractive. A little makeup and some clothes were proving otherwise.

"I just hope she stays away from me," I said, seething.

"Don't let her get under your skin, Didi," Roxanne said.

"Yeah," Jolene agreed. "Don't let her get under your skin. The best thing to do is to ignore her. Act as though you are totally happy, carefree. You could care less about her."

I nodded, resolving to do just that.

Minutes later, the crowd was moving. As I walked with my girlfriends up the long ramp leading to the ship, I suddenly remembered my mother's warning.

Be careful. Remember what happened to Ashley Hamilton. Stay with your friends at all times, and don't associate with any strangers. Promise me.

I exhaled slowly, then looked around to take in the tropical surroundings of the port of Miami.

And there was the jerk from the plane, staring at me. He grinned.

Not the kind of grin meant to make a girl feel special; rather, the kind meant to incite fear.

And I did feel fear. Most definitely.

Part Two

Who holds his peace and gathers stones,
will find a time to throw them.

—PORTUGUESE PROVERB

Chapter Eight

A LITTLE OVER an hour later, Jolene, Roxanne, and I had boarded the ship, settled our bags into a room that looked much smaller than it had in the brochure, and were now checking out the rest of the luxury cruise ship. Jolene had walked with us through the main lobby area with the glass elevators and spiral staircase, and past the casino and gift shops before telling us that she was going to head upstairs to the top deck to call Scott on her cell phone. Once we were on the open seas, it would be an exorbitant rate to make a call from the ship's phones. Around twelve bucks a minute, from what I understood. You'd have to be crazy to make a call at that price—or completely desperate.

There were so many areas to the ship that I knew it would be easy for the week to pass without seeing them all.

"You look like your dog just died," Roxanne said, slipping her arm through mine as we came to the top of a staircase that opened to a casual eating area.

"I don't have a dog," I replied, being cheeky.

"You know what I mean. You hardly look in a festive mood, and we're supposed to be celebrating. Come on. Let's head to the bar on the top deck and get something to drink."

I let Roxanne lead me through the crowd. There was a good mix of people. Adults. Seniors. Young kids. But definitely a good number of college students who obviously had the same idea we had: to let loose for the last week of winter break before heading back to school.

I wondered how many other women were nursing broken hearts. How many others had booked this trip with their boyfriends but had since broken up.

"Smile," Roxanne instructed me, plastering a syrupy grin on her own face in an effort to guide me. "For God's sake, you're on vacation."

I smiled.

"Pathetic, but that's the idea. Keep trying."

I managed another smile, this one genuine, if faint. I appreciated Roxanne trying to cheer me up. She was right. I was in Miami, it was winter break, and I was about to cruise the Caribbean and see five different islands.

I couldn't let my problems with Drake keep me from enjoying something I was about to experience for the first time.

Roxanne and I finally reached the top deck, where it seemed almost everyone else had congregated. People were lined up at the ship's rail, looking out at the port of Miami. Some people on the ground were already waving at us, even though the ship had yet to set sail.

"What are you having to drink?" Roxanne asked me. "I'm buying."

"Whatever you're having."

"Let's go inside and see if there are any special drinks to toast the occasion."

"Aren't we waiting for Jolene?" I asked.

Roxanne shrugged. "She said she'd find us."

"If she's still on the phone, then things must be going well with Scott, which is good. I'm glad he's coming around after the abor—" I stopped abruptly, catching myself.

"What?" Roxanne asked.

"Nothing," I said quickly. Too quickly.

Roxanne's eyes narrowed. "No. You started to say abortion, didn't you?"

Shit. Shit. Shit. I hadn't been thinking. Jolene normally shared everything with both of us, which was why I'd been about to speak freely.

"Jolene had an abortion?"

I couldn't very well lie now. "Look, you can't say anything. In fact, forget you even heard that. It was a tough decision for her, a real mess—"

"And she told you, but not me."

"Because—"

"Because what?"

I groaned, silently cursing my stupidity. "She'll kill me if I tell you. So *please,* you can't let on that you know."

"I won't," Roxanne snipped, her tone making it clear she wasn't happy to have been left out of this news.

"She was seeing someone else. Scott found out, but she also

ended up pregnant, didn't know who the father was. An abortion made the most sense, but she's feeling down about it. She wasn't planning to tell me, but I'm her roommate and she was falling apart, so I guess she had to tell someone. Please, Roxy—"

"I won't say anything," Roxanne said. "It's her life. She doesn't have to tell me anything." As if to drive that point home, she plastered on a smile. "Come on. Let's get a drink."

Feeling like the world's biggest fool, I followed Roxanne to the ship's upper bar. It was crowded with people doing the same thing we were; starting the trip with a drink in hand.

I trusted Roxanne. She could keep her mouth shut. But I felt like crap for having betrayed Jolene's confidence.

"Oh, look," Roxanne said, pointing to the board above the bar. She sounded upbeat. Not at all upset. "There's a drink called Bon Voyage. I think I'll order that one."

"I'll try it, too."

There were a good number of bartenders working, so it didn't take all that long to get our drinks. The Bon Voyage was a signature drink exclusive to the SunSeekers Cruise Line, and consisted of vodka, a splash of peach schnapps, lemonade, and cranberry juice.

I tasted it, and it reminded me of everything I considered the Caribbean to be. Refreshing and intoxicating.

The ship jerked, and everyone was thrown to the left. At first, we were startled. Then we realized the boat was moving, and there was a collective chuckle among the crowd.

"We're on the move." Roxanne smiled brightly. Too brightly. Damn it, she was pissed.

"Look, Roxy—"

"Whatever, Dee. Don't sweat it. I always thought Jo and I

were close, but I'm not all that surprised she would leave me in the dark."

"It wasn't about leaving you in the dark. She's hurting. She didn't want to share such a personal decision with everyone."

"I tell you both everything. Same as you tell us everything."

Roxanne gave me a pointed look, but I said nothing. I was thinking that we all had some secrets we told no one. I definitely had mine.

"Secret boyfriend, pregnancy, abortion?" Roxanne went on. "For her to keep all that to herself . . . I don't know. Sometimes I get a vibe about Jolene. I think she's sneaky. The kind of person you can't really trust."

I wouldn't have been more baffled if Roxanne had said she believed that Jolene had had a sex change.

"Seriously, Roxy. Don't you think you're being a bit harsh?"

Roxanne shrugged.

It was the hurt causing her to speak this way. Hurt at not hearing Jolene's major news from Jolene herself.

Me and my big mouth. I'd hoped to start this vacation off in a fun, stress-free way.

Instead, it was starting with drama.

Chapter Nine

IT DIDN'T TAKE LONG for the Miami skyline to recede in the distance, and soon there was nothing but vast ocean before us. Behind us, the glow of the Miami Beach strip's lights was still visible, an array of neon colors in the now darkening sky.

I'd walked around the ship with Roxanne, but there was still no sign of Jolene. After Roxanne's comment, I had to admit I was starting to wonder where Jolene could have gone off to.

Which was ridiculous. She was probably looking for us the way we'd been looking for her, all of us missing each other the way people do in those comedies where one person goes through a door moments before another person enters through a different door.

The other option—and I considered this quite likely—was that the conversation with Scott hadn't gone as well as she had hoped, and Jolene was back in the room, looking for some quiet alone time.

The day had been fairly warm, but thanks to the strong breeze on the upper deck, I was feeling a chill. "Maybe we should head inside," I suggested.

Roxanne led the way toward the front of the ship, and just before we approached a set of doors, she halted. "Is that Rudy?"

"Where?"

She pointed and we both advanced.

And sure enough, it was Rudy. He was currently passed out on the ground between two lounge chairs on the pool deck, snoring as if he was in a comfy bed.

Already in a drunken stupor . . .

Rudy, one of the more outgoing seniors on campus, was known for being the guy who drank too much at every gathering where alcohol was served. In three and a half years of college, one would expect that he'd have learned how to hold his liquor, but apparently he hadn't.

"Oh God," Roxanne said with a chuckle. "Look at his face."

I looked at his face and chuckled as well.

His thin lips were smeared in a bright red shade of lipstick. Sparkly blue eyeshadow covered his eyelids. His cheeks were rosy, and his fingernails were painted a fuchsia pink.

I snapped a picture with my camera phone. So did Roxanne.

"He's gonna be pissed when he wakes up," Roxanne commented.

"He should be used to it by now," I pointed out. "The guys are always playing tricks on him when he gets this drunk."

"I don't think Rudy gets embarrassed anymore, otherwise he would have stopped drinking. Remember the time the guys left him butt naked on the front lawn?"

"Tell me about it." Recalling the photos that had spread like wildfire via e-mail, a laugh erupted in my throat.

"At least you're laughing," Roxanne said.

And she was right. My mood had brightened substantially.

Hopefully a good omen of things to come for the rest of the trip.

"Don't look now," Roxanne began, "but there are two *really* hot guys checking us out."

Instinctively, I began to turn my head in the direction she was looking, and Roxanne said in an urgent whisper, "I said don't look!"

It was too late. I saw the attractive, tall, dark-skinned man smile at me. So did the man next to him, who looked to be his brother.

I quickly averted my gaze.

But the effort had been wasted. Because Roxanne decided to wave at them.

"Roxanne," I admonished, "what are you doing?"

"They're cute. We should hang out with them."

"You're not serious."

"Why not?" She looked at me as though she was clueless.

I made a face. "You know what I'm talking about. Obviously I'm hoping to reconcile with Drake."

"Oh." She forced a smile.

"And what about Rick?"

"We're not serious yet," Roxanne replied. "And he's not here."

"Roxanne . . ." I began, frowning. But I didn't get to complete my statement, because the two guys were suddenly beside us.

"Hey," one said, his smile charming.

As I looked at both of the men, I realized that they weren't just brothers, they were twins. One was a little more buff than the other, and the buffer one was also bald, but they were definitely twins.

"Hi." Roxanne was all smiles, definitely flirting.

"I'm Devon," the buffer one announced. "This is my brother, Javen."

"I'm Roxanne, and this is my friend, Didi."

I wanted to roll my eyes. I didn't want to engage in conversation with these guys as if we were hoping to hook up.

"Where are you all from?" Devon asked.

"Philly," Roxanne replied. "Well, close to it. We go to Lan-U."

"You had that missing girl last year," the guy said, narrowing his eyes. "The one who went to some island on spring break and never returned."

"Yeah," I chimed in. "Talk about scary."

"Did you know her?" Devon asked.

Roxanne and I shook our heads in unison. "No."

We may not have known Ashley personally, but her disappearance had rocked all of us at Lan-U.

"Can I get you another of what you're drinking?" Devon asked, and it was clear he was talking to me.

"Um," I hedged. "Actually, I've got a boyfriend."

Devon chuckled. "That's a new drink. Haven't heard of that one before."

My face flamed.

"It's an ex-boyfriend," Roxanne chimed in.

I glared at her, wanting to throttle her. "We're working things out," I explained tactfully. "I just don't want to lead anyone on."

"It's only a drink," Devon said, flashing that charming smile. "Not a marriage proposal."

The comment stung, though it shouldn't have. "All the same, I want to check in on a friend of mine. She's not feeling too well."

It wasn't a lie. Jolene was still feeling glum over her decision to terminate her pregnancy. She could have been in the room, depressed, for all I knew.

Roxanne made a face at me, one that showed her disapproval, but I didn't care. She hadn't been big on me trying to repair my relationship with Drake, especially since he'd been the one to officially dump me. But it was my life, not hers, and I wasn't about to have a holiday hook-up simply because my relationship status was in limbo.

"Nice to meet you Devon, Javen." I looked at Roxanne. "See you later."

The frown that marred her lips was slight, but it was there nonetheless. Yet she didn't protest.

Turning, I made my way through the happy crowd and down to the lower level. For the first time since we'd boarded, I saw Drake. He was outside, standing at the railing.

My stomach fluttered. I was nervous, I realized.

But why? Drake and I had been a couple for five years. It was ridiculous for me to fear running into him on the ship.

In fact, I decided to go and speak to him. How would we ever patch things up if I didn't?

I continued down the steps, then stopped abruptly when I saw a girl standing beside him at the railing.

Directly beside him. Which meant they were chatting.

I could see her face from her profile. She was thin with breasts unnaturally large for her frame. Spanish-looking. Long, curly black hair.

Gorgeous. And coincidentally, she looked a lot like Rachel Jepson.

Quickly, I averted my gaze, unable to deal with watching them together.

I hurried down the hallway in search of my room.

My room was not as easy to find as I'd thought it would be. The various hallways and corridors of the massive ship were like tunnels in a maze, each exit leading me to a place that looked familiar, yet different. More than once, I'd ended up back in a common area that I had already passed.

I had no idea people could get lost on a cruise ship, but I was discovering that it wasn't that easy to get around.

"Should have left a bread crumb trail," I mumbled.

"Didi?"

At the sound of Jolene's voice, I turned around. She was near a door that led to a stairwell, one I had decided to walk past. Her eyes lighting up, she hurried toward me.

"Where the hell is our room?" I asked.

"You're lost, too? So was I."

"I need a map," I said. "Or better yet, a trail of bread crumbs."

"I was heading to the casino," Jolene said.

"Definitely that way," I said, pointing behind her. "And up the stairs, I think two levels."

"Why don't you come with me?"

She looked happy, not at all like a woman who'd had a bad

conversation with her boyfriend. I couldn't help thinking that if Roxanne let it slip that I'd spilled her secret, the smile on Jolene's face would disappear mighty fast.

"Sure." I had been hoping to find Jolene in our room, hang out with her for a while as Roxanne flirted to her heart's content with Devon and Javen. But here she was, and the evening was young.

We made our way to the casino, which was packed with people. Slot machines were pinging everywhere. From old ladies to young college guys, the floor was packed with people dropping coins into whatever machine they were at. The crowd appeared as happy and carefree as the people had in all the promotional photos.

And then I sensed eyes on me. Slowly, I looked in that direction. A dark-skinned black man in a SunSeekers uniform—black blacks, black vest, white shirt—was smiling at me.

I quickly looked away. I hadn't wanted to give Devon and Javen the impression that I was available, and they were cute college guys. I certainly didn't want to give a man who was probably in his forties any encouragement.

I went back to surveying the floor, and after several seconds I spotted Drake. My stomach sank when I saw that the dark-haired bombshell was still with him.

But it was the sight of two other people, standing about ten feet away from Drake, that made me suck in a sharp breath.

A cold sensation prickled across the back of my neck—and then spread all over my body.

Chapter Ten

TROUBLE WAS BREWING.

I sensed it. Sensed it the way an animal senses a lurking predator.

Rooted to my spot on the floor near the entrance, I watched the guy who clearly wanted trouble. He and his friend were circling Drake the way two lionesses circled a wildebeest.

Drake was oblivious, sitting at the slot machine and chatting to the bombshell, not even noticing his surroundings.

"Shit, Jo—those are the guys I told you about from the plane. I think they're looking for trouble."

Jolene frowned. "I think you're right."

"Should we go over there?" I asked. "Try to . . . I don't know . . . diffuse the situation?"

"Well, they haven't done anything yet. Maybe they won't. Maybe they're just . . . watching him."

For what purpose? If they were watching him, there was a reason. The way I saw it, they were biding their time.

And then it happened. The guy from the plane moved up to the slot machine next to Drake's, which had just been vacated. As he did, he accidentally-on-purpose dumped his draft beer on Drake's crotch. Drake shot to his feet, brushing away the liquid from his clothes. He didn't immediately realize who had done this to him, that it had been calculated.

But I saw in his body language the moment he connected the dots. His back grew rigid. His chest puffed out. He suddenly seemed larger.

". . . fucking problem?" Drake yelled.

The guy's response was to plow a shoulder into Drake's chest.

A collective gasp erupted from the crowd as Drake violently bumped into a woman at the slot machine on the other side, causing her to spill the bucket of change she had been clutching.

"Shit!" I uttered, and sprang forward.

Drake punched the guy in the face. The guy reeled backward, losing his footing, and as he fell, he grabbed at the Hispanic woman's flowing skirt, yanking it down to her knees as he landed on the floor.

A high-pitched scream erupted from her throat, and she simultaneously grabbed at her skirt and jumped backward.

She was embarrassed, not hurt.

Now the guy's friend got into the mix. He hooked his arm

around Drake's neck from behind. I jumped onto him, pulling at his dirty-blond hair. "Leave him alone!" I screamed.

My back was rammed backward against a slot machine—hard—knocking the air from my lungs. I tried to hang on, but an elbow to my solar plexus caused me to release my hold on the guy.

I heard Drake curse, and then the guy whose back I'd jumped on was doubling over in pain.

As I lay on the ground trying to catch my breath, I saw that the first guy was ready for more. But now, so was Kent, one of the friends Drake was now rooming with. He must have been nearby. The brawl seemed to last several minutes, but I'm sure it was less than sixty seconds before security ran into the room, quickly getting in the middle of Kent, Drake, and the two losers and subduing them.

I was still on the ground, taking it all in. Drake wrestled his arm free from the security guard holding him, and when the man protested, Drake snapped, "Let me help my girlfriend."

Girlfriend . . . It was amazing how the word lifted my spirits, even as a piercing pain stabbed at my ribs.

Drake stepped toward me and offered me his hand. I gripped it and he pulled me up.

"You okay?" he asked, looking me over.

I nodded. "Yeah."

"Sir." It was the security guard.

"What?" Drake snapped.

"You'll need to come with us."

"Why?" Drake asked, the expression on his face saying he wanted to strangle somebody.

"You need to come with us," the security guard reiterated. Firm. No room for questioning his authority.

I nodded at Drake, encouraging him to go ahead. I figured it was a formality. A report had to be filed about the incident. Then I faced the security guard. "Look, if you need me to be a witness, I saw what happened."

I wasn't sure if the security guard heard me and ignored me, or if he hadn't heard what I said. But I decided not to press the matter when I saw him take Drake by the arm and lead him toward the exit of the casino.

Other security personnel were leading the other men, including Kent, out the doors. I could see angry arms flailing and hear raised voices, but other than that the men didn't refuse to go.

"Are you okay?"

At the sound of the male voice, I turned. The man in a Sun-Seekers uniform who had been staring at me when I'd first entered the casino was now standing in front of me.

"Yeah," I said, a little curtly. I wasn't interested in engaging in conversation with him. "I'm fine."

"I'm not too sure about that." Angling my head to the right, I saw Jolene. Her eyes were focused on my abdomen.

I realized then that I had both hands on my upper abdomen. It was an unconscious gesture, but I suddenly realized just how much my rib cage hurt.

I lifted my blouse. My fair skin had a dark bruise.

"You should get that checked out," Jolene suggested.

"It's just a bruise," I protested.

"I would listen to your friend," the man said. His name tag read "Greg." "A nurse can examine you."

But his eyes said that *he* wanted to examine me.

"I'm fine," I reiterated. "It's just a bruise."

"What if you have a broken rib?" Jolene countered.

I said nothing. In one part of my brain, I acknowledged that she was right. But the other part of my brain was remembering my mother's fear, her insistence that I be careful because of what had happened to Ashley Hamilton.

I hadn't expected to encounter any problems. But the fight between Drake and those guys from the plane proved otherwise.

The cruise had gotten off to an unpleasant start.

I couldn't help wondering if it was going to get any worse.

Chapter Eleven

I STAYED IN the vicinity of the casino, guessing that Drake would show up there after he was released by security, to let me know what was going on. I figured in half an hour or forty-five minutes, the matter would be settled. Probably all men involved, regardless of who had started the fight, would be reprimanded and warned, but ultimately released. It wasn't like anyone was truly hurt. But when an hour came and went, I became really concerned.

"You really ought to go see medical," Jolene said.

At her comment, I realized I was still holding my rib cage. It hurt, but I had blocked the pain, hoping to see Drake.

"Seriously," Jolene continued. "What if you've got a cracked rib or something?"

"All right," I said. We had been waiting on the cushy chairs outside of the casino, passing most of the time talking about what had happened. "I guess I can go get checked out, then come back here."

"I'm sure Drake will find you. He'll let you know what happened."

I nodded. Obviously, Jolene's idea of fun wasn't to sit around waiting for Drake to show up.

She went with me in search of medical attention, where a nurse examined me and deduced that I had a bruised rib. She gave me Tylenol, an ice pack, and instructed me not to do any kind of physical exercise that would aggravate the area.

All I could think about when she was examining me was that every minute I spent with her was a minute I couldn't be looking for Drake.

An hour after I'd finished seeing medical, which was a good two hours after Drake had been taken by security, I still hadn't seen him or Kent. I went back to the casino area with Jolene, but fifteen minutes later, she suggested we walk the ship in search of Drake instead.

But after walking around for nearly half an hour, there was still no sign of Drake.

"He shouldn't be out there," Jolene said as we stood on the inside of a door that led to the pool deck. It was dark, and the only people on the deck right now were couples snuggling and kissing.

"No," I said. But I couldn't be one hundred percent sure.

"For all we know, he's back in his room," Jolene went on.

"You're probably right."

I was scanning the shapes on the lounge chairs, trying to see if any of the silhouettes looked like Drake. Not seeing him, I faced Jolene again. Saw that she was frowning.

I quickly threw my gaze toward the pool deck, thinking she must have spotted Drake. And then she spoke.

"Something's been bothering me," she said.

I faced her again. "What?"

"Those guys. The ones who were fighting with Drake. I don't know why, but they looked familiar."

My stomach fluttered. I knew she was on to something. "Yes," I agreed. "I thought the same thing when I saw them on the plane. That I knew them from somewhere."

"Where?" Jolene asked.

The memory tickled at my brain, light as a feather. But it wouldn't come to me. "I don't know."

"There you are!"

Jolene and I turned at the exact same time. Roxanne was rushing toward us.

I closely watched her interaction with Jolene. Earlier, she'd said some pretty unflattering things about someone I'd believed to be one of her best friends. Now I watched for any sign of tension. But Roxanne smiled brightly, and first hugged Jolene, then me.

"Where have you been?" she asked.

She was tipsy. Heck, she was probably three sheets to the wind.

Jolene glanced at me, and then gestured to say that I should go ahead.

So we all sat on the nearby chairs and I filled Roxanne in on what had happened in the casino and the fact that we hadn't seen Drake since, or the other guys.

"You don't think they've arrested them, do you?" I asked my friends.

"I can't imagine them arresting anyone for a fight," Roxanne said. "They've probably given everyone a talking-to and sent them on their way."

"Then where's Drake?" I asked. I didn't expect an answer. The question was rhetorical.

I was considering going to the ship's security office when Kent entered through the door that led to the pool deck. Immediately, I sprang to my feet and hurried toward him.

"God, Kent, what happened?"

He made a face. "A whole lot of bullshit. There was an 'incident' report," he explained. "And stern warnings to stay out of trouble or we'd be escorted off the ship immediately. I wanted to ask if they planned to stick us in one of those inflatable boats and make us paddle back to Miami." Kent chuckled mirthlessly. "It boiled down to them telling us to stay away from each other." He shrugged. "That was pretty much it."

"Where's Drake?"

Kent shrugged. "He was heading off to get a burger when we left. I went straight to the bar. I haven't seen him since."

"How long ago?"

"An hour, I guess."

An hour. And Drake hadn't come to find me.

I soon found out why.

Because when I went to the burger joint—the last place I had expected to find him and therefore hadn't searched it—I saw him.

And he was with that gorgeous Hispanic woman I'd seen him with earlier.

One minute, he's calling me his girlfriend. The next, he's hanging with that other woman.

I turned abruptly, needing to get away. And bumped right into Greg, the member of the cruise staff who'd been checking me out in the casino.

"Excuse me," I said, and made a move to sidestep him.

But he clearly didn't want me to walk away, because he matched my movements, blocking me.

He grinned at me. "Hello."

"Hi," I said, not meeting his eyes. I got the feeling he was interested in more than being cordial.

"I'm Greg," he said, sounding cheerful and professional. "Did you go see the nurse?"

I nodded. "Yeah, I did. I have a bruised rib, but I'll be fine. Now—"

"I'm one of the ship's Program Coordinators, so if you need anything, I'm here to help," Greg went on.

"Oh." I relaxed. In fact, I felt a bit silly for having been on edge. "Thank you."

"What's your name?"

"Didi," I replied. And then I looked back through the doors of the burger place, noticing that Drake and the other woman couldn't stop smiling at each other.

I wanted to puke.

"Who's the guy?"

My eyes flew to Greg's at the question.

"The one you've been staring at," he said by way of clarification.

It wasn't that I needed him to clarify anything. It was that I was surprised he had known I was staring at anyone.

Was it that obvious?

"Ex-boyfriend?" he supplied.

"No one," I lied. "Look, my friends are waiting for me." Which wasn't a lie. My instincts were telling me to get away from this guy. He seemed pleasant enough, but he was creeping me out for some reason.

This time when I tried to sidestep him, he let me pass. Relief washed over me.

Paranoia? Perhaps. And also likely some anxiety over everything that had happened today.

But I walked briskly away nonetheless, not daring to look back.

I found my room in only twenty minutes, which I considered miraculous. No doubt drunken people wandered the ship aimlessly at night, completely lost, unable to find their way to their cabins. I had a feeling people ended up sleeping on the deck or elsewhere because they couldn't locate their cabins and simply gave up. Heck, some probably passed out in the hallways.

I found Jolene in our room, getting dressed for a night in the disco. Roxanne had apparently gone to the karaoke session with Devon and Javen. I had a suspicion that Roxanne would end up in bed with both of them, just for the experience of sleeping with twins.

It was the least of my concerns. I was in a funk over Drake, and as Jolene applied makeup to her eyes, I couldn't help bitching about him and his new friend.

"Why would he call me his girlfriend in the casino, then be hanging with this other girl all evening?"

"For whatever reason, he's still not ready to get back together with you."

"If he sleeps with her . . ."

"Will it be over then?" Jolene asked. "Is that your breaking point? An affair?"

There was a sarcastic edge to her voice. Staring at her, I scowled. Her comment was meant to hit me below the belt—and it had. Because she knew about Drake's affair with Rachel, and the fact that I hadn't dumped him.

"What's with the bitch attitude?" I asked, knowing I sounded like a bitch myself.

"It's just . . ." Jolene began, and stopped.

"Just what?" I asked, a hint of a challenge in my voice.

"Just . . . you keep worrying about Drake. Searching for him. Thinking about how he is. And now, wondering if he's going to sleep with someone else. I bet he's not worrying about you."

A sharp pain seared my chest, and it had nothing to do with my bruised rib. "Thanks, Jolene," I quipped.

"What do you want me to say?" she asked. "That you wandering around the ship like a love-sick puppy is appealing? God, Didi. I had an abortion before winter break. I'm still having a hard time with that. Yeah, I know you're having a hard time right now, but you're not the only one with issues."

"I know that," I said, more harshly than I'd anticipated. "You've been through a hard time, too, but you're the one who—"

One of Jolene's eyebrows raised. "Who what? Who slept around and got pregnant? So I brought my pain on myself?"

Exactly. She'd made certain choices, and now had to deal

with the consequences of those choices. I hadn't done anything to bring on my current misery.

But I said, "At least the whole world doesn't know you had an abortion. Everyone thinks my boyfriend is a friggin' rapist."

"So it's a competition?" she asked angrily. "You have to be the one suffering more?"

"Don't be stupid," I snapped. And when I saw her crestfallen expression, I quickly apologized. "I'm sorry. God, why are we even fighting?"

Jolene's eyes flashed fire. Dropping her brush, she grabbed her purse and stormed toward the cabin door.

"Jolene," I said, keeping my voice calm. But she was out the door a moment later, slamming it shut.

I plopped my head down on my pillow. Now Jolene was mad at me.

That made strike two for shitty things that had happened on my vacation so far.

Fuck.

Chapter Twelve

I FELT LIKE SHIT all night. I didn't bother going out to the disco. Seeing Drake with his new friend would depress me even more.

Jolene didn't understand. She had never loved Scott the way I loved Drake. Seeing him with someone else, and knowing we might never work things out, was *killing* me.

About three in the morning the cabin door opened. My head was in that direction, so I cracked my eyes open. Saw Jolene. I promptly closed my eyes, pretending to be asleep.

Roxanne, I noted, did not return to the cabin all night.

She probably spent the night screwing those hot twins. I

felt a twinge of jealousy. Not because she'd had two hot guys, but because she was able to enjoy herself on this cruise. She wasn't experiencing life-altering heartbreak.

Shortly after seven, I decided to get up. I'd barely slept anyway, so I may as well head out and get some coffee. Nassau was our first port, and we had either arrived or would be arriving shortly.

Even after I had showered and dressed, Jolene didn't wake up. Or perhaps she had, but she was pretending, like I had during the night, to be asleep.

No matter. It was probably better this way. I wanted today to be a better day. Taking a morning stroll around the ship to reflect and center myself was a perfect idea.

But as I headed to the door, something caught my eye. There was a slip of paper on the ground.

I lifted the paper and unfolded it. A note was written in block letters.

YOU THINK YOU CAN TRUST YOUR FRIENDS.
I'VE GOT NEWS FOR YOU. YOU CAN'T.

Huh?

I read the note again. And again. But each time, it made no sense.

It hadn't been addressed to me. It hadn't been addressed to anyone. Had someone put the note under the wrong door? Or was it a silly prank?

The moment the thought came to me, I knew who was behind it.

Natalie.

Somehow she must have learned the room we were in and

slipped this note under the door. What the hell was her game plan?

Vowing to put Natalie out of my mind, I left the room. She had hurt me once. I wouldn't let her hurt me anymore.

I entered the first cafeteria I could find and promptly found an empty booth. The place was half occupied. At this hour, people were either sleeping in after partying late into the night, or opting to forgo breakfast and eat on the island.

The first order of business for me was coffee. I used to hate the stuff, but found that as I rushed to get papers done at school, I had come to like it. I'd gotten used to the good stuff. Like Starbucks, or Seattle's Best. The ship's coffee left a lot to be desired, but I hoped it would provide the caffeine jolt I needed.

I couldn't have been more surprised to see Drake enter the cafeteria—alone. At first, he didn't see me. He was on the opposite end from where I was, and took his time going through the buffet. With his plate piled high, he turned.

And then he saw me.

My heart accelerated. Again, I noted that things had truly changed between us. Never before would I have been so anxious at seeing Drake.

I feared he was going to avoid me, as he'd pretty much done since telling me we needed to take a break. But once he saw me, he started in my direction.

"Hey," he said softly, placing his plate down on the table. "What's up?"

"Nothing much." My heart was pounding furiously.

"Not eating?" he asked.

"Not yet. I wanted coffee first."

Drake nodded. He knew I could go for an hour or two without breakfast, as long as I had my coffee.

Drake sat across from me in the booth and began to devour his breakfast. Scrambled eggs. Bacon. Pancakes smothered in syrup. He could consume thousands of calories a day and maintain his great shape.

I wasn't sure what to say to him. The last thing I wanted to do was say the wrong thing and cause him to get up from the table. So I opted for small talk.

"Are you and the guys doing any excursions on the island?"

"We're just gonna hang around Atlantis," Drake said. "Chill."

"Yeah, I'll probably do the same."

A minute or so passed. I watched Drake eat. A part of me was desperate to ask him about the Hispanic girl. But I didn't want to act jealous, or give him a reason to get pissed off. In my heart, I felt that had he spent the night in bed with her, he wouldn't be up right now and in the cafeteria.

"Hey," Drake suddenly said, his voice soft and low, the kind of tone that made my body shiver with anticipation.

"Yes?" *This is it,* I thought. *He's finally gonna tell me he still loves me and can't live without me.*

"Have you gotten . . ." His voice trailed off, and his forehead furrowed, as though he wasn't sure if he should say what was on his mind.

"What?" I asked.

He glanced around the cafeteria before speaking. "Have you gotten any weird e-mails? Or phone calls?"

"What do you mean?"

"Before we came on this cruise." He shrugged. "I was just wondering if you got anything that seemed odd."

I frowned. "You mean about Natalie?" When he didn't answer, I went on. "Sure, there's been all kinds of crazy shit since she said what she said. Some of it has been downright vicious.

People have been nasty. Concerning you and concerning me. But it'll pass, Drake. And if it doesn't, well, in a matter of months, we're graduating. Screw Natalie. Screw everyone at Lan-U who wants to get a kick out of talking trash about us."

Drake glanced around the cafeteria again. I did the same—following his line of sight, and wondering what he was looking at.

"Have you seen those guys since last night?" I asked him.

"No. Thank God."

"What the hell is their problem?" I asked. "Are they pissed because of what happened on the plane?"

Drake didn't answer. He shoved a huge piece of pancake into his mouth. When he finished chewing, he said, "Everything sucks. One minute my life was great, now it sucks."

My first instinct was to tell him that my life was pretty sucky at the moment as well, but I remembered my fight with Jolene last night, her comment about me making our pain a competition. So I refrained from talking about myself, instead supporting Drake as he got his feelings off his chest. He hadn't really talked to me after the accusation, and I was glad he was finally opening up to me.

"No, Drake." Reaching across the table, I patted his arm. "Don't say that."

"It's true. What if this rape accusation follows me for the rest of my life? You think I'll ever play in the NBA with the reputation of being a rapist? Or get hired as an intern at a TV station?"

"No one believes Natalie," I said. "You can still have a career in the NBA, or in sportscasting. Whatever you want." If Drake's dream of playing professionally didn't pan out he hoped to work in television. I still wanted our dream—him involved in sports in some capacity, me working at a humanitarian organization.

"Yeah, right," he scoffed.

I looked at Drake, hesitating before I spoke. "You know I will always be there for you. No matter how tough things get, whatever you're going through, I'll be there for you."

"I don't even know if you believe me," he said quietly.

"I do," I said without hesitation. "Drake, you can't know how sorry I am for what I said. I was hurting, and I guess I wanted you to hurt, too. But not for a second do I believe what Natalie said. I wouldn't still love you if I did."

I stared at him, and he at me, my words hanging heavily in the air between us. I hoped that he would say what I was desperate to hear—that he still loved me—but he said nothing.

This time, I didn't just stroke his hand in support, but placed mine on his in a gesture of affection. "You supported me through . . . through that night." My throat constricted at the memory of that awful night nearly four years ago, months before we'd left for college. "There is no way I wouldn't be there for you now."

Drake held my gaze for a long moment, then he pulled his hand away. I tried not to read too much into the gesture, because he lifted his fork. But he didn't resume eating.

"About that," he began. He stopped. Sighed. "Sometimes I think that's the whole reason we're still together. That if not for—"

"*No,*" I said firmly. "I'm with you because I love you."

"But if that hadn't happened . . ." Drake's voice trailed off, leaving his statement incomplete. But what he didn't say I still heard loud and clear.

"That's not the only reason I love you," I stressed. "It's part of it, sure. But not the main reason."

Drake shrugged. "I'm not so sure anymore."

"Well, I am."

"You have no doubts at all?" he asked. "No doubts that if that night had never happened, we might have gone our separate ways already?"

Drake's words crushed me. Emotion clawed at my throat, and I had to fight not to cry.

"Come on," Drake said. "Don't tell me you've never considered that. Not even when you saw Chris?"

There was a note in his voice I couldn't identify when he said Chris's name, and I knew that part of his doubt had to do with having seen me with him at the airport. Maybe that's what his whole flirting-with-the-hot-chick routine had been about—a way to get back at me.

"No." I spoke quickly, without doubt. But the truth was, he was right. There were times when I had thought about just that. What happened that night nearly four years ago had bonded us—for more than one reason. We'd loved each other, yes; but we also shared a secret.

One we would take to our graves.

But after his affair with Rachel, I began to wonder about how strong our relationship was. Drake said Rachel had been a fling, meaningless. And I had ultimately forgiven him. We continued to be the super couple Lan-U had known us to be.

But secretly I had wondered. Wondered if we didn't have this secret between us, if I would have still forgiven him.

"Well, maybe it's something you should think about," Drake said quietly.

Tears filled my eyes. I had my doubts—that was normal—but I honestly could not even imagine my life without Drake.

In response to my tears, Drake moved over to my side of the booth and pulled me into an embrace. "It's not that I don't love you," he said softly. "It's just . . . sometimes I think we both need some time apart so we can heal. Put what happened behind us and then see if we still see each other in the same light."

"No," I said, shaking my head. "I already know."

And if Drake wasn't there for me, who would be?

Who would love me after what I had done?

Chapter Thirteen

I WASN'T SURPRISED when Jolene kept her distance from me that day. When I returned to the room, I found her gone, but Roxanne was there, as bubbly and happy as ever.

"You slept with them, didn't you?" I asked.

"Not them," Roxanne replied, a silly grin playing on her lips. "Devon."

"Oh."

Roxanne giggled. "You sound disappointed."

"No, no of course not." No point telling her I was convinced that she'd gotten her freak on. "But what about Rick?"

"We're not serious yet. And I think he's still got a thing for his ex, so . . ." She shrugged.

"Roxanne," I tsked, shaking my head. Then, "Was it good?"

"Girl, it was great!"

I let myself get caught up in Roxanne's adventure, living vicariously through her story. Lord knew I needed something to help get my mind off my own reality.

I had no clue where Jolene was when Roxanne and I left the ship and made our way to the famed Atlantis resort. And I told myself I didn't care. She had to understand what I was going through, that with the extra stress in my life, I wasn't quite myself.

The temperature was in the mid-seventies, and the sky was a clear, deep blue. Roxanne and I were planning to head to the beach at the Atlantis resort to lounge around even if we didn't end up in the water, but first we stopped to browse the shops at Marina Village, an outdoor village of stores en route to the Atlantis hotel. We window-shopped, perused the tables of goods in front of the stores, and strolled through the various boutiques—more to pass the time than because we were interested in buying anything. I did see some cute tote bags and crafts, and figured I would buy something for my parents when we headed back to the ship.

"This is really cute," I said, lifting a straw tote bag that had the image of a turtle embroidered on one side, and the words "Nassau, Bahamas" beneath it.

Roxanne approached me from a table a few feet away. She checked out the bag I was holding. "Yeah, cute," she agreed. And then, "Do you ever wonder? Ever wonder if he did it?"

My hands stilled on the bag. The question had come out of

left field. Though I knew what she had to be referring to, I asked, "Did what?"

"You know . . ." Roxanne shrugged. "Do you ever wonder if what Natalie said was true? That she was—"

"Stop," I said, holding up a hand. "Don't even repeat that vile allegation."

Roxanne strolled to the other side of the table as if she hadn't just tried to ruin the mood, picking up a black bag this time. She held the bag up, examined it. Then she asked, "So you never wonder?"

"No!" I couldn't help shouting the word. It was bad enough that the rest of the Lan-U students had judged my boyfriend. But to have my best friend thinking the worst about him, too?

I glanced around, anxiety making my pulse pound. No one was within earshot. Certainly no one we knew from Lancaster.

"I can't believe you would ask me that," I said.

"Natalie's pretty insistent about what happened."

"You *talked* to her?" I asked.

"I saw her last night," Roxanne explained. "In the disco."

"And you decided to talk to her about her ridiculous allegation?" I couldn't believe my ears. And I couldn't help remembering that note slipped under the door.

YOU THINK YOU CAN TRUST YOUR FRIENDS.
I'VE GOT NEWS FOR YOU. YOU CAN'T.

Was there something to those bizarre words?

"She came up to me," Roxanne explained. "She was trying to get away from some guy who was talking to her. Get this: She's got bigger breasts now."

"She got breast implants?"

"Yep. She was wearing a dress with a high neckline, but it was very clear that the boobs are definitely bigger."

"Where the hell did she get the money for that?" I asked.

Roxanne shrugged. "Who knows. But she's had a serious makeover. She actually looks good."

I didn't want to hear about how good Natalie now looked. I was pissed that Roxanne would spend any time indulging her delusion that my boyfriend would have ever been interested in touching her with a ten-foot pole.

"Well, whatever makeover she had, she's still the biggest loser on campus. She only wishes a guy like Drake would want to touch her."

"Okay," Roxanne said, her tone conciliatory. "I'm not saying he did. I . . . I just wondered, ya know? Sometimes we think we know a person, but—"

"*No buts,*" I interjected. "I know Drake."

Roxanne nodded. "You know him better than I do. I was just asking."

"I do know him," I said, stressing the words. "And Drake isn't the kind of guy to assault a woman like . . . like that. Not any woman," I amended.

Drake was honest and decent.

Honorable.

Roxanne didn't know Drake the way I did, and I would never tell her the one thing I knew would change her mind.

Roxanne had made the statement that we both had shared our deepest secrets with each other, and I hadn't corrected her. Yes, she'd told me the humiliating truth about her mother—that she had been convicted of DUI and was currently serving out a sentence in jail. But there was no way I could tell her my darkest secret.

"Oh my God," Roxanne suddenly uttered, looking behind me. "Talk about not knowing people."

I whirled around. The air left my lungs in a rush, as surely as it had when I'd been elbowed in the gut the day before.

Jolene was walking toward us.

With Natalie.

She didn't see us right away. And when she did, she halted. It didn't take a trained psychotherapist to see that she was trying to decide what to do.

Natalie quickly veered to the right. After a few beats, Jolene continued walking straight, in our direction.

I think she's sneaky. Roxanne's comment sounded in my mind.

Anger pumped through my blood, as hot as fire. What was Natalie trying to do? Plant seeds of doubt in my friends' minds about Drake?

"Since when were you and Natalie so chummy?" I demanded, marching toward Jolene.

"Didi—"

"Did you invite her on this cruise?"

"Of course not!"

"You're walking with her as if you're the best of friends," I went on.

"Calm down."

"I'm not going to calm down. That bitch turned my life inside out and now she's trying to turn you and Roxanne against me!"

Roxanne and Jolene shared a glance. I studied the both of them, wondering if there was some secret they were keeping from me.

Or had that been Natalie's plan? To put that note under the

door, hoping I was the one who found it, then befriend my friends in an attempt to make me paranoid?

"I was getting off the boat at the same time she was," Jolene explained. "She just . . . started talking to me."

"About Drake?" I asked.

"Eventually, yes. But—"

"And you had to walk with her, talk with her, listen to her bullshit!"

Jolene said nothing.

"I realize you're pissed with me, Jo, but do you have to turn against me?"

"You're jumping to conclusions."

"Like hell I am."

And then I stalked off.

I was livid. The two people in the world I would expect to spit in Natalie's face had *listened* to her spew crap about Drake. They were playing right into her plan. Clearly, she had come on this cruise as a way to cause more chaos in my life.

And to that end, she was succeeding.

I all but ran toward the Atlantis hotel.

"For God's sake, Didi . . . wait up."

Only when I'd rounded a curve in the marketplace did I stop. I didn't realize how fast I'd been walking until Roxanne caught up to me, her breathing ragged.

Mine was ragged, too, but not because I'd exerted myself. Suddenly, it seemed the rug was being pulled out from under me at every turn. I didn't know what to think anymore.

"What are you going to do—spend the day on the beach pissed off?" Roxanne asked. "Just calm down."

"Easy for you to say. Your life hasn't gone to hell."

Roxanne's chest rose and fell with a heavy breath. "We're here in paradise. Can't you just try to be happy? I mean, just because Natalie talks to any of us doesn't mean we believe her."

"Twenty minutes ago you were asking if I thought Drake did it."

"I know. And . . . and I shouldn't have. It's just . . ."

"Just what?"

"Nothing," Roxanne quickly said. "Just a dumb question."

I narrowed my eyes, not sure I believed her. But moments later, I decided I didn't care. I didn't want to talk about Drake with her or anyone else.

"Look," Roxanne began, "can we go to the beach and have a good time? Please?"

Several moments passed. And then I said, "Fine."

It was a beautiful day. I was in paradise. On the vacation I'd been looking forward to for two years.

It was time I tried to enjoy myself.

The Atlantis resort was absolutely stunning. The grounds spanned acres and were spectacular, with dazzling waterfalls, lush greenery, lagoons filled with marine life, and even a dolphin cove.

The Royal Towers were the focal point of the resort, and actually looked like five buildings fused together. The buildings ascended in height from the far left and right sides to the middle. A suspended archway connected the two tallest buildings. Magnificent was the only way to describe the peach-colored structure.

The shops at the Royal Towers consisted of high-end stores,

like Cartier, Gucci, Ferragamo, and more. Roxanne and I enjoyed window-shopping en route to the beach. Nothing like a bit of bling and designer clothing to get a girl into a better mood. I couldn't afford a single thing in any of the stores, but the jewelry and shoes were certainly nice to gawk at.

By the time we wound our way along the pathways to the beach, I was missing Jolene and feeling guilty for snapping at her. Roxanne had also spoken to Natalie, and I hadn't gotten so mad at her that we weren't talking.

We had all booked this trip together. We should all have been hanging out together.

I vowed to apologize if I saw her. But thus far, I hadn't seen her along the stretch of beach.

I did, however, see Drake again. And that girl I now thought of as *the other woman.* She and her friends had planted themselves close to Drake and his buddies. It was clear to me that she was after my man.

Thankfully, there was no sign of the two guys who had given Drake problems. I hoped our paths didn't cross again for the rest of the trip.

Roxanne and I chatted for a while, but at some point I must have drifted off, because I was jarred awake when I heard, "You bitch!"

My eyes popped open. Standing above me—her hands planted on her hips and an angry scowl on her face—was Jolene.

"Jo?" I said, confused by her wrath.

"*You* did this," she snapped.

Now I sat up. "Did what?"

"This," she said, jutting her iPhone forward. "The latest *gossip* from The Gossip Hour."

I glanced at Roxanne, whose expression said she was as confused as I was.

Then I looked at Jolene again. She was extending the phone toward me, almost like a dare.

I took it, shaded the screen so I could see better, and began to read.

And then my stomach sank.

Hot piece of gossip today, folks. Guess which female basketball star recently had an abortion? Dark skin, short hair. Just shy of six feet. You can figure it out. Not *that* shocking, I know. But how about the fact that she killed her baby because she didn't know who the daddy was?

"Oh my God," I uttered. There was no point saying that we couldn't be sure the rumor referred to her, because we both knew otherwise.

"How could you do this to me?"

I got to my feet. "I didn't, Jo. Honest to G—"

"Bullshit!" she snapped.

"Come here," I said, taking her by the arm and leading her several feet away where hopefully no one would hear us. As it was, we'd gotten the attention of those around us.

Tears spilled down Jolene's face. She was both devastated and livid.

"I never did this," I reiterated. "I promise you."

"Yes you did. You did it to get back at me because you're pissed that I was talking to Natalie!"

"How long have you known me, Jo? You know I would never hurt you like that. You took me into your confidence, and . . ."

My voice trailed off. I suddenly realized that I couldn't finish my sentence.

"And you told someone," Jolene surmised, picking up on what I hadn't said.

"I . . ." I swallowed. "I only told Roxanne."

"Nice. I told you not to tell her. Not to tell *anyone*!"

I glanced beyond Jolene to Roxanne, who was still sitting on her towel, but watching us curiously.

"I don't think she said anything. Certainly not to The Gossip Hour."

"No, I'm pretty sure you did that, since you're the one who can't be trusted." Jolene's eyes flashed fire. And then she began to weep uncontrollably.

I didn't know what to say. I *had* betrayed her confidence. But I was certain someone other than Roxanne had to be behind The Gossip Hour news. After all, Roxanne and I had been together all morning. When would she have had the chance to leak this news?

Besides, why would she?

"Never in my wildest dreams would I have thought you would do something so . . . so evil."

"I swear, Jo."

She shoved me. Hard. I stumbled backward, twisting my ankle as I fell onto the warm sand.

There was rage in Jolene's eyes as she stared down at me. Unadulterated rage.

And then she stalked off, leaving me sitting on the sand, feeling embarrassed and confused.

Chapter Fourteen

ONE DAY, and the trip had gone totally to hell.

Back at my beach towel, I explained to Roxanne what had happened, and I couldn't resist asking, "Did you say something? To anyone?"

"You think I leaked the story of Jolene's abortion to The Gossip Hour?"

"I'm not saying that," I said carefully. "But maybe you said something to someone . . . accidentally? Kind of like I did with you?"

"No. I didn't."

I frowned. "Then Jolene must have told someone else. Or

someone overheard us." I groaned. "Not that Jolene will believe me. Especially after she learned that I told you."

"She'll calm down," Roxanne said. "Give her time. She'll realize you wouldn't do something like that to hurt her."

Would she? I couldn't be sure. I'd never seen her so irate before.

I was in no mood to enjoy the sunshine, but stayed where I was on the beach. I wanted to go back to the ship and my room, but Jolene might have been there, and I knew that Roxanne was right. She needed time to realize the truth.

But I couldn't help wondering how her story had come to be on The Gossip Hour. And I couldn't help wondering if something more sinister was going on.

Hours later, we were back on the ship and heading toward Jamaica. I didn't return to the room, fearing another confrontation with Jolene if she was there. So I went to the upper deck for some alone time, found an empty lounge chair near a railing, and began to read the novel I'd brought with me.

But my mind couldn't retain a single word. The last thing I could do was escape into a good story when my dream trip had turned into a nightmare.

Lowering my book, I eased my body up. There was a jogging track several feet from the edge of the pool, and I was amazed that people were actually in running gear, getting some exercise. When I first saw the track, I thought it was a wasted addition to a luxury cruise liner that had gambling, several bars, a casino, and karaoke to occupy people's time. But there were clearly some die-hard fitness fanatics out there.

Standing, I walked to the nearby railing and looked out at

the ocean. For a long time I stared forward, thinking about how my reputation had gone to hell after that rumor on The Gossip Hour. Would the same thing happen to Jolene?

In the midst of my thoughts, a chill crept across my shoulder blades—and it had nothing to do with the breeze on deck.

Someone was watching me.

Knowing it with absolute certainty, I was almost afraid to look around. But I tried to be casual as I turned and glanced over my shoulder.

Panic gripped my body from head to toe. The two guys from the plane were standing near the hot tub about twenty feet away from me. Staring at me.

They didn't even look away.

I glanced around, doing a quick survey of how many people were near me. There were a good number of people milling about, some in one of the two hot tubs, and some frolicking in the pool. Certainly these guys wouldn't dare hurt me up here.

But I moved to my right nonetheless, scurrying in the opposite direction from where the guys were. When I got to the far end of the deck, I saw that they were still watching me. Not moving, just watching me.

I walked briskly, and when I got to a door that would lead me inside, I all but jumped in.

And then I ran.

I ran to the steps and charged down them, my breathing ragged from fear. When I reached the bottom of the stairs, I looked up to see if they were following me. I heard the sound of the door opening upstairs and started to sprint.

The first place I reached was the casino, and I quickly ducked inside. The fast-paced dinging of the bells on a slot machine matched the fast staccato beat of my heart.

I walked down the first aisle of slot machines and turned the corner, hoping to be out of view of those men if they showed up in here. I sat down at an available machine, but wondered if I should keep going to the far back of the casino and really stay out of sight.

But what could those guys do to me with all the people inside here? I should be able to dance on a black jack table and not encounter any problems. Surely they wouldn't be so stupid as to want to hurt me after the trouble they'd gotten into with the ship's security for their antics yesterday.

Nonetheless, I didn't want to chance seeing them again.

They scared me.

"Miss, are you using that machine?"

At the question, I looked up into the face of a man who appeared to be in his sixties. He held a large plastic bucket of change.

"No," I said, rising. "You can have it."

I began to stroll the casino floor, moving deeper inside, farther away from the door. The place was like a maze of tunnels, and I went from one to the next, fearing that I'd find my pursuers each time I rounded a corner at the end of a bank of slot machines.

What I needed was another place to sit down. And it would probably be best if I started to play.

Looking at the slot machines in front of me, I saw that they were all dollar machines, and I wasn't interested in playing a dollar a spin. So I continued to peruse the floor.

I heard the laugh before I saw her. And when I rounded yet

another bank of machines, I glanced to the area on my right. As I'd suspected, I *had* heard Roxanne's laugh. I could see her back as she sat on a stool at the edge of the slot machine one lane over.

Relief flooded me. I no longer felt alone and pursued. With Roxanne by my side, I would feel less vulnerable.

As I moved toward her, she laughed again, and I realized that she was with someone. Someone sitting in front of the slot machine who I couldn't see. Jolene?

No. She couldn't be with Jolene. Because Roxanne suddenly leaned forward and extended a hand as if touching someone's leg. Maybe she was with that Devon guy she had slept with.

As I reached her, rounding the edge of the slot machine where she was sitting, I saw the person she was hanging out with.

Drake.

In a nanosecond, I took it all in. The hand on Drake's knee. The low-cut shirt Roxanne was wearing that showed off her breasts. How she was leaning forward so Drake could see those breasts without impairment.

My head swam. I couldn't believe my eyes.

Drake's eyes connected with mine. Mid-giggle, Roxanne finally realized that someone was standing over her shoulder. She whipped her head around to look at me.

I saw the surprise register in her eyes, but a moment later, she plastered a smile on her face. "Hey, Didi. Did you get your relaxation time in?"

My eyes flitted between Roxanne and Drake as I desperately tried to assess the situation. Was something going on between them?

"Can I talk to you a minute?" I said to Roxanne. My tone was brusque.

Roxanne's eyes registered concern. "Sure." She turned to Drake. "Hey, you better win my money back."

My head was swimming. Anger was boiling inside of me. There was no way Roxanne could actually be making a play for my man . . . Could she?

I led the way, moving briskly, and Roxanne followed me. When we were well out of earshot of Drake, she asked, "What is it, Didi?"

"This way," I said, and then I turned and headed toward the casino exit. I didn't want to have spectators as I had it out with her.

I noticed Greg then, saw that he was staring at me. I felt a moment of alarm, but didn't break stride.

When I was outside the casino door with Roxanne, I whirled around to face her. "What are you doing with Drake?"

She laughed airily, as though trying to convey to me that there was nothing for me to be worked up about. Which meant she knew exactly why I was upset—and in my mind, that made her guilty.

"Just hanging out, having some fun."

"With *Drake*?"

She shot me a disbelieving look. "What? You think there's something going on with me and him?"

"Roxanne, you're *my* friend. I don't expect you to be flirting with Drake. Even if we are broken up, he's still off-limits."

Roxanne's lips tightened ever so slightly. "Obviously. Now, will you calm down and stop jumping to conclusions?"

Maybe I *was* jumping to conclusions. But I couldn't forget the note that had been slipped beneath my cabin door. Though it hadn't been specifically addressed to me, I felt that it had been left for my eyes.

YOU THINK YOU CAN TRUST YOUR FRIENDS.
I'VE GOT NEWS FOR YOU. YOU CAN'T.

"And did it ever occur to you that I might be talking to Drake about forgiving you?" Roxanne added, and now a smile played on her lips.

I eyed her warily.

"You're so suspicious," she said good-naturedly. "Sheesh."

"You were talking to Drake about forgiving me?" I was doubtful and hopeful at the same time.

"Uh huh." Roxanne grinned with pride. "You know I've got your back, girl."

"What did you say to him?"

"I told him he's got to see your side of things. Understand how hard this has been on you."

And just like that, I felt guilty. Guilty for doubting my friend. "Thanks, Roxy."

"Don't mention it," she said and winked. "By the way, why don't you go in there and talk to him?" She elbowed me playfully. "I think he might be ready to hear you out."

My heart began to beat fast. I never would have imagined that one day I would be nervous about talking to Drake, not after how close we'd been. "You think so?" I asked.

"Go." Roxanne gave me a little push. "You want him back, don't you? Go in there and tell him."

I nodded jerkily. Roxanne was right. If I still wanted Drake, I needed to go after him. What we'd had was real. After dating for five years, he *had* to still have feelings for me.

I smiled at Roxanne, both a thank-you and an apology. Then I went back into the casino and found Drake where I'd left him. His eyes flitted in my direction as I neared him, but then they went back to the slot machine, as if he was trying to pretend he hadn't seen me.

I sat on the seat beside him, the one Roxanne had vacated. "Hey," I said softly.

"Hey," he replied, then fed more money into the machine.

Several moments passed. I watched Drake lose several rounds before speaking. "Having any luck at this machine?"

"Not really."

The conversation was strained. How had we gotten to this place? Once, we had talked about everything with ease.

"Look," I began. "Can we talk? Maybe out on the deck where it's not so loud?"

Drake looked at me then, really looked at me. And I saw in his eyes the same sadness I knew mine held. We both needed to get over the issue already and move on.

" 'Kay." He pressed a button on the machine, and coins began to fill the steel bin. While I knew it was his money, the sound of the coins hitting the metal was intoxicating. I could see how people became addicted to gambling.

He scooped all the quarters into a bucket and stood, and I felt a little patter in my chest. I always did when I looked at him—even after five years.

Drake exchanged his coins for bills. Then I led the way toward the exit, seeing couples laughing and holding hands as they gambled and wishing that Drake and I were experiencing that at the moment. Hopefully by the end of the trip we would be.

I stepped through the casino doors, and almost instantly there was silence. Thank God. I was glad to escape all the noise.

I kept going and opened one of the nearby doors that led to the middle deck. The sea air wafted over me, a gentle breeze that was a little on the chilly side.

I went to the railing. Drake came up beside me. I wished for nothing more than for my man to put his arms around my waist and snuggle with me, for both of us to take in the romantic view.

I looked at him. He was staring off into the distance, a troubled expression on his face. I drew in a deep breath and spoke. "Drake."

Slowly, he faced me. "It's not that I don't love you," he said without preamble. "It's just—"

"That you need time."

"That I can't be sure you really trust me. I saw the look on your face when you saw Roxanne with me."

I couldn't deny that, but still, he had to understand how things had looked from my vantage point. "I do trust you."

"It's not just the trust issue," Drake said, but then he didn't complete his statement.

"What is it?"

Not looking at me, he sighed heavily.

"You don't love me anymore?" I asked, despite what he'd said a moment ago.

"I do love you," he replied, and sounded adamant.

Thank God, I thought. Then said, "If you love me—"

"It's not that simple."

"Why not?"

He looked conflicted, as though something serious was weighing him down. Not for the first time, I got the sense that there was something Drake wasn't telling me.

"Rachel's sister, Lydia, came to see me at Christmas."

At the mention of Rachel, I felt conflicting emotions. That irrational spurt of jealousy because he'd slept with her, but also sadness at her tragic death. Was this what had Drake on edge—Rachel's death?

"How's she doing?" I asked.

"Not well, under the circumstances. But she gave me an update on the coroner's findings."

"What'd she say?" I asked, suddenly anxious.

"The autopsy showed that Rachel had ingested a large amount of sleeping pills."

"Sleeping pills?" I paused briefly. "So they think she left the party, downed sleeping pills, began to drive, and drove off the road once the pills kicked in?"

Drake nodded. "Rachel's death has officially been classified a suicide."

There was a "but" to his statement. I could hear it in his voice. "But Lydia doesn't believe it," I said.

"No," Drake said. "No one ever believes a loved one will commit suicide, right?"

I was silent for a long moment as I thought about what Drake had told me. "Does it make sense to you that she would run off to her car to make a clean getaway, then stop to take sleeping pills? And did she have them in her car?"

"Obviously, she did. She was upset. But Lydia thinks the toxicology report is wrong. According to her, Rachel never even liked to take aspirin."

I was trying to read between the lines of what Drake was telling me. Did he believe there was something suspicious behind Rachel's death?

So I looked at him and point-blank asked him, "Do you think she was murdered?"

Chapter Fifteen

"MURDERED?" DRAKE ASKED, as if my question had come out of left field.

"Based on what Lydia told you—"

"Rachel obviously killed herself. I didn't think she'd do it, but—"

"But what if she didn't?" I interjected. "What if someone *gave* her those sleeping pills?"

"How?" Drake asked doubtfully.

"Perhaps in her drink," I answered.

"Why?"

"Because she knew something. Something that someone

wanted to keep quiet." I didn't know where this idea was coming from, but the idea had taken on a life of its own. Maybe deep down I had always believed there was something fishy about Rachel's untimely death.

"Did Rachel talk to you?"

"About what?"

"Did someone say something to you?"

My stomach tickled. Was I on to something? "About what, Drake?"

"You're the one who mentioned murder."

"I . . . I don't know why. It was just a feeling. Maybe she had proof about Seth's cruelty toward animals, proof that could get him arrest—"

"Didi, *stop*." Drake spoke firmly. "Now you're accusing Seth of *murder*?"

Was I?

"I know you don't like him," Drake went on, "but can you please stop throwing around accusations about Seth?"

"You're the one who mentioned what Lydia said about the sleeping pills."

"Because it means that Rachel killed herself," Drake said.

I stared at him, trying to study him. Did he truly believe that?

"Now you're jumping to conclusions and accusing someone of murder—and for what reason?" He gave me a long look, full of disappointment. Or something else?

"Please, babe," he continued. "Just stop. And whatever you do, don't go around telling people you think Seth is a murderer."

"I won't. I was only thinking out loud because of what Lydia—"

"Well, stop." Drake groaned with frustration. "Please."

"All right," I said, resigned to dropping the matter. Somehow we had gotten off track. I didn't want to fight anymore. Not about Seth. Not about Rachel. I just wanted things back to the way they were.

I stared at the sun dipping into the horizon. A beautiful, romantic view, and yet Drake and I were at odds.

"It kills me that we're both here and we're not together," I went on, my voice cracking. "It just kills me."

And then Drake did something that surprised me. He pulled me into his arms. And Lord, it felt so good.

"I want things back the way they were, too," he said softly. "And maybe we can get there. I hope we can."

It was the first promising thing he'd said to me in forever. "Can we hang out this evening?" I asked. "Just you and me, like we used to?"

At first, Drake didn't respond. Then he slowly nodded. "All right. But it will have to be later. I've got plans with the guys, and I don't want to blow them off. How about we meet at midnight? On the upper deck, by the pool?"

Midnight. A time for lovers. We would meet at midnight, then end up in his cabin making love . . .

"Midnight's perfect," I said. "See you then."

Drake went back inside through the door we had come through to stand at the ship's railing, and I watched him go. A few seconds later, he glanced at me through the glass and smiled. I waved.

Gazing out at the horizon once again, I felt more hopeful than I had in weeks.

Smiling, I walked to the left, my hand trailing along the length of the railing as I continued to stare out at the ocean. In the morning, we would be arriving in Jamaica—and the possibilities were endless.

I finally looked directly in front of me. And drew up short.

My heart slammed into my rib cage. Was I actually seeing what I thought I was seeing?

Natalie . . . with that creep from the plane?

Her back was to me, but I recognized the sleek ponytail and the clothes she'd been wearing earlier. The guy from the plane had a good few inches on her, and I could see his face as he looked at her.

I quickly ducked into the nearest door. After standing still for several seconds, not daring to breathe, I was certain the guy hadn't seen me. Natalie and the guy from the plane chatted, oblivious to the fact that they were being watched.

I crept forward, keeping my eyes on them, as though that alone would tell me what they were talking about. They were standing front-to-front at the ship's railing, about a foot apart.

Stopping to stand behind a large palm plant, I stared at them through the glass. What were they doing together? Was the guy simply trying to pick her up?

Or did they already know each other?

The thought made my entire body go tense. If they knew each other, then his being on the cruise . . . her being on the cruise . . .

"Oh my God," I uttered.

The man looked my way then, as if he'd heard me. His dark eyes connected with mine instantly. His lips moved, and then Natalie whirled her head in my direction.

I took off down the hallway, fear coursing through my veins

like liquid ice. I found a stairwell and raced down it, not stopping until I was two levels lower.

Opening the door, I sprang into the hallway. But I instantly remembered that Natalie had found my room to leave me that note, so heading to my room right now might not be the smartest thing.

I spun around to head back to the stairwell.

And ran smack into someone.

Chapter Sixteen

For a moment, I was stunned. One minute I'd been running. The next I came up against the wall of a human body.

In an instant, my eyes focused. I realized that Greg was standing before me. Holding me by my upper arms.

"Hey," he said, looking concerned. "What's going on?"

My fear intensified. Where had Greg come from? Had he been following me?

"H-how . . . w-what are you d-doing . . . ?" I could hardly get my words out. I was beyond flustered.

"I saw you running. I came to help."

I gasped in air. Found it hard to breathe.

"You don't look okay," Greg went on.

He seemed genuinely concerned, but I was wary of him.

I don't know why. It was his sudden appearance. The way he'd looked at me before that made me uneasy.

I shrugged out of his grasp. "Is that why you followed me?"

"Of course. I want to make sure the ship's patrons are safe."

"I'm . . . I'm okay."

"You look upset," he said, eyeing me warily.

"I'm fine," I lied, wondering if my heart would ever calm down.

"Okay," Greg said slowly, as if he didn't quite buy what I was saying. "I hope you're not unhappy that I followed you. You don't know how many people I've seen become upset about something who end up jumping overboard."

My eyebrows shot up. "What?"

"Suicide," Greg clarified.

I must have looked mortified, because he said, "It happens a lot, Didi. More than is ever reported. People get drunk on a cruise—they suddenly think they can fly. Or they become upset because their boyfriend is flirting with someone else. They make a rash decision to end it all the easy way—by jumping into the ocean."

Greg was giving me a pointed look. Was his last scenario describing me? Did he think I was jealous and distraught and capable of suicide?

"I'm fine," I insisted, and I forced a smile. I didn't want him thinking I was about to end it all by jumping into the ocean. "I'm just a little tired. I'm going to lie down."

Greg nodded. "Let me walk you to your room."

No. That was what I wanted to say. But he was a SunSeeker

employee. If I was scared, surely I could confide in him, let him help me.

"Sure," I told him.

Greg walked with me down the hallway, stopping with me as we reached my cabin. I slipped my key card into the lock and quickly opened the door. "Thanks," I said. "I'll be out later."

I got the feeling that Greg wanted to come into the room with me, but I didn't give him the chance. I quickly shut the door behind me and bolted the lock.

And then, for good measure, I dragged the chair from the desk and positioned it against the door's handle.

A feeling of unease settled over me. I stayed in the room, waiting for Roxanne or Jolene to arrive so I could tell them about Natalie and the guy from the plane. But three hours passed and neither had shown up.

Midnight was approaching, and the last thing I would do was miss my date with Drake. I would tell him about Natalie, about the guy from the plane, and warn him. I had the feeling we both needed to watch our backs where they were concerned.

I planned to stay in my cabin until shortly before midnight, but hunger got the better of me, and I ventured out around ten-thirty. The burger joint was fairly packed, mostly with twenty-somethings hanging out eating fries and greasy burgers. Nervous, I glanced around the establishment, but relaxed when I saw no one I considered a threat. A small group of Lan-U students was on the far side of the cafeteria. I recognized them, but didn't hang out with them at school. I was afraid they'd invite me to join them, given that I was a fellow student.

Thankfully they didn't notice me—I wasn't in the mood to be social.

I got myself a burger and fries and took a seat on the opposite side of the restaurant, knowing that to those around I must look like a loner. Let them think what they wanted. At my table, I sat so that I could face the entrance and see whoever was entering.

Paranoid? Maybe. But I couldn't shake my feeling of anxiety.

I was still trying to make sense of what I'd seen—Natalie and that guy from the plane. Had the guy seen Natalie for the first time on this trip? Was he being a typical guy and making a play for a woman he found attractive?

Or did they know each other from before? Was there a nefarious reason for them being on this cruise?

If they *had* come to cause trouble, how stupid could they be? Natalie could easily be identified, as could the guys who'd gotten into the fight with Drake.

Maybe Natalie's goal was simply to make me sweat.

The burger and fries quelled my hunger, but I was too fretful to enjoy the food. As eleven-thirty rolled around and I saw no further sign of Natalie or the guys from the plane, I began to feel marginally better.

Paranoia had to be getting the better of me.

I'd had the foresight to bring a novel with me, so I spent the next twenty-five minutes reading. Like before, I found I wasn't truly retaining what I'd read, but it was a way to pass the time until midnight.

For the umpteenth time, I glanced at my watch. Finally, it was eleven fifty-five. I closed my novel, got up, slipped my key card into the back pocket of my jeans, and started out of the restaurant.

Then I made my way to the upper deck, my stomach fluttering with nerves.

The deck was dark. Not pitch black, thanks to a couple of lights around the pool area, but it was still a little too dark for comfort. Shadows seemed to be dancing all around me, creating a sense of eeriness, not romance. But I was certain that once Drake arrived and took me in his arms, I would feel differently. Then, I would embrace the darkness.

Absolutely no one was on the deck. Without the warmth of the sun, it was actually quite cold. I hugged my torso, aware that the chill was only partly because of the climate.

It was also because of fear.

It was being out on the deck all alone, in the darkness. Where was Drake?

Three minutes passed with no sign of anyone. I walked across the width of the deck, checking one side of the ship, then the other. I was certain Drake had said to meet right here, but it was possible he'd forgotten the exact spot.

My wandering proved fruitless. Drake wasn't on either side of the pool. I pulled my cell phone out of my jeans' pocket and checked the time. Twelve-eleven. Certainly Drake should have been here by now.

He's coming, I told myself. *He has to be.*

I wandered to the ship's railing on the side where I expected Drake to show up. Staring out into the darkness, I was struck by the vastness of the ocean. It was more profound at night than it was in the day. For the first time, I thought of how truly small one person was in the context of the huge world.

Hearing a sound, I spun around. I didn't immediately see anyone. But I *knew* a door had just opened.

And that's when I saw the shadow. The form of someone on the left side of the boat walking toward me.

"Drake?" I called.

No response. But as the person got closer, a chill kissed the back of my neck.

I recognized the silhouette. And it wasn't Drake.

It was Greg.

Swallowing hard, I contemplated trying to make a quick getaway. He knew I was here—no doubt about it. The question was whether or not he had seen me come out here earlier. Had he seen me, watched me from inside the ship, waiting to see if someone was going to join me?

Again, I couldn't help wondering if he was following me.

Every cell in my body screamed, *Run!* But my brain told me not to show fear, and running would tell Greg that I was afraid. So I stood, paralyzed. I was alone on deck with a man who gave me the heebie-jeebies. And after what he'd told me earlier about people falling and jumping overboard, I was even more creeped out.

"Didi," Greg said. His face became illuminated as he stepped under a light.

"Hey," I said, hoping to sound casual. But an alarm was sounding in my brain. One that said I should get away from Greg as quickly as possible.

"What are you doing out here?" he asked as he came to stand beside me at the railing. "All alone?"

"I'm . . . I'm waiting for someone."

"Maybe for me," he said, and chuckled.

I forced a smile, one I hoped conveyed to him no unease

whatsoever. "My boyfriend—he's supposed to meet me out here."

Greg looked around, almost making a show of doing so, bringing home the point that we were the only two people out here.

"I'm sure he'll be here any minute," I went on.

"The guy you were talking to in the casino?"

I don't know why, but it bothered me that he knew. Bothered me because I got the sense he'd deliberately been watching me.

"Yeah," I answered.

"You sure he's your boyfriend?"

"Excuse me?"

"It's just . . . I've seen him with so many other women on this ship. And in the casino, I could have sworn he was dating that girl with the long, curly hair. I saw them about twenty minutes ago."

"You did?" I asked.

"At the disco. And they seemed very . . . close."

My stomach tightened. Was Drake planning to show up? Or was he so preoccupied with that damn girl he'd been hanging with that he had completely forgotten about me?

"No." I shook my head, not wanting to believe it. "He was supposed to meet me. Right here at midnight."

"Well, he's not here," Greg said, stating the obvious.

I turned around, toward the railing, feeling ill. After the chat I'd had with Drake earlier, could he truly have forgotten our planned meeting?

When I felt Greg's fingers stroke my neck, I lurched forward in shock, then whirled around, my eyes bulging.

"Shhh," he cooed, and reached for my face. "Just relax."

"What are you doing?"

"You're beautiful."

I stepped backward hastily. But he advanced, slipping an arm around my waist and pulling me against him. And the next thing I knew, his lips were on mine, his tongue slipping into my mouth.

I was too stunned to react.

Too afraid.

A sound suddenly registered in my brain. Had someone just come onto the deck?

I pushed against Greg, freeing myself, and darted my gaze toward the door leading inside. It was slowly closing, but no one had come out onto the deck.

Drake. Panic clawed at my throat. Drake must have come outside, seen me in Greg's arms, and quickly taken off.

"Forget him," Greg said, moving toward me once again. "He's not even thinking about you."

I glared at Greg. "Don't you touch me!" I pointed a warning finger at him. "Stay away from me or I'll report you to the captain for harassing me."

My threat had gotten through to Greg, because he stood where he was. Thank God. Obviously, he didn't want to get in trouble for making unwanted sexual advances.

Slowly, I took a few steps away from him, wanting to make sure he wasn't going to come after me. Convinced that he wasn't going to follow me, I sprinted toward the door, fearing Drake had seen what had happened and had misconstrued the truth.

I had to find him.

Chapter Seventeen

I COULDN'T find Drake.

A search of the casino, the disco, and the various bars on the ship proved futile. My calls to his room went unanswered.

Defeated, I went back to my room after an hour and a half of searching. A part of me felt stupid. I was wasting time searching for Drake, holding on to the illusion that we would get back together. I was supposed to be having fun, but instead I was completely miserable.

I'd seen Jolene and Roxanne dancing up a storm on the dance floor. Unlike me, they were having a great time. I should have joined them—and almost did. Until I spotted Greg on the dance floor as well. I didn't want to be anywhere near that creep. Thankfully, he'd been too involved with a striking redhead to notice me.

As I plopped myself down on my bed, Greg's words haunted me. *I could have sworn he was dating that girl with the long, curly hair. I saw them about twenty minutes ago. They seemed very . . . close.*

Was Greg right? Was Drake with that girl right now? In her bedroom? Making love to her? Doing things to her that I liked him to do to me?

He can't be, I told myself. But I was no longer sure.

I wanted to go back out, search the ship for Drake again.

But I didn't, because I was afraid of what I might find.

Him in the arms of that other woman.

I slept fitfully. By the time the first beams of sunlight began to spill through the cabin's circular window, I was wide awake.

Glancing at the clock, I saw that it was just after six-thirty. We'd be arriving in Jamaica soon.

Before this trip, I had been so excited about this particular destination. And yet I almost didn't want to get out of bed. Didn't want to get off the ship. Didn't want to head into the port at Ocho Rios and explore any of the island.

What was the point, when Drake wouldn't be with me?

Drake and that other woman . . . All night, I had imagined what he might have been doing with her. Had she worked her own brand of magic on him that would have him never coming back to me?

And if he had betrayed me with someone else, did I want him back?

You have no doubts at all? No doubts that if that night had never happened, we might have gone our separate ways already?

Remembering Drake's questions had me instantly anxious. Maybe he'd been trying to tell me that he didn't want a relationship with me anymore. He had tried to let me down gently, but I wouldn't listen.

Suddenly, I wanted to know. Needed to know if Drake had spent the night with another woman.

Because if he *had* spent the night with that beautiful Hispanic woman, then our relationship was over. I had been holding on to the hope that we would repair our relationship and come out stronger than ever before. But if it wasn't to be, then I may as well learn the truth now. And accept it, no matter how hard it would be.

Roxanne and Jolene were both still sleeping when I left the room shortly after seven. My hope was that I would find Drake in the cafeteria as I had the morning before.

The cafeteria was again sparsely populated.

I didn't see Drake, but I did see Kent and Reid, his roommates. Sitting at a table in the middle of the cafeteria, they both had plates with heaping mounds of scrambled eggs, bacon, and toast.

As I approached the table, Kent saw me. He smiled as he met my gaze. "Hey, Didi."

"Hey," I replied in greeting, nodding at both Kent and Reid. "Where's Drake at?" I asked, getting to the point. "Sleeping?"

Kent's eyes narrowed slightly. "Why are you asking us?" he asked with a chuckle.

My stomach sank. Oh God. If they didn't know where he was, that meant he was with that woman.

"I thought you might have seen him recently," I said, trying to be nonchalant.

"We got up early," Reid explained. "About an hour ago. Hit the gym, then the track. Drake might have returned to the room after we left."

Returned to the room . . . I felt ill. "When was the last time you saw him?" I asked.

"What's with the tight leash?" Kent asked, chuckling.

"Leash?" I echoed.

"You spent all night with him," Kent went on. "He's probably getting some rest before we head onto the island."

I stared at Kent, confused. "I . . . I didn't spend the night with him."

Now Kent was the one who looked confused. "The last time I saw Drake, he said he was heading to meet you. Probably around eleven forty-five last night."

Dumbfounded, I stared at Kent for a long moment, a myriad of thoughts running through my mind. I heard what he was saying, and yet I didn't understand.

"He was heading to see me?"

"You never hooked up last night?" Kent asked.

I shook my head. "I went to meet him on deck as planned, but he never showed up."

"When he left the casino, he said he was heading to meet you." Kent looked at Reid. "Right, Reid?"

Reid nodded. "That's what he said. We were trying to get him to go to the disco, but he wasn't having it."

Greg told me that he'd seen Drake in the disco with that Hispanic girl close to midnight. Had Greg been lying?

My stomach was in knots, but I wasn't sure why. On one hand, I was happy to learn that Drake had gone to meet me after all. He hadn't stood me up. But it meant that what I feared had likely happened. Drake had come onto the deck at the same moment that Greg was harassing me, and he'd gotten the wrong impression about what was going on. Had he ended up in bed with that beautiful Hispanic girl as a way to get even with me?

"Oh God," I muttered.

"Hey, don't worry," Kent said. "I'm sure he'll turn up. Probably spent the night with Michael in his cabin. Or with another one of the guys. No big deal."

Kent was trying to reassure me as though he thought I was a jealous girlfriend. There was a time in my relationship with Drake where there would have been no need to make excuses for him.

But that had all changed.

"He might have decided to lay low because of that guy," Reid offered. "The one from the plane who he got into the fight with."

I hadn't considered that. Suddenly, my heart filled with hope. Maybe Drake was trying to avoid that guy. Who knew if the guy had followed Drake to the deck last night, or gotten into an altercation with him somewhere else. Maybe Drake had opted for safety as opposed to conflict.

"Yeah, you're probably right." My relief was like a living, breathing thing. "That must be what happened."

"What are you going to do?" Roxanne asked.

It was shortly after eight-thirty, and I was standing with Roxanne at the side of the ship's walkway, watching to see if

Drake disembarked. Jolene, still pissed with me, had already headed off the ship with some other Lan-U students. I tried not to let it bother me, as my bigger concern was Drake. Among the hundreds of people filing off the ship, I had yet to see him.

"I . . ." My voice trailed off. "Wait a little longer, I guess."

A little longer turned into another half an hour, by which time most people had left the ship. Only a few people were trickling out.

"Maybe we missed him," Roxanne said.

I frowned. I didn't know what to say, what to do. But I had an odd feeling. The feeling that something was wrong. "It's like I've seen absolutely everyone *but* Drake."

Roxanne sighed, and there was something in her tone that I didn't like. I met her gaze.

"What?" I asked.

"Nothing."

"No, what were you going to say?"

"You said you think Drake saw you on deck with Greg. I'm betting you're right. Don't you think he found the first available woman to drown his sorrows with?"

I scowled at her. "You were the one telling me to work it out with him."

"Yeah, but if he saw you with Greg . . . He's a guy, Dee. Where do you think he is right now?"

I didn't want to answer that question. Because my suspicion was that Roxanne was right.

For some reason, I looked to the left. And spotted Greg. Was I mistaken, or was he glaring at me?

"Come on," I said, suddenly grabbing Roxanne by the elbow.

"You don't want to wait anymore?"

"No." I started to walk with her. "I'll catch up with Drake sooner or later."

Roxanne looked over her shoulder. And then she halted. "That's Greg."

"I know. That's why—"

Roxanne pulled her arm from my grasp. "I'm gonna go talk to him."

"No. Don't."

"After what you said he did to you last night . . ." Roxanne shook her head. "Someone's gotta tell him to go to hell."

"Leave it alone, Roxy."

But she marched off toward Greg despite my protest, and I buried my face in my hands.

Moments later, I looked in their direction. Greg stood where he was, about a hundred feet away, as Roxanne marched toward him.

I heard raised voices, saw her hands flailing. And soon after it had started, Roxanne was whirling around on her heel and marching back toward me.

My gaze connected with Greg's. He looked pissed.

"Damn it, Roxy. You should have left well enough alone."

"No way. Someone messes with my friends, they don't get away with it." She smiled sweetly, then looped her arm through mine. "We're in Jamaica, mon. Let's go have some fun."

Chapter Eighteen

DRAKE AND I had planned to go to Dunn's River Falls, along with a group of students from Lan-U. I had hoped for a day of romance and fun. The romance part was shot to hell, but I could still have fun with Roxanne.

The jury was out on when Jolene would be ready to talk to me again . . . or if she ever would be.

"Jolene hates me, doesn't she?" Roxanne and I were sitting in the back of a taxi that was about to leave the port and take us to Dunn's River Falls.

"Don't worry," Roxanne said softly. "Jolene will come around."

"I guess," I said. She couldn't very well never see me again.

Sooner or later she'd see the truth—that I would never hurt her by leaking her news to The Gossip Hour.

"This is Jamaica!" Roxanne went on. "Look at that landscape. The mountains, all that greenery. It's beautiful here."

I nodded, but my heart wasn't in it. It was the last day of the year, and I didn't want to think that the clock would strike midnight without me reconciling with Drake. That a new year would dawn without my man back in my life.

I had been looking forward to this trip for a long time, and on so many levels it had gone horribly wrong.

And it wasn't just Drake's likely involvement with that other woman.

"Remember that guy who fought with Drake the first night—the one who I told you was on the plane with us?"

"Yeah."

"Have you seen him with Natalie by any chance?"

Roxanne shook her head. "No. Why?"

"I saw Natalie with that guy last night, on deck."

"And?"

"And . . . I don't know if she just met him on this cruise, or if they knew each other from before."

Roxanne made a face. "You think they know each other?"

"I don't know. But what if they do? What if that explains why Natalie is on this cruise?"

"You mean payback?"

"Maybe," I whispered.

The taxi driver slowed, then turned left. Moments later, we were at the entrance to Dunn's River Falls.

We'd had the option of climbing the falls with a tour guide. Online, I'd seen the photos of people holding hands as they ascended the six-hundred-foot-high waterfall. But doing it on our own, Roxanne and I could take as much time as we wanted.

Before we could climb the falls, we had to descend a winding path lined with lush foliage and tropical trees in order to get to the beach. The stretch of pristine beach and turquoise water was postcard picturesque. To the left of the path we'd descended, there was a small inlet of shallow water where the base of the waterfall was. I couldn't help thinking of Drake, wishing that he was here with me to experience this.

"Hey, look who it is!"

At Roxanne's exclamation, I looked at her. Saw that she was pointing in the direction of the beach. I followed her finger.

And then I saw them. Devon and Javen. Rising from the water, they waved to us in unison.

"Shit," I mumbled.

"Nuh uh. You're not going to be antisocial today."

Devon and Javen were making their way toward us. Roxanne skipped toward the edge of the water, clearly elated to see Devon.

I watched them share a hot kiss. In my peripheral vision, I saw Javen approaching me.

"Hey." His grin was warm. Inviting. "You two gonna climb the falls?"

"That's why we're here," I said flippantly.

If Javen noticed my tone, he ignored it. "Let's all climb together."

I glanced at Roxanne, who had her arm around Devon's waist. The two were laughing like teenagers in love.

It was obvious we were now going to be a foursome. So I faced Javen and said, "Why not?"

. . .

We began our climb on the left side of the waterfall, where large stones formed a sort of natural staircase. Gazing upward, I could see people frolicking in what appeared to be shallow pools of water formed by the rocks within the falls.

We arrived at the first such shallow pool, about ten feet wide by five feet. I instantly bent my knees, submerging myself into the cool, fresh water.

"Take a photo of us?" Roxanne asked Devon. She passed him her waterproof camera, then moved beside me. I stood, posed with her, and Devon snapped a photo.

We continued upward. We arrived at another landing, this one much larger than the first one. It was around forty feet wide, with people swimming in the natural pool. Roxanne squealed, and I saw that Devon had pulled her into the water with him.

When I felt the cold water splash against my back, I whirled around. Javen, grinning at me, splashed me again. And I made my decision in that moment to let go and have a good time. So I splashed him back, but it was harder than I'd intended, because I got him with a full face of water.

"Oh, it's like that, is it?" he asked.

Javen lunged for me, and I screamed and tried to escape him. But he slipped an arm around my waist, preventing me from getting away.

He pulled me against him, my back pressing against his slick chest. And then he was turning me in his arms, and suddenly we were staring at each other, both of our breathing ragged.

And then he planted his lips on mine.

He kissed me, and I let him. Partly because I was angry with Drake. Partly because I needed a distraction. And partly because it felt good.

He knew how to use his lips and tongue, and for those moments when his lips were on mine, I forgot everything else.

Javen was the one to pull away, and when he did, he was smiling at me the way a guy does when he thinks there's the possibility of a relationship blossoming.

Sobering, I looked away. "Javen—"

"I like you," he said. "I really do."

I felt guilty. Javen honestly seemed sweet, but I couldn't lead him on. Emotionally, I couldn't let myself explore a relationship with him. Not even a fling.

"And I like you," I said softly. "Which is why I don't want to lead you on. I'm . . . I've just broken up with someone." Getting those words out was like trying to swallow a rock. Difficult and painful. "And I—"

"I get it," he said, his tone saying he was totally cool. "But nothing wrong with being friends, right?"

"No." I offered him a smile, almost wishing he'd get pissed with me for rebuffing him. He truly seemed like a nice guy and I almost felt stupid for being hung up on Drake, especially if he was off somewhere with that Hispanic hottie. "Nothing wrong with being friends."

Hours later, when we set sail from Jamaica, I sat on a deck of the ship overlooking the island. Roxanne and Devon had taken off, and I was given strict instructions not to go to the room. She did allow me to get a few things first, so I picked up the novel I had barely been able to read.

I was pissed with Drake, but feeling marginally better. Javen's interest in me had helped remind me that I was desirable, and had gone a long way in helping brighten my mood. So much so that I was able to lose myself in the world of the hot romance novel I was reading.

I'm not sure how much time passed when I looked up from the pages of my novel. But when I did, I noticed the mane of long, curly black hair instantly. And knew to whom it belonged.

Lowering my book, I stared at the woman I was certain had spent the better part of last night and today with Drake.

She was with the friend I had seen her with before, and the two were laughing as they stood at the railing, chatting about something.

And though I'd told myself that I was going to forget about Drake for the rest of the trip, I couldn't help looking around to see if he was within the vicinity.

He was nowhere.

Was he finally back in his room, resting after exhausting himself with this other woman? It still burned me how much she resembled Rachel, made me wonder if he had lied to me about his feelings for her after their fling.

At least if he wasn't with her, I could finally confront him. I found myself getting up. Heading to cabin 4889. When I got there, I halted, listening for any sound inside.

I heard none.

Knowing he might be sleeping, I raised my hand and rapped on the door nonetheless. We didn't have to get back together, but I wanted to have it out with him.

Call it closure. Call it pathetic. But I needed to hear him say that our relationship was over.

Several seconds passed, and no answer. I knocked again,

and more seconds passed with no answer. I heard no shuffling inside, no sound of anything to indicate that he was in there.

Where the hell is he?

And suddenly, I thought of Natalie. And those guys from the plane. I had seen neither of them today.

An uneasy feeling settled over me.

Something's happened. It was like someone whispered the words in my ear.

My chest tightened.

I pounded on the door this time, but again, no one answered. Someone opened the door across the hallway and stared in my direction.

I quickly walked off down the hallway. "Check the ship," I found myself saying. "Check it one more time."

So I did. I went on every single level, checking the casino, every bar, every restaurant, every casual eatery. Some people stared at me curiously as I strode by with purpose, peeking my head around every corner. Clearly, people were wondering what I was up to.

This time, when I saw no sign of Drake anywhere, the feeling in the pit of my stomach told me that there was a reason for it.

A reason I didn't want to contemplate in my wildest dreams.

Chapter Nineteen

ON MY SEARCH of the ship, I'd seen Kent and Reid hanging out with a couple of women in one of the bars. On a mission now, I started back there. I had to find out if they had seen Drake. If they had seen him, then I could put to rest the horrific suspicion rolling through my mind.

But as I was jogging up the stairs to the upper level, Jolene was heading down. I halted, and so did she. Several seconds of awkward silence ensued, both of us staring but not saying a word.

I was the one to break the silence. "Jolene, I—"

"I have something to tell you," she said, cutting me off.

Her tone had a serious edge. Apprehension emanated from her eyes. Both put me on guard. "Okay."

"Those guys who started the fight with Drake. I've seen them before."

"What?"

"Remember I said they looked familiar?" she asked.

"Yes. I told you the same thing."

"I swear, I feel like I've seen them at Lan-U. Maybe one night when we were out at The Goose Egg?"

The words niggled at my memory. I couldn't exactly place where I had seen them before, but the idea that it had been at Lancaster clicked. At the bar we liked to frequent?

Yes. The word sounded in my brain. Jolene was right.

"It just came to me. I don't know how I even remembered. It's just . . . the one guy, the one who dumped his drink on Drake? I saw him this morning when we were leaving the ship. Made eye contact with him. And I felt . . . I swear to God, I felt a chill. And I felt it the first time I looked at him, that night at the bar. That's what made me remember who he was."

My chest had constricted. I found it hard to inhale.

"I saw Natalie talking to one of them," I managed to say. "The one who spilled his drink on Drake." I sucked in a ragged breath. "Oh shit. It wasn't a coincidence."

"I saw Natalie with both of them," Jolene said. When my eyes widened, she continued. "Yesterday morning when I was eating breakfast."

"Before we got off the ship?" I asked for clarification.

"Mmm hmm."

"But you never said anything."

"Because you got pissed when you saw me with her and

walked away from me. You never let me tell you what I was talking to her about."

"You said she was talking trash about Drake."

"Yes, but I didn't care what she had to say about him. I wanted to find out what was up with her and those guys. At the time, I didn't recognize them, but I knew they'd started that fight with Drake. So after I saw her sitting at a table with them eating breakfast, I had to confront her."

"What did she say?" I asked, my voice merely a rasp.

"She said she didn't know those guys, that they just sat at the table with her because they wanted to hit on her. I believed her, so I didn't press the matter. Especially once you got mad at me. But now that I'm sure I saw those guys at Lan-U . . ."

"Natalie knew them before we got here," I concluded. Those guys weren't Lan-U students. I knew that much. Their being at The Goose Egg wasn't a coincidence. Nor, I was sure, was their being on this cruise.

And shit, they'd been on the plane with me and Drake.

None of it was coincidence.

Nausea swirled inside of me.

They'd been scoping Drake out for weeks. Maybe even me.

And if that was the case . . .

"Have you seen Drake?" I asked, my voice tinged with dread.

"No." Jolene's eyes narrowed with concern.

"When was the last time you saw him?"

Jolene shook her head. "Um, not since yesterday. Some time in the evening, I think."

"Oh my God," I uttered. I doubled over as pain pierced my belly.

Jolene rushed to my side. "What, Dee?"

I couldn't speak. All I could think about was the unfathomable thought that had entered my mind earlier.

Drake had been missing all day . . .

Was he alive and well and somewhere on the ship? Or had he met with foul play?

Jolene went upstairs to the bar with me where Kent and Reid confirmed that they hadn't seen Drake since last night. They hadn't run into him on the island, and hadn't seen him in the room. In fact, they didn't think his belongings had been touched.

My head was swirling. So was my stomach. I rushed out of the bar and went to the ship's railing, gripping it tightly as I stared out at the ocean.

Jolene came to stand beside me, saying, "I'm sure he's somewhere."

"Where?" I asked. My gaze was riveted on the dark, infinite ocean. Drake couldn't be lost out there, could he?

"Well . . ."

I looked at my friend. "Trust me, Jolene, if Drake is locked in a room with some other woman, I'll be relieved. Better that than the alternative."

"I'm just saying, don't freak out. Yeah, I agree that it's freaky Natalie and those guys are here on the cruise, but maybe she was dating one of them and that's why they were at Lan-U."

"And that's why they were on the same plane as me and Drake?" I asked skeptically.

Jolene's lips parted, but she didn't speak. I knew she didn't have an answer for that.

"I'm just saying," she finally said, "we can't jump to conclusions."

"For two months, Natalie's been saying that Drake raped her. Now she's here, and she's with two guys who made sure to pick a fight with Drake. And suddenly he's nowhere to be found."

I closed my eyes tightly. The argument I was making supported the very idea I didn't want to believe.

"We'll find him," Jolene said.

"I hope so," I said, staring out at an ocean that could swallow a person whole and leave no evidence. "I really, really hope so."

I tried, for the sake of my sanity, to believe Jolene was right. That we would find Drake by the time the evening was over. Perhaps I would share my crazy theory with him and we'd laugh about it. Or perhaps I would keep my paranoid delusions to myself.

"Let's split up," Jolene suggested. "You search one side of the ship, I'll search the other, and we'll meet right here in one hour."

It was a smart idea, and I agreed. It was entirely possible that Drake and I were simply missing each other. If Jolene and I split up, we'd have a better chance of running into him.

"What about Roxanne?" Jolene asked before we parted. "Should we get her involved? Or even Drake's friends?"

I contemplated the idea for a moment, then dismissed it

with a shake of my head. With it being New Year's Eve, I didn't want to disturb Roxanne's special celebration with Devon. As for Drake's friends, I would involve them later if tonight's search proved fruitless. For now, I didn't want them thinking I was overreacting. Or worse—an untrusting girlfriend.

"If we run into Roxanne, fine," I said. "But I don't want to disturb her love fest."

"And we won't need to, because we *are* going to find Drake." Jolene smiled softly, then squeezed my hand in support.

We went off in different directions then. I walked slowly, perusing every open spot I could find. People were decked out in cocktail dresses and tuxes. There was a lot of glitter and sequins and New Year's Eve hats. Everyone was ready to ring in the New Year in grand style.

Given that everyone was ready to celebrate, I knew that running around the ship in search of Drake, I had to stand out like a sore thumb. People openly gave me curious looks. If they'd seen me wandering around before, they had to be wondering why I wasn't relaxing somewhere with a drink.

With each minute that passed and no Drake, I became more and more anxious. Somewhere along the way I realized that I hadn't seen Natalie or either of the guys from the plane. I didn't think they had jumped or fallen overboard.

The ship was massive. Clearly, it was harder than it seemed to find someone.

I clung to that thought, knowing that it was possible Drake was in the room of someone I didn't know. I kept hoping that I would round a corner, and there he'd be, and I would feel both incredibly stupid and incredibly relieved.

I took the back end of the ship and searched the video arcade, the outdoor golf area, the sports court, the kids' beach area, library, Internet café, and the various dining areas on the various decks. There were fourteen decks in total, and I searched every public area from top to bottom, then started to make my way back up again.

On deck seven, when I entered the library for the second time, I found it empty. No one wanted to be curled up on a sofa with a book on New Year's Eve. I plopped down onto one of the many oversized leather chairs. The room featured warm, beige colors and had lots of lighting. It was the kind of library one might envision in their dream house.

I glanced upward, to the second level. And it occurred to me that I hadn't searched the upper level the first time. There'd been a few people milling about, and I had done a visual sweep of the room, figuring that Drake wasn't in here.

Now I made my way to the spiral steps that led to the upper level. The second level had a huge, circular cut-out in the floor from where one could look down onto the sitting area below.

It was as I reached the second level that I heard a sound. I paused, straining to listen. The sound of a door clicking shut traveled to my ears. Someone had entered the library.

My heart rate quickened. Easing toward the railing, I glanced below.

And jerked backward at what I saw.

The SunSeekers uniform . . . the dark skin and bald head.

It was Greg.

Now my heart beat even faster. *He's following me* was the thought that popped into my mind.

Taking quiet steps backward, I took cover behind a tower of books and watched Greg. He was moving slowly, quietly—almost creeping, if I wasn't mistaken.

Looking for me? Hoping to sneak up on me?

I saw the moment his head began to angle, and I quickly darted backward. Had he seen me? I couldn't be sure.

There were two staircases leading to the second level, and Greg was closer to the one I had just ascended. Every instinct in my body told me that he was going to head upstairs. If I wanted to get downstairs without him seeing me, I would have to get to the second staircase. But it was a good fifty yards away, and I would have to run for it, which would definitely alert him to the fact that I was up here.

But if he was following me, he would know that I had come into the library. And if I wasn't on the first level, then I had to be upstairs.

Daring to peek my head forward, I glanced below—and didn't see him.

I took off, charging for the second staircase. I was halfway down it when I saw him on the second level. Our eyes connected, and in that nanosecond, I saw his surprise.

Surprise that he hadn't been able to come upon me unawares.

I propelled my legs as fast as I could to the main level, noticing that Greg was now running toward the stairwell I'd gone down. Not stopping, I raced for the library's exit. As I got to the door, I glanced over my shoulder and saw that Greg had now reached the main level.

My pulse racing out of control, I sprinted into the hallway and ran straight ahead. No one was on this deck. Thousands of people on this ship, and there was not one other person here!

Greg was behind me. I knew he had to be. But thank God, a corner appeared. I rounded it, and it led me to the doors for the restrooms.

I darted into the women's restroom, and then into a stall.

The only sound I could hear was the sound of my pulse thundering in my ears. Had Greg seen me enter the restroom? Or did he think I had gone ahead to the nearest stairwell?

I waited several seconds, my ears strained for any sound.

And then the bathroom door squeaked open.

Chapter Twenty

As quietly as I could, I stepped onto the toilet seat. Terrified, I knew I couldn't afford to make a sound. Drawing in a deep breath, I held it.

A stall door opened next to me. Greg?

My lungs began to burn, but I didn't dare breathe.

There was some shuffling, then a moment of silence. And then the sound of someone urinating.

Another woman. It had to be.

But I had to be sure. Silently getting off of the toilet seat, I peered beneath the metal wall. The feet I saw were decidedly female—in low-heeled sandals with bright red toenails.

Only once the woman in the stall flushed her toilet did I do the same. She exited her stall, then I exited mine. If Greg was following me, my only chance to escape him was to have someone around as a witness. He wouldn't dare harass me—or worse—in the presence of someone else.

The woman, probably in her late thirties, smiled at me as we both approached the sinks. She was wearing a strapless black evening dress that stopped just above her knees. I returned her smile, hoping that I looked cordial, and not utterly terrified.

And once we were both done washing and drying our hands, I followed her out of the bathroom.

Terror gripped me as I did, the fear that I would run into Greg more intense than anything I'd ever experienced. But, thank God, the hallway was empty.

The woman went to her right, heading upstairs. I followed her, not daring to go anywhere else.

When the woman reached the top of the stairs, she went into the main dining hall. After a quick glance around to make sure Greg wasn't in the vicinity, I went to the next stairwell that led up. At least there were people around on these decks, unlike at the library.

My heart was still beating a mile a minute when I sat on a lounge chair near the pool, where I'd promised to meet Jolene. Still no sign of Greg. A number of people were milling about, both in the pool and out, so I felt safe.

For the moment.

I was never more relieved than when I saw Jolene appear on the pool deck. But my relief was short-lived when she shook her head as she approached me, silently letting me know that she hadn't seen Drake.

Jolene sat on the lounge chair beside mine. "Short of searching all the individual rooms, I looked everywhere, and I didn't see him at all."

"Me neither." I worried my bottom lip. "What should I do?"

"If you're really concerned, then you have to report him missing. But if you think he's maybe passed out in someone's room, well, you could wait a while."

I didn't speak. I wasn't sure what the best course of action was.

"What does your heart say?" Jolene asked me.

"That something's wrong."

She gave me an odd look, and then she said, "You're scared. Did something happen?"

I groaned, dragged a hand over my face, and then told her about Greg.

"Are you sure he was following you?"

I thought of how I hadn't seen him in the hallway when I was running to escape. Maybe he *hadn't* been. "I . . . I'm not sure. All I know is that the guy freaks me out." I paused. Sighed. "But he's hardly my biggest concern right now. I keep thinking about Natalie and those guys and the fact that Drake hasn't been seen since last night. By the way, did you see Natalie while looking for Drake?"

Jolene shook her head. "No."

Silence passed between us. We were both trying to make sense of the situation.

"Thanks," I said after a long moment. "For helping me."

Jolene offered me a small smile. "About The Gossip Hour . . . I know you didn't tell them about my abortion. You wouldn't."

"Never, Jo." For her to help me look for Drake, I knew she wasn't still mad at me, or feel I was responsible for something so hurtful. But it was nice to hear her say it out loud.

"It could have been Scott," she said to me. "I was thinking about that all day. Maybe he's not ready to forgive me." She shrugged.

"You think so?"

"I don't know. And you know what—I'm already past caring."

Again, we were silent. My brain was going a mile a minute. I kept thinking about the fact that Kent and Reid hadn't seen any evidence that Drake had been back in the room.

As if to add to my anxiety, the woman who had been hanging with Drake suddenly appeared on the pool deck. She and her friend were dressed in identical thigh-high white robes—the same ones that were hanging in our cabin closet. I watched them as they wandered to the hot tub closest to where Jolene and I were sitting. They slipped out of their robes, revealing skimpy black bikinis.

I swallowed hard, jealousy hitting me like a slap in the face at the thought of Drake having been with this woman. Her curly hair was pulled into an unkempt ponytail, but it wouldn't matter if she were bald—she was gorgeous.

"Should I talk to her?" I asked Jolene.

"Why?"

"To ask her if she's seen Drake." But as I said the words, I was rising. And then I was strolling across the pool deck to the hot tub.

Mid-laugh, the woman suddenly noticed me. The smile on her face faltered, and her eyes grew wide with alarm.

Perhaps she thought I wanted to beat her pretty face to a

pulp because she'd been flirting with my man. So I tried to put her mind at ease by speaking in a conciliatory tone.

"Excuse me," I began. "Can I ask you a question?"

The woman met her friend's gaze, as if seeking her opinion. Then she faced me and shrugged. "Sure."

"The guy you were hanging out with yesterday and the day before—six-foot-four, really hot." *My boyfriend,* I added silently, but didn't say. "Drake."

"Oh, yeah." She smiled tightly. It was obvious she didn't know what to make of my intentions. "What about him?"

"Have you seen him recently?"

Slowly, she shook her head. "No."

"When was the last time you saw him?"

She made an expression like she was thinking hard. "Hmm. Sometime yesterday."

Was she lying? I couldn't tell.

"You didn't spend the night with him?" I went on, not sure where I'd gotten the guts to be so bold.

Her eyes widened again. "No. I did *not*."

"I'm sure you already know that I'm his girlfriend," I said. "So you might think you have to lie to me. But if the two of you were together . . . if he's in your room now . . . all I want to know is that he's okay."

"I already told you I haven't seen him," she said, definitely testy. "If you can't keep tabs on your boyfriend, that's not my problem."

"Please . . ." I'd wanted to remain strong, but my voice cracked. "I just want to know where he is . . ."

The hard edge to the woman's gaze softened. She studied me. She must have decided that my distress was real, that I wasn't a jealous girlfriend lashing out at her.

"Honestly," she said, her tone calm. "I haven't seen him. Not since yesterday. He said he was supposed to meet his girlfriend at midnight."

My first reaction was happiness. But it was quickly followed by despair.

I was happy that Drake had told this woman about me. Because if he had, then it was clear that he hadn't formed a romantic connection with her.

But my God, if he *hadn't* formed a romantic connection with her, if he hadn't spent the night in her room . . .

Where was he?

"Thanks," I said, then quickly turned, despair and confusion fighting for control of my emotions.

I made my way back to Jolene. "She hasn't seen him," I said.

"You believe her?"

I opened my mouth to speak, but found that I couldn't. So I nodded.

"Dee, you look awful."

"Something's wrong," I managed. "Something's h-happened . . ."

"You don't know that," Jolene said.

But I did. I knew.

Knew it in my heart.

Chapter Twenty-one

HAVING DONE ALL I could possibly do, I knew there was no other option than to report Drake missing.

Jolene and I went to Guest Services, where I told the woman behind the desk that I had an emergency and needed to speak with someone.

"What is the nature of your emergency?" she asked me.

"My boyfriend's missing," I explained.

"Missing?"

"I haven't seen him since yesterday."

"He hasn't been back to your room since yesterday?"

"Actually, we're not in the same room. He's rooming with

his male buddies, I'm rooming with my girlfriends." *Why does this matter?* I wanted to ask. "But his friends say he hasn't been back to the room either."

"I can page him for you," the woman offered.

"Page him?" I asked, sounding a bit incredulous. I had already determined that Drake was missing. What good would it do to page him? As far as I was concerned, it was time to organize a search team to sweep the entire ship—and beyond.

Clearly picking up on my misgivings, the woman said, "It's the standard first step. Paging a passeng—"

"Yes, of course," I said, nodding. Paging him *did* make sense. It was possible that Drake was *somewhere* on the ship, and that I just couldn't find him. He could be laying low in someone else's room, for example, trying to avoid Natalie's goons.

I had to cling to the possible, not envision the worst-case scenario.

Putting on a brave face, I turned to Jolene. "Now we wait."

"Paging Mr. Drake Shaw. Paging Mr. Drake Shaw. Will you please report to Guest Services on deck four?"

Jolene and I waited on a sofa in the Guest Services office. And waited. After half an hour, the woman paged Drake again, but as the next thirty minutes rolled around, he still didn't show.

My anxiety grew with each passing second. I was too worried to engage in any sort of small talk with Jolene. We both sat, still and silent, hoping against hope that Drake would enter the office sooner rather than later.

Nearly twenty-four hours had passed since I'd last seen Drake. Should I have reported him missing earlier?

Would it have made a difference?

As I sat, hunched forward, my head heavy with emotion, my mind wandered back to the talk I'd had with Drake when deciding on the room we would book for the cruise. He hadn't wanted a stateroom with a balcony for fear of falling off the ship. He had spoken in jest, and at the time, I'd found the seemingly unfounded concern funny.

Not anymore.

Because now I couldn't help wondering if his comment had been a premonition of what would come.

After Drake failed to respond to any of the pages, the staff captain—second in command of the ship—was summoned. His name was Roman Musgrave, and he was a tall man, around six foot five, with a full head of salt-and-pepper hair and striking blue eyes. I explained to him my concern, the last time I had seen Drake, and that I was especially worried because of the altercation he'd been in the first evening aboard the ship.

The staff captain authorized a search of the entire ship. Given the late hour and the New Year's celebrations under way, I knew it would be an inconvenience to many of the guests, especially those with young children. But it had to be done. Jolene and I were advised to return to our cabin to get some rest and await word, since it would take hours to search the entire ship.

Roxanne was in the room, decked out in a black mini dress. Seeing me and Jolene, her eyes filled with concern.

"What's going on?"

So I told her. And then I said to both her and Jolene, "I'm not going to the disco. I-I can't. But you two feel free to go ring in the New Year without me."

"As if," Jolene said.

"We're not going to leave you until we learn what happened to Drake," Roxanne added.

"Thank you." Despite my anxiety, I smiled. I was glad to have my two friends with me.

I lay on my small bed and closed my eyes. All I could do now was wait.

Shortly after two in the morning, the staff captain came to our room to report the bad news to me. It had taken a little over three hours to search the entire ship, but there had been no sign of Drake.

The news rendered me numb. "What now?" I asked.

The staff captain explained that they would search the ship's computers to determine when Drake had last disembarked the ship. It was possible that he was still in Jamaica. That he hadn't made it back to the ship before it left port.

"You need to have a helicopter searching the ocean," I said, frustration overwhelming me. "All this time has been wasted searching the ship, while Drake could be lost at sea . . ."

"It's more likely he's in Jamaica," Roman Musgrave explained. "It happens a lot—people are late getting back to the ship and end up stranded. Often, they'll fly to the next port where they can get back on board. Don't worry. We'll track him down."

"They'll find him," Roxanne said from her bed, closest to the cabin's small window, once Roman Musgrave had gone. "Drake probably went to some local hang-out on the island, found some guys with weed, got stoned, and lost track of time."

"Absolutely," Jolene agreed. "You know how much Drake loves his weed."

Drake did love smoking marijuana—too much, as far as I was concerned—and it was something I'd always gotten on his case about.

Had he done what Roxanne had hypothesized? Gone in search of some "good stuff" on the island, then gotten stoned?

I wanted to believe that. Lord knew I did. But the truth was, I doubted that Drake had ever gotten off the ship in Jamaica. And if he hadn't disembarked, yet he wasn't currently on board, then he was lost at sea. And the longer it took to search the water, the less likely he was to survive.

If it isn't too late already . . .

That thought was there in my mind, strong and persistent. But I did my best to keep it tamped down. Because I only wanted to entertain the positive, not the negative.

If I allowed myself to think that the worst had happened, I would lose it. Completely.

Besides, even if Drake was somehow lost at sea, it didn't mean he was dead. How many stories were there of people who walked away from totally wrecked cars with only a scratch? Of those who survived plane crashes, helicopter crashes, gunshots to the head. Not to mention all the people who had been trapped under the earthquake rubble in Haiti for several days, only to emerge alive—against all odds.

Drake was strong, athletic. If he had fallen overboard, I didn't doubt that he could tread water for hours. And with salt water, he could easily float. Better still, he might have found something in the water he'd been able to hang on to in order to keep afloat with ease.

Far-fetched, perhaps. But not impossible.

I had to cling to the possible.

. . .

I didn't hear from the staff captain until six the next morning. He called my room and requested that I head to his office as soon as possible so we could speak privately.

My heart pounded every step of the way there. It was pretty clear to me that if Drake had been located, the staff captain would have relayed that to me over the phone.

Don't give up hope, I reminded myself. *Maybe Drake* has *been found.*

But when I arrived at Roman's office, the news went from bad to worse.

According to the ship's computerized records, Drake had not disembarked in Jamaica. He had last scanned his card when he got onto the cruise liner after the stop in The Bahamas.

Despite my resolve to cling to the positive, I burst into tears.

"I'm very sorry, miss," the staff captain said to me, coming around to my side of the desk to put a hand on my shoulder. It was just the two of us in his office.

"Will the Coast Guard do a search now?" I asked.

"Unfortunately, there's a lot of ocean to cover since we left The Bahamas," he replied, sitting back down.

His words hit me like a rock in the head. "Are you saying you won't search for him?"

"No, that's not what I'm saying. In fact, we've turned the ship around in an attempt to search for Drake," the staff captain continued. "At seven o'clock, we'll be announcing that over the P.A. system, once most people will be up and preparing to disembark."

I had noticed, en route to the office, that there was no land in sight. I'd figured we were just a short distance away from Grand Cayman. But knowing that the ship had turned around . . . Relief surged through me, renewing my hope.

"We've contacted the U.S. Coast Guard, the Jamaican Coast Guard, the Royal Bahamas Defense Force. Search-and-rescue teams are hard at work right now to find your boyfriend."

"Thank you," I said, tears filling my eyes. Some people would no doubt be pissed that their cruise had been interrupted, but if they were in my shoes, they'd want SunSeekers to do the same for their loved one.

"The problem is that no one reported Drake missing until last night, which, as I said, leaves a vast area to be searched. What we need to do next is question everyone who had any interaction with Drake. Narrow down a specific time frame that will give us a better idea of where Drake might be lost so the searchers can target that area. As we speak, security personnel are going through the video footage from the ship to find the last time Drake was caught on camera."

Suddenly this was all too real. I supposed that even as I'd gone to Guest Services yesterday evening, I'd thought that Drake would turn up somewhere. But he hadn't, and my worst fear was coming true.

"The last time you saw Drake was . . . ?" Roman asked me.

"The night before last, around six in the evening. We were outside on deck ten, near the casino, talking for a bit. We made plans to meet on the pool deck at midnight. I showed, he didn't."

Roman nodded, scribbled notes. "We know that Drake was rooming with Kent Stevens and Reid Preston. They're being questioned now. But who are Drake's other friends and acquaintances on board this cruise?"

"There are a number of students from Lancaster University. We're not all friends, per se, but we definitely know each other." I named all those I could think of, saving Natalie for last. "And this may be important: Natalie Laymon accused my boyfriend of . . . of raping her. Back at college. It's not true, Drake would never do that, but still, Natalie could want to cause trouble. Those guys my boyfriend got into a fight with . . . I think they're her friends. I've seen her with them, and so have my friends. You'll have those guys' names from an incident report the first night after their fight in the casino. If something happened to Drake, I think Natalie and those guys are behind it."

"Wes Brewster and Geoffrey Laymon," Roman said, referring to his notes. "They're being questioned now as well."

"Good."

"Anyone else?" Roman asked.

"Wait a minute. Did you say Geoffrey *Laymon*?"

The staff captain nodded. "Yes."

"Laymon . . . he must be related to Natalie." I was speaking more to myself, the picture in my mind becoming clearer. "If Geoffrey is related to Natalie, then he must have come on this cruise to get back at Drake . . ."

"As I said, they're being questioned right now. And security is reviewing video footage." He paused briefly. "Anyone else your boyfriend may have befriended on the cruise?"

I was about to say no. And then I remembered. "Actually, there was another woman Drake was hanging out with. Someone he met on the cruise. I saw them together a few times. The first time was in the casino, before the fight."

Roman leaned back in his seat, studying me with his striking blue eyes. "Were you and Drake having problems?" he asked. My expression must have relayed my shock, because he went on. "You weren't sharing a room, and you mentioned arranging a time to meet. Given the allegation of rape, and now this other woman—"

"I didn't say he was involved with this other woman."

"But you suspect she was a romantic interest." It was a statement, not a question.

Was there something in my expression, or in my tone, that had caused the staff captain to deduce that? "I don't . . . I don't understand."

"Didi, I've been doing this job for many years. People go on vacations all the time and get involved with individuals who are not their romantic partner. Especially if there are problems before they head on the cruise. I've seen honeymoons end in disaster when one partner caves to temptation." He paused briefly, held my gaze. "While it certainly isn't common, I've seen jealousy lead people to jump overboard."

"Jump overboard?" I repeated, aghast. "Is that what you think happened?"

"It's my job to examine every possibility," Roman said gently. "Sometimes misadventure leads one to fall overboard. A person gets drunk, then decides to try a balancing act along the railing. But more often than not, I've seen jealousy lead people to act rashly. As well as despair."

"*Despair?*"

The staff captain regarded me with a tender expression before speaking. "You said your boyfriend was accused of rape before he came on this cruise—"

"*Accused.* But he didn't do it."

"Add to the stress over such an allegation, the two of you were having problems."

"He didn't jump!" I insisted. "There's no way he would have jumped overboard because of anything Natalie said." My breaths were coming in hot, angry spurts. "If he *did* end up overboard, then he was pushed. By Natalie and her goon friends, or relatives or whoever the hell they are. No one from Lan-U likes her. Why would she even come on this cruise? For vengeance, that's why. And it appears she got it."

The staff captain held up a hand. "Please, Didi. Calm down."

"I can't calm down! Drake is out there, lost, and you want to treat this like a suicide!"

The staff captain regarded me with an expression so kind, it was actually painful. "Didi." He sighed wearily. "I'm not saying that's what happened. And perhaps I shouldn't have said anything, not until we know for sure. I know how hard it is for loved ones to ever think that someone they've known for years would ever take their own life. But it does happen."

And suddenly I was thinking about Rachel, about the pills she had apparently taken and how her sister didn't believe she had taken her own life. Had she? Had Rachel, overwhelmed with despair, deliberately planned to kill herself?

All the evidence in the world might point to that, and her family would likely still cling to their belief that Rachel wasn't the type, that she would never do such a thing.

Was I deluding myself? Was the staff captain right? Was Drake depressed about the allegation, and perhaps about our failing relationship, to the point where he'd decided to take his own life?

No. I wouldn't believe it. I couldn't.

But I thought also about the moment Greg had forced

himself on me, and the fact that Drake might have witnessed that. Seeing the woman he loved in the arms of someone else could have been the proverbial straw that broke the camel's back.

I kept that bit of information to myself, not wanting to give the staff captain further reason to think Drake was suicidal.

"Do you know the name of this woman you said Drake was spending time with?"

I didn't answer right away. I had to force myself to draw in steady breaths before I could speak. "No," I finally told the staff captain. "But I asked her last night if she'd seen Drake, and she told me she hadn't. I can pick her out in any video you might show me," I added, realizing that it was a good idea for the ship's security staff to dot all their *i*'s and cross all their *t*'s. It was possible, though doubtful, that the Hispanic bombshell might have some information that could help lead to Drake. Something she'd unwittingly heard or witnessed.

"That will be helpful." The comment was gentle, and it struck me anew that Drake was missing, likely overboard in the middle of the ocean. And I lost it again.

"We'll also ask for any witnesses to what may have happened to come forward," Roman explained.

I nodded, unable to speak.

The staff captain offered me a small smile. There was compassion in his expression, but also pity.

And I suddenly wanted to ask him about the success rate of finding people lost at sea. How many people had been retrieved—alive—after Herculean efforts to find them.

But I didn't. Because I couldn't.

I didn't want to know.

If I asked the question and was told that one hundred percent of people lost at sea for more than twenty-four hours were never found alive, well, to know that would kill all hope.

And I wasn't ready to do that.

On the first day of a brand-new year, I wasn't ready to believe that the man I had planned to spend my life with was never coming home.

Chapter Twenty-two

HALF AN HOUR LATER, I was sitting crossed-legged on my bed, when there was an announcement letting the passengers know that the ship was now back on course, heading to Grand Cayman.

My stomach sank.

The announcement went on to say that unfortunately due to the delay, there would only be a few hours for people to explore the island, meaning that scheduled excursions would have to be canceled. A full refund would be issued to those affected by the delay. There was an apology for the inconvenience.

"Why would they turn around when they haven't found him?" Jolene asked.

"They've got a ship full of people they don't want to *inconvenience*," I said sourly.

"But the Coast Guard is out there searching," Roxanne pointed out. "They'll be able to do a much better job finding Drake than a cruise liner can."

Roxanne was right, and I clung to that.

But I was aware that every second that passed with no news meant bad news.

Nearly two hours after I had returned to the room, the cabin phone rang.

Roxanne, closest to the phone, looked to me as if seeking permission to answer it. Too numb to move, I nodded.

She picked up the receiver before the phone could ring a third time. "Hello? Yes, she's here. One second." She met my gaze, saying, "It's for you."

"Hello?" I said cautiously. It felt as if two people were inside my body, playing tug-of-war with my intestines. I hadn't been able to eat a thing all day, and felt nauseous.

"It's Staff Captain Roman Musgrave. Can you return to my office?"

"Sure," I said. "I'm on my way."

"Did they find him?" Jolene asked, her eyes alight with wary hopefulness.

"I don't know." I looked at her, then Roxanne. "He only said that he wants me to go to his office."

"You want us to go with you?" Roxanne asked.

Saying nothing, I shook my head and headed for the door. Whatever the staff captain had to say, I wanted to hear it in confidence.

When I got to the staff captain's office, the look on his face told me that he had something serious to say.

"What?" I asked, fearing the worst. "What's happened?"

Roman wore a grim expression as he settled into the seat opposite me. "There's been some news," he said.

Oh God. Please no. "You . . . you found Drake?"

"No. But in light of the ship-wide search, a guest has come forward with some information. Apparently in the early hours of Tuesday morning, the very night you believe Drake went missing, the guest heard the sound of something crashing into the water. At the time, she thought it odd, but dismissed it as a wave crashing against the boat. Now that she's had time to reflect, she feels what she heard may have been a body hitting the water."

"And she's only saying something now? If I heard what I thought was a body hitting the water, I wouldn't wait two days to report that."

"Like I said, at the time she wasn't sure what she heard. But her room is several decks below the pool deck—where you were supposed to meet Drake. And . . ." Roman's voice trailed off, and he inhaled deeply. "Upon further inspection of the area, we've found a trace amount of blood on one of the railings."

My stomach sank. "Blood?"

"Yes. It's a small amount. That's why we missed it before now."

God, no. What had Drake endured that night? Had Natalie's goons cut him? Beat him, then pushed him overboard?

"If there's blood," I said, raising my gaze to face the staff captain, "then that means there was a struggle. Blood is proof that he didn't kill himself."

"I'm inclined to agree."

"Natalie and those two guys." My lungs constricted, making it hard for me to inhale any air. "They did this. They're behind this."

Roman didn't respond, just stared at me for a long moment. I got the sense he was trying to scrutinize me.

"I spoke to Drake's mother," he finally said. "Mrs. Shaw."

"You told her?" I asked, my voice raising an octave. It made sense that he had to, although there was a part of me that wished he hadn't contacted Drake's mother. Not until we had some definite answers.

"Given the circumstances, I needed to call her."

My temples began to throb with the weight of the situation. I knew Janine Shaw very well, knew that she would have broken down upon hearing the news. News that would be even more devastating after losing her husband in the summer.

"How is she?" I asked.

"Distraught. Understandably." The staff captain paused. "But she told me something worthy of note, Didi."

"Okay," I said slowly, warily, sensing something in his tone. "What did she say?"

"Drake had an interesting talk with his mother before he left for the cruise. He told her that if anything were to happen to him, it wouldn't be an accident. That she should make sure any tragic mishap involving him be investigated as murder."

Several beats passed without me breathing.

Drake *knew*? He knew that someone was after him?

Suddenly, I could see it. The last times I'd spoken with him,

I'd sensed that there was something he wasn't sharing with me. Something that was weighing heavily on his mind.

Why didn't you tell me, Drake? After our five-year relationship, I thought he could, and would, tell me anything.

Instead, he had shared his disturbing fear with his mother. And he'd done so before we'd ever set sail.

I felt as if I were shrouded in dense fog. Somehow I kept my voice calm as I asked, "Did he say who he thought would hurt him, and why?"

"In addition to the list of suspects you provided," Roman said, "Mrs. Shaw felt there should be one more."

"Who?" I asked, desperate to know.

The staff captain leveled a long, hard look at me and said, "You."

One word, but it changed everything. "*Me?*"

"She feels that after the breakup of your relationship with her son, you may have been angry. Unable to let go."

"You're not serious. You don't think I had anything to do with Drake going overboard?"

"I'm wondering why you weren't honest about the nature of your relationship with Mr. Shaw."

Mr. Shaw? "Drake was my boyfriend. But we were having some problems. We talked about that."

"Mrs. Shaw believes there was a lot more animosity between you two than you let on to me."

What the hell? She'd always liked me . . . or so I thought. "Mrs. Shaw is standing on the outside looking in. She doesn't know what happens in my relationship with Drake. And right now, her grief is clearly getting to her, causing her to not think logically."

The staff captain said nothing, his eyes unreadable.

"I loved Drake," I stressed. "All I wanted was for us to get our relationship back on track. I wouldn't kill him."

Roman said nothing. Did he believe me? Was he going to pursue charges against *me*?

"The FBI is headed to Grand Cayman," the staff captain said. "They'll need to speak to you when we get there."

A distress signal went off in my brain. "Me?"

"And anyone else who may have information about this case," Roman went on.

"Oh," I said, relaxing. Not that I had anything to worry about, but I didn't want the investigation sidetracked with the police looking into me as a viable suspect when I knew I'd done nothing wrong.

"It's strictly procedure," the staff captain explained. "All ships that leave ports out of the United States fall under the jurisdiction of the FBI if a crime is committed. Not that there *was* a crime," he amended. "Right now, we can only speculate as to what happened. The FBI will make their determination based on the evidence."

I nodded. "Right."

"I'm going to have to ask that you don't disembark. You or your friends. The FBI will want to question all of you. The same is true for everyone else who had a connection to Drake on this cruise, and anyone who feels they have information that can help in the investigation."

"How long before we get to Grand Cayman?"

"Another three and a half hours. We should be there by twelve-thirty."

A lot could happen in three and a half hours.

Drake could be rescued.

Or his body could be found.

. . .

Rushing out of the staff captain's office, I rounded the corner and started down a long hallway.

And then I stopped dead in my tracks when I saw who was walking in my direction.

Natalie.

She was alone. In fact, no one else was in the corridor.

Our gazes connected. And then my blood began to boil.

I started toward her with determination. Natalie's eyes widened with alarm, but she seemed too stunned to move.

"You killed him!" As I reached her, I shoved her. "You killed Drake!"

"No!" she protested. "That's not true."

I wanted to punch her. Seriously. "You came on this cruise for one reason only. To get revenge."

"I didn't!"

"And why? Because Drake wouldn't return your affections? Were you so obsessed with him that you lied about him raping you as a way to lash out at him for not being with you?"

"I didn't lie," Natalie said, stressing each word.

I raised my hand. Balled it into a fist. Natalie raised her hands to block her face, cowering.

Maybe it was the fear I saw in her eyes. Fear that made me realize just how out of control I was. Instead of striking her, I lowered my fist.

"The FBI will get the truth out of you. As soon as we get to Grand Cayman, they'll question you and you'll go down." I had no doubt that Natalie would wither under the pressure of a police interrogation, and within minutes, she would be admitting to her hand in what had happened to Drake. "You lied about Drake, and now he's dead!"

"I didn't. I swear."

Again, I was tempted to smack her, but somehow refrained. "How dare you say that to me?"

"Because . . . because it's true," she said, her voice cracking. "I told the truth as I knew it. I *didn't lie*."

"What do you mean: the truth as you knew it?"

"I *was* raped," she insisted. "But . . . but now I don't think it was Drake who did it."

Her words were a bombshell. My knees buckled as though the very ground beneath me had moved.

"What are you saying? You told everyone who would listen that Drake was the one who raped you. You went to The Gossip Hour, and not only did you destroy Drake by going public, you destroyed our relationship."

"That . . . that wasn't my plan. I didn't mean to hurt you. And now that I know Drake wasn't the one who raped me, I feel awful."

"You *know*? How could you not know before?"

She looked around before speaking, and seeing no one, continued. "The room . . . it was dark. I couldn't be certain who was the one on top of me. All I know for sure is that Drake was in the room . . . in the beginning."

"You crucified Drake with your allegation of rape," I said, incredulous. "Now you're saying you were never sure?"

"There was more than one of them," she said, her voice lower but more urgent, as if that justified her accusing Drake of such a horrific crime. "I'm not sure how many."

"You were gang-raped?"

She nodded jerkily, her eyes misting with tears. "I was out of it. Someone put something in my drink. "I was woozy, and didn't really remember some details until later. And when I did, I distinctly remembered Drake taking me up to a room so I could sit down in private because I was feeling weird. He got me some water, I think. The next thing I knew, I was waking up to someone on top of me, and other guys were in the room, laughing."

"You never said that you were gang-raped. You specifically said that Drake raped you. Now it sounds like you're saying he tried to help you?"

"I know what I said."

She was spinning a ball of new lies. Trying to distance herself from what had happened to Drake by pretending she no longer had a bone to pick with him. "And that's what you believed," I said sharply. "You came on this cruise for one reason: to get even with Drake! And you got your vengeance."

"I came on this cruise because someone told me I should!"

Natalie's eyes were as round as saucers. Her chest heaved with each breath.

"What did you say?" I asked, certain I hadn't heard her correctly.

"Someone told me to come on this cruise," she went on. "Paid my way."

I scowled. "Who?"

"I don't know. At first I thought . . . I thought it was Drake."

"And you jumped at the chance of going on a cruise with a man you said had raped you," I said, my tone making it clear I thought she was a first-rate liar.

Natalie said nothing.

"Or were you hoping that you'd both literally sail off into

the sunset?" When Natalie didn't speak, I nodded. "Yes, that's it, isn't it? You *were* obsessed with Drake."

"I wanted an apology. *That's* why I came on this cruise. And in the letter I received that included my itinerary for the cruise, Drake said he wanted to make amends with me—"

"You expect me to believe *Drake* paid for you to come on this cruise?"

"That's what I thought. And no, I didn't jump at the opportunity. But I wanted an apology. I wanted closure. My therapist said that closure would go a long way in terms of my healing. So I figured why not go on a free vacation? But I wasn't dumb enough to come on this cruise without people with me. Just in case Drake was planning to hurt me. Thanks to him providing his full itinerary in the letter with the ticket, I knew when he'd be flying out of California. I told my brother and cousin, and lo and behold they arranged to be on the same flight as Drake. I guess they wanted to keep their eyes on him, as much as possible, every step of the way."

"I've heard enough." If I didn't get away from her, I *would* hurt her. She was the reason Drake was missing, maybe even dead. "You're an evil, scheming bitch."

Again, Natalie looked around, clearly uncomfortable. An elderly couple was approaching from the far end of the hall.

"Let me finish," Natalie whispered. "Please."

I said nothing. And for some reason, though I didn't care to hear another word she had to say, I stayed rooted to the spot.

Natalie continued. "My brother and cousin were pissed because they thought Drake had raped me. So yeah, they started that fight with him. But they didn't kill him."

"You really expect me to believe that?"

"It's the truth. Especially when I told them I no longer believed that Drake was the one who raped me."

I should have turned and walked away. Not listened to any more of the bullshit Natalie was spewing.

And yet something about it didn't seem like bullshit. As crazy a story as she was spinning, it had the ring of truth.

But still I said, "You sound insane. You know that, right?"

"Trust me, I know. But hear me out. I spoke to Drake after the fight in the casino. I asked him why he'd wanted me on this cruise. That's when I found out he didn't pay my way. He said he had no clue what I was talking about—and I believed him. But he told me something else, and it's made all the difference."

"What?"

"He told me that he didn't rape me, but that he knew who did."

The next few seconds passed as if in slow motion. I wasn't sure how to process what she was saying.

"Who?" I finally asked. "Who raped you?"

"He didn't say. *Wouldn't* say." She paused. "He said he would tell me only when he got the proof."

"Proof? What kind of proof?"

Natalie shrugged. "I don't know. And maybe this doesn't make sense, but I got the feeling that he was scared."

This was a wild and crazy story. Incredible. But hadn't I had the exact same impression? That Drake was scared of something?

"I've wracked my brain to figure out what's going on," Natalie went on. "And the only thing that makes sense is that someone clearly wanted me on this cruise. Went as far as to pretend Drake had sent me the ticket. Someone who believed I would possibly want revenge against Drake for hurting me. Or at least have a motive for wanting him dead. And now he's missing." Natalie stopped. Inhaled sharply. "I think someone planned to kill Drake before we ever got on this cruise. And they wanted me here as a scapegoat."

Suddenly, Natalie's eyes widened as she glanced at something behind me. I whipped my head around in time to see a wisp of movement at the far end of the corridor, but didn't see an actual person.

"Trust no one," Natalie said. A definite warning. "*No one.*"

And then she spun around and hustled down the hallway.

Chapter Twenty-three

RATIONALLY, I KNEW I shouldn't have believed a thing Natalie said. And yet her words left me terrified.

She had done a complete about-face. She no longer believed that Drake had raped her, but she was maintaining that she *had* been raped.

He said he would tell me only when he got the proof.

Proof? What kind of proof?

It would be so easy to believe that Natalie was lying. I had already written her off as a woman who'd made a false allegation. I figured that she'd lied for attention, or perhaps because she was delusional.

So why was I even considering her story as truth now?

The story was crazy. No doubt about it. But I hadn't detected any deception as she'd relayed it. Instead, she had clearly been afraid.

Something bigger was going on than the obvious. Something I didn't understand.

There was one thing I could think of. The one thing that made a morsel of sense.

Seth had raped Natalie. Drake knew the truth, but didn't want to cross him. He had insisted that I not level any allegations against Seth, and I'd thought that it was because he didn't want me stirring up dirt.

But what if it was because Drake had been afraid? Afraid of what Seth would do?

Suddenly, I was remembering Drake's words after I'd threatened to report Seth for the kitten incident. Drake had been adamant that I keep my mouth shut. Because he wanted to protect Seth . . . or protect me?

Had Drake been afraid that if he spoke out against Seth, his friend would retaliate against him?

And was it possible that Rachel had witnessed the rape, or learned of it, and had been killed to ensure her silence?

My stomach began to flutter. God help me, the idea made sense.

But Seth wasn't on this cruise. As far as I knew, he was in St. Bart's. Did he have someone on this cruise do his dirty work?

He was loaded. He could easily be the one who'd paid Natalie's way. Especially if he wanted to set her up . . .

Hearing a sound, I whirled around. Saw no one.

The cruise line's administrative offices were at the end of a long corridor on the fourth deck, away from the well-traveled areas. If you were in this area, it was to deal with Guest Services or other administrative staff.

So now that Natalie was gone, I was alone.

I started down the hallway, planning to go to the stairwell at the far opposite end of the ship. My cabin was two levels up, on the sixth deck. But as I neared the elevators, I sensed eyes on me.

Felt their chill.

I spun around. Saw nothing. Was I simply paranoid, scared because of what Natalie said?

I continued down the hallway, my feet moving quickly now. The very first exit I got to, I opened the door and rushed into the stairwell. I charged up the stairs, fear fueling my every step.

Don't stop, I thought when I got to deck six. Exiting one deck up would provide me with better safety. The main dining hall was on deck seven, and hence, more people were bound to be there.

I was panting when I got to deck seven and threw the door open. The main dining hall was opposite the stairs. A handful of people were inside the entryway, walking about. Beyond the entrance to the dining hall was a wide set of stairs that led to the level below. The Kids' Club was down there. As was the library.

Glancing around, I saw no one exiting the stairwell. I *was* being paranoid, I decided. Natalie's story had gotten to me.

I moved toward the wide staircase, but halted at the top. I had a stitch in my side from having charged up three flights, and I pressed a hand against my side to alleviate the pain.

My neck prickled as something penetrated my brain. The faintest sound of a foot—

Suddenly, I was thrown forward. My hands flailed, grasped for purchase on the railing. Failed.

And then I was tumbling, rolling head over feet down the steps.

Unable to stop.

The seconds that passed seemed like hours. I lay, dazed, my mind a blur. I could grasp that something was out of sync, but I didn't know what.

And then I heard the voices. The panic.

"My God, are you okay?"

"Can you hear me?"

My eyes focused. I saw the face of a woman, concern obvious in her gaze. I flitted my eyes to the right, saw another woman's face.

"Excuse me," a man said. Then the two women eased back, and another face appeared between them. It took a second for my brain to process that the man was Greg.

Alarm gripped me from head to toe. My memory returned in a flash. In an instant, I knew what had happened.

I had been about to go down the steps. Then someone had pushed me.

Meeting Greg's gaze again, I tried to sit up.

"Stay still," the woman said. "You might be hurt."

"Someone pushed me," I said, looking at the woman. Then I once again stared at Greg.

What was he doing here, at this exact moment?

Coincidence?

"Pushed?" the woman asked, sounding doubtful. "No, dear. You fell."

"No," I disagreed.

"I rushed to the stairs the moment I heard the commotion," the woman said. "I didn't see anyone behind you."

"Someone pushed me," I insisted. As I sat up, Greg put a hand on my shoulder.

I shrugged away from his touch. My neck hurt, and I was winded. But I was okay.

At least I would be, once I got away from Greg.

"I think you should go to Medical," Greg said. "Get checked out."

"You might have a concussion," the middle-aged woman chimed in.

Greg studied my eyes. "I can't be sure, but your retinas appear normal. Do you feel any tingling in your arms or legs?"

"No," I said. I didn't want to make another trip to see the cruise nurse. "I'm fine."

"That was quite the fall," one of the women said, speaking in general to the small crowd that had gathered.

Had I fallen? Was I so fearful because of my conversation with Natalie that I'd imagined being pushed?

No . . .

This wasn't coincidence, Greg's being here. I was certain that I'd felt hands on my back, shoving me hard.

Someone in a SunSeekers uniform pushed through the crowd. The man wore a look of grave concern. "What happened? Are you okay?"

I didn't want to make a big deal out of this. What I wanted was to get out of here. So I stood and rolled my neck, stretched my back. There was definitely pain in my neck, but I would live.

"I'm fine," I announced, and added a chuckle for good measure. "I'm such a klutz."

People around me began to chuckle as well, clearly relieved that I seemed to be okay.

"You're sure?" the other SunSeekers employee asked me.

"Definitely. I'm tough."

Then I began to walk away, taking steps backward at first. I kept my eyes on Greg, making sure he was staying put.

Certain that he wasn't coming after me, I finally turned and started down the hallway. And when I reached the first stairwell, I disappeared inside and made my escape.

But I couldn't help remembering Natalie's words, and Drake's mother's.

Someone had been out to get Drake. He had known that before coming on this cruise.

Was someone also out to get me?

When I got back to the cabin, Roxanne and Jolene looked at me anxiously. "Well?" Roxanne asked.

Sighing wearily, I plopped down on my bed. And then I filled them in on what the witness had heard, how she'd thought nothing of it at the time, but now realized she may have heard Drake crashing into the water. "According to the staff captain, there's a small amount of blood on the top deck's railing in the area above that woman's room."

"Oh God," Jolene uttered.

"That only proves he fell into the water," Roxanne said, trying to be encouraging. "He could be alive out there."

She didn't sound convinced of her own words. But how could I blame her? Even I was starting to doubt that we would find Drake alive. How could I hang on to hope given all the time that had passed? If the witness who'd heard the splash was correct, then the Coast Guard hadn't started searching for Drake for a full twenty-four hours after he'd gone missing. What were the chances of him being alive in the raging waters of the ocean?

Jolene must have sensed my thoughts, because she said, "Remember that story last year of the kid who survived that plane crash in Africa? Everyone else died, but miraculously, he survived. Don't give up hope, Dee."

"The FBI will be in Grand Cayman when we get there. They'll want to question all of us. Anyone who knew Drake or came into contact with him on this cruise."

Roxanne nodded.

We were all quiet, the three of us no doubt thinking about the devastating predicament at hand. My mind went back to Natalie, what she'd said about someone paying her way on this cruise and her suspicion that she was here as a scapegoat.

I opened my mouth to tell my friends about it, then promptly closed my lips.

Trust no one. That had been Natalie's warning.

Clearly, she was the one who slipped the note under my door. The one advising me not to trust my friends.

Silent, I looked at Roxanne and Jolene in turn. Roxanne was resting her face against one palm, pensive. Glum. Jolene lay on her bed staring at the ceiling, the edges of her mouth curled downward. They both seemed as upset as I was.

Trust no one.

Not even them?

But a moment later, I dismissed the idea as ludicrous. Roxanne and Jolene were my best friends in the world. There was no way either one of them would do anything to hurt me.

Seth was behind this. Somehow, some way, Seth had gotten someone to come on this cruise and do his dirty work. And he had the perfect alibi. He was hundreds of miles away in St. Bart's.

"I ran into Natalie when I was leaving the staff captain's office," I said without preamble. That got Roxanne and Jolene's immediate attention. "She had quite the story to tell."

"What?" Jolene and Roxanne asked in unison.

I told them, leaving out nothing.

"Do you believe her?" Roxanne asked. "I mean, this is the same girl who trashed Drake at school. Now she's saying she believes he didn't rape her? You ask me, she's come up with a new story to pretend like she doesn't have a reason to want Drake dead."

Thinking, I said nothing. Roxanne could very well be right. It was highly conceivable that at the time Natalie had hatched her plan for revenge, she hadn't considered how easily the police would connect her to any foul play where Drake was concerned. But now that Drake was missing, she had seen the obvious hole in her plan and was changing her story to absolve herself of any culpability.

"Her brother and cousin were on the plane with you and Drake," Jolene added. "That couldn't be coincidence. Then they show up on the cruise. They start a fight with Drake in the casino. Now Natalie thinks she can pretend she had no reason to want him dead?"

Good arguments. Absolutely. But it was the look in Natalie's eyes. And the fear I had sensed in Drake when I spoke to him the last time.

"Someone pushed me down the steps shortly after Natalie spoke to me."

"What?" Jolene shrieked. Roxanne's eyes widened in horror.

I rubbed the back of my neck, which was definitely sore.

Maybe I ought to see Medical, after all. "I think it was that guy, Greg. The one who was hitting on me. As I was lying on my back, he appeared out of nowhere."

"Did anyone see him?" Roxanne asked.

"Some people came to help me after I fell. They claim I fell. But they didn't see me fall, only heard me and rushed to help me once I was sprawled out on the ground."

"Asshole," Roxanne quipped.

"Why didn't you tell us that when you first came into the room?" Jolene asked.

I shrugged. "Because I'm more concerned about Drake. And I'm not really hurt." I moved my neck from side to side. "Well, a little. But I'll be fine."

"You should report him," Jolene said.

"I would, but I can't really prove it. Besides, I don't want time wasted on me and a complaint about this guy. I want all resources dedicated to finding Drake."

"I told him where to go," Roxanne began, "but obviously that didn't work."

"Which is why you should tell security about your fears," Jolene insisted. "Who knows, maybe he had something to do with what happened to Drake."

At the comment, my eyes met Jolene's. Held. Could she be right?

"Because he was jealous?" I asked. "Jealous that I was with Drake?"

"Stranger things have happened," Jolene said.

My stomach fluttered as I considered the idea. But a moment later, I dismissed it.

Drake had been afraid *before* we'd ever set sail. Before I'd ever met Greg. His mother's story was a testament to that.

No, whoever had thrown Drake into the ocean was someone who had had an issue with him before.

The two questions that remained to be solved were who, and why?

Chapter Twenty-four

THE SHIP ARRIVED in Grand Cayman at twelve-thirty, just as the staff captain had said it would. Before anyone disembarked, all those deemed to have any information about Drake and what may have happened to him were instructed to meet in the large dining hall.

A team of FBI agents boarded the ship soon after we docked, and made their way to the dining hall to explain what would happen next. We would be escorted, a few people at a time, to the executive offices where we would have privacy as we were questioned.

I was among the first people called, as was the woman who'd heard the splash in the water. She was in her mid-forties, with short black hair and at least forty extra pounds of weight on her five-foot-five-inch frame.

Special Agent Rafael Diaz introduced himself to me, then led me to the fourth deck. He was five-foot-eight at the most, with a lean frame and a crew cut. His firm, probing gaze screamed "law enforcement."

I found myself sweating by the time I reached the staff captain's office, fearful of the questions that would come, even though I had done nothing wrong. Perhaps it was the seriousness of the situation, coupled with my dwindling hope.

Special Agent Diaz was cordial as he sat opposite me at the staff captain's desk.

"Didi Randall, right?" he asked for clarification.

"Yes," I responded.

"Can you tell me the nature of your relationship with Drake Shaw?"

I told him, leaving out nothing. Told him that we'd been together for five years, but that Natalie's allegation of rape had driven a wedge between us. I told him also that Natalie was someone I believed would want revenge, but that she had only today changed her story, saying she no longer believed Drake had raped her.

Special Agent Diaz listened to my story, took notes. And then he asked me about the last time I'd seen Drake.

"It was Monday evening. We were on the exterior deck, outside of the casino. Like I said, we'd been sort of taking a break from each other after the rape allegation, but we still cared about each other. There was no anger between us."

"Even though Natalie Laymon accused him of rape?"

"I never believed her," I said. "I knew Drake would never do something like that."

"What time was it that you last saw Drake?"

"Hmm, about six. We talked for a bit, then made plans to meet at the main pool deck at midnight. He said he was going to be hanging with his friends for the evening, which is why he wanted to meet me later."

"And he never showed?"

I shook my head.

The agent produced a sketch. "This is the main pool deck. Point out to me where you were waiting for Drake."

I looked at the sketch. And then I pointed to the left side of the ship. "Right there. Sort of diagonal to the door that led back inside," I added, using my finger to illustrate.

The agent marked an *X* on the sketch. Then he continued. "How long did you wait before leaving?"

"I . . . I don't know."

The agent's eyebrow shot up. "You don't know?"

"Maybe five minutes," I hedged. I hadn't considered that the police would ask me this. I had kept the whole truth from the staff captain, and I suddenly wondered if that would come back to haunt me. If I told the entire truth now, would they deem that I had something to hide?

"Only five minutes?" The agent looked doubtful. "If I thought this was the moment I was going to reunite with a five-year love, I would wait more than five minutes."

"It was late," I explained. "I . . . I got a little scared outside. I was all alone, and I didn't feel safe."

"No one else was on the pool deck?"

Special Agent Diaz's steadfast gaze was my undoing. He

appeared to be in his late thirties or early forties, which meant he had a lot of years as a cop under his belt. He probably had a bullshit detector as keen as any of the most elaborate radar detectors.

"Okay, here's the deal," I began, and noted that the agent's eyes widened with interest. "I went to the pool deck as planned. Only as I was waiting, someone else came onto the deck. This guy who works for the cruise line, named Greg. He . . . he made unwanted sexual advances. And as he did, I heard someone else come onto the deck. But by the time I got Greg off of me, I didn't see anyone. I think . . . I think Drake came onto the deck and saw me, and misconstrued what he saw."

"According to the notes from the staff captain, you never mentioned this before."

"I didn't mention it because I don't think it has anything to do with what happened. And . . ." My voice trailed off.

"And what?"

"And because I didn't want to give Mr. Musgrave more reason to believe that Drake might have killed himself." When Special Agent Diaz didn't speak, I continued. "He was telling me how people who are depressed on cruises often jump overboard, and he figured with Drake being accused of rape, and our relationship being at odds, he had reason to be depressed. I know Drake would never kill himself, so that's why I didn't tell him about what happened with Greg. What if he stopped searching for Drake because of what I said?"

The agent said nothing, merely nodded and jotted down more notes.

"Did you want your boyfriend dead?" Special Agent Diaz asked, startling me.

"Dead?"

"Yes, dead. Were you angry with him because he was accused of rape?"

"I already told you I didn't believe Natalie."

"Yet you were both at odds."

The interview had gone from cordial to accusatory. I suddenly felt like I was defending myself against a charge of murder.

"Not because of me. I believed Drake. But because of the stress he was under."

"It had to be stressful for you, too."

"It was. But I wouldn't kill him."

"Yet you were the one who planned to meet Drake on deck, at midnight, which, it turns out, is the approximate time he went missing."

"I told you what happened. That guy Greg showed up. Scared Drake away. In fact . . . Someone pushed me down the steps earlier today. I think it was Greg."

"You're alleging that someone who works for the cruise line pushed you down the stairs?" The agent's tone couldn't have been more doubtful.

"Yes," I said. "And maybe . . . maybe he was the one who killed Drake."

"A SunSeekers employee?"

"One of my friends said that maybe he was jealous. Jealous that I was with Drake."

"One minute you believe that Natalie Laymon and her family members are behind what happened to Drake. Now you believe it's a cruise ship employee?"

"I don't know what to think. I'm throwing out options because I'm as baffled as you are."

"What does Greg look like?"

"He's black. Dark-skinned. About six feet tall. Bald. Maybe forty-five."

The agent made notes. Then he studied me for several seconds, not saying a word. It unnerved me.

Finally, he stood, saying. "Wait here."

As he left the room, I dropped my head onto the desk. A sob erupted in my throat. Did he truly believe I had something to do with what had happened to Drake? Or was he simply trying to fluster me?

The minutes ticked by. Five minutes turned to ten. Ten to fifteen. But when forty minutes rolled around with no sign of the agent, I was truly starting to sweat.

Innocent people were convicted of crimes all the time. And the first ones suspected were always the ones who had a relationship with the victim.

Was the FBI agent off somewhere with his colleagues right now, building a case against me?

When the door flew open, I jumped from fright. Special Agent Diaz entered the room, followed by Roman Musgrave.

"Sorry to keep you waiting," the agent said, and sat opposite me once more.

"It's okay," I replied, my voice meek.

"Two things of note," the agent said, all business. "One: We discovered that the video on the pool deck was tampered with. The very one that would have taped you where you said you were standing."

"Tampered with?" I asked, aghast.

"The lens was covered with black spray paint."

Though I knew it had to be true, I looked at the staff captain, who nodded his confirmation.

"Oh my God," I uttered. "So someone definitely planned this. Planned to murder Drake."

"It's not the first time video equipment has been tampered with," Roman said. "We've seen it before, when couples want to make love outside without the security staff's prying eyes on them."

"Is that what you think happened?" I asked. "That someone tampered with the video camera because they were making out?"

"We can't be certain," the agent advised me. "But it does seem a suspicious coincidence."

A lump lodged in my throat. I tried to swallow it away, but couldn't. "And the second thing?" I asked. "You said there was something else."

The agent exchanged a look with the staff captain before facing me once more. "You mentioned someone named Greg had been sexually harassing you."

"Yes, that's right." I looked at Roman. "One of the ship's employees."

Again, the agent and the staff captain shared a look.

"What?" I asked. "What is it?"

"There's a slight problem with your story," Special Agent Diaz said to me, again staring at me with that dark, probing gaze. "There are two men named Greg employed on this ship. But neither is a dark-skinned black man."

My eyes narrowed. "What are you saying?"

"I'm saying, Miss Randall," the agent began, "that the man you described doesn't exist. Now, are you ready to stop bullshitting me and tell me the truth?"

Chapter Twenty-five

Several seconds passed before I was able to speak. "Wh-what?" I croaked.

"There are two men named Greg who work on this ship," the agent elaborated. "Both are white. Now, if you don't start telling me the truth, I'm going to think you had something to do with what happened to your ex-boyfriend."

"No . . ." My voice was a mix of horror and fear. This couldn't be true. It was impossible.

I threw a frantic gaze at the staff captain. "You have to know him. About six feet tall, dark-skinned. Bald. Greg. Maybe Greg is his middle name. I don't know. All I know is that he works for this cruise line. I believe he said he was a program coordinator." When Roman said nothing, I continued, my words coming out quickly. "You *must* know him. For God's sake, he's been walking around in a SunSeekers uniform since day one."

"There is no one named Greg who fits the description you gave," the staff captain concurred.

What was going on? There had to be some mistake. "Someone, then. Someone who matches the description I gave you. Hell, he was there today when I fell down the stairs. People saw him. Ask for witnesses. Give me photos of every person on staff. I'll pick him out for you."

Neither the special agent nor the staff captain said anything.

"If you were having an affair," the staff captain began gently.

"An *affair*? Are you serious? I came on this cruise to reconcile with Drake. Why would I have an affair?"

"People do all kinds of things one would never expect," Roman said.

"You're out of your mind. I just told you I'd go through the photos of all the men on staff and point Greg out to you. Or whatever his name really is. Show me the security video. I'll pick him out."

But it hit me then, what the agent had said. My God, could it be true? Was there really no man matching the description I'd given them who worked for the SunSeekers cruise line?

"He's the one," I said, horror filling me. "He's the one Seth hired. He came on this ship, pretended to work for the cruise line. Got close to me. To Drake. And he threw Drake overboard. It had to have been him!"

"Slow down," the agent said. "What's this latest theory?"

I hated that he'd said *latest theory,* as if I was guilty and making up stories to cover my ass. "I don't know what's going on," I said, slowly, clearly. "All I can do is speculate. Give you options to pursue. And Natalie Laymon—the one who said Drake raped her—told me a different story this morning."

With both men listening intently to what I had to say, I explained to them the conversation I'd had with Natalie, how she now felt that Drake may not have been the one who raped her, and that she possibly could have been invited on this cruise as a scapegoat. Then I told them about Seth, how I hated him for cruelly abusing animals, how he likely hated me for confronting him about what he'd done, and ended with the theory that maybe he had raped Natalie, and Drake knew it, and therefore he wanted to silence Drake.

Even if the FBI agent and the staff captain weren't looking at me as if I'd grown another head, I would have realized how ridiculous my story sounded. After I'd finished my long, convoluted assumption, I was left feeling as though I'd made a bigger fool of myself than I had when describing a man who apparently had been passing himself off as a SunSeekers' employee.

"What's Seth's surname?" the agent asked. And then he turned to Roman. "If you can track him down so I can question—"

"Actually," I interjected, then paused. I almost didn't finish my statement, because I knew I would sound like a total nut. "He's not . . . he's not on this cruise."

The agent's eyebrow shot up again. "Excuse me?"

"His name is Seth Downey, and he's not on this cruise." The scenario might be ludicrous, but I may as well share it. See it through. "Right now, he should be in St. Barts."

"Miss Randall, I'm confused."

"He's rich," I explained. "He's got the resources to pay someone to come on this cruise and do his dirty work. I know this sounds crazy, but what if that's exactly what happened?"

The agent looked at me doubtfully. He didn't believe me. And I couldn't blame him.

Special Agent Diaz looked at Roman. "Will you excuse me and Miss Randall?"

"Certainly," the staff captain agreed, then left the room.

"Miss Randall," the agent began once the staff captain was gone, "I'm not about to go on any wild-goose chases. I appreciate your theories, but I've got to investigate what happened on this ship." He paused. Gave me a hard stare. "You were seen lurking outside Drake Shaw's cabin. Can you tell me why?"

Lurking outside of Drake's cabin? I hadn't been lurk— "Oh," I said, understanding. "You must mean after we left Jamaica. I went to his room to see if he was there. I wasn't *lurking*."

"You are seen glancing around the hallway several times, putting your ear against his door."

"Because I was worried that he was in the room with . . . with someone else," I admitted. "I listened at the door, heard nothing, then knocked." I swallowed, remembering my jealous fear that Drake had been screwing that Hispanic bombshell. "Obviously, if I'd killed him the night before, I wouldn't need to be outside of his room *lurking*. I would know he wasn't there."

"Unless you were trying to keep up appearances," the agent said. "Make it look as though you would have no clue that Drake wasn't there, when you clearly did."

"I hadn't seen him all day," I said testily. "That's why I went to his room. And when he didn't come to the door, well, that was the first inclination I had that something was wrong."

Special Agent Diaz said nothing.

"Do you think I did this?" I asked him, point-blank. If he thought I was lying, then it stood to reason he would assume I was lying to hide my own guilt. "I'm five feet six inches. Drake's six-foot-four. Do you really think I could throw him overboard?"

The question weighed heavily between us in the seconds that followed. If the agent's intention was to make me sweat, he had succeeded.

"I follow the evidence, Miss Randall."

"And the evidence is telling you I killed my boyfriend?" I asked, sarcasm dripping from my voice. I was tired of playing nice. This was bullshit.

"Right now, I'm trying to determine if Drake was a victim of foul play or if he jumped."

I remained silent, meeting the FBI agent's gaze dead-on. I wanted him to look deep into my eyes and see the truth. The truth that I would never—*could* never—hurt Drake.

"I can tell you this," Special Agent Diaz said. "You were seen on the videotape footage rushing into the ship from the exterior deck. Of course, with the exterior video camera tampered with, there's no way to tell what happened on deck."

I wanted to leap out of my chair and scream that I was innocent. Instead, dread made my muscles as heavy as concrete, preventing me from lifting even a finger.

The agent's words registered with startling severity. Suddenly, I could see where this was going. I was seen rushing inside from the deck, perhaps looking like a woman fleeing a crime scene. "I was running inside because of that guy Greg," I said, desperate now to make him understand. "Because he'd come on to me and I was trying to get away from him. And because I thought Drake had maybe seen me with him. So I had to find Drake and make him understand."

"Which is something the video footage confirms."

I stared at Special Agent Diaz, confused. "What do you mean?"

"At the time you must have been out on deck, Drake appeared at the door. We have footage of him pushing the door open, but then he suddenly hurries back inside."

"Oh my God," I uttered, a hoarse whisper. "He saw me. He saw me with Greg."

"There's footage of him entering the disco," the agent went on, "but about ten minutes later, Drake returns to that same door you exited through. This time he heads outside."

To confront me? I wondered. After seeing me with Greg, he must have assumed the worst. Figured I was getting hot and heavy with someone on the pool deck. Upset, he had run off. Perhaps after some time to calm down, he decided to head back to the pool deck to have it out with me.

Had he run into Greg? Had they fought over me? Had Greg thrown him overboard?

A strangled sob seeped past my lips. I felt ill. Ill with the thought that in Drake's last moments, he had likely believed that I had been screwing around on him.

I started to cry. "And after that?" I asked, though I knew. I knew.

"So far, that's the last footage of Drake Shaw we've been able to find. He exits the door to go onto the pool deck, and then he vanishes. He disappears into the night without a trace."

Part Three

"Bush get ears and dutty get tongue."

Translation: Sometimes you think that what you do or say nobody sees or hears, but yet your secrets are known.

—GUYANESE PROVERB

Chapter Twenty-six

Without a trace.

The haunting words left me chilled. I kept imagining Drake seeing me with Greg, the shock and betrayal he must have felt. And I imagined him going back to the deck to confront me. Instead, he confronted Greg.

And Greg had killed him.

That was the scenario that seemed the most likely. Add to that the fact that "Greg" had impersonated a SunSeekers employee, well, it was obvious.

But had he come onto the cruise with the specific intention of killing Drake? Or was he some kind of sexual predator who found cruises to be fertile hunting ground? Had he set his sights on me by chance, and sought to get Drake out of the way?

How had Greg been able to masquerade as an employee of the ship? Were people so single-mindedly absorbed with their own positions that they hadn't noticed someone who didn't belong?

It was baffling, but I guess it proved the theory that if you made yourself look like you belonged, no one doubted that you did.

To me, it made sense that Greg had had something to do with what happened to Drake. Yet the kicker was what Drake had told his mother. That if anything should happen to him, it would be murder. Drake knew someone was targeting him, and he'd expected an attack at some point. That was the one thing that shot a hole in my theory that the fight between Greg and Drake had been a spontaneous one.

Unless someone *was* after Drake, but by the strangest of coincidences, someone else had killed Drake first.

My head hurt from all my hypothesizing. So many scenarios, no real answers.

There was one thing I knew for sure: I couldn't continue on the cruise. How could I sail on to Cozumel as though my world was fine?

With the permission of the FBI, I got off the ship in Grand Cayman. Roxanne and Jolene left with me. They couldn't carry on with the cruise if one of their best friend's boyfriends was lost at sea.

I led the way down the ramp and off the ship, inhaling a deep lungful of the salty, island air. As I gazed around at the beauty of the place, a pang of pain hit me so hard, I almost burst into tears. Drake and I had planned to visit Stingray City here on the island. You could see the tame creatures through glass-bottomed boats, or you could go scuba diving with them, or you could enjoy them while snorkeling. We had chosen the snorkel option—something I'd always wanted to do, and unlike scuba diving, you didn't need lessons in order to do it. Instead of our fun-filled excursion, I was stepping onto Grand Cayman with the knowledge that Drake was likely dead.

And not just dead. Murdered.

I wasn't aware of having stopped walking until Jolene placed a hand on my shoulder and asked, "Are you okay?"

I faced her. My chest hurt with every breath I inhaled. "Not really," I said, aware that I was the farthest thing from okay. Somehow I was hanging on, though, maybe until I was able to get back to Lan-U. In the comfort of my own room, I knew I would totally break down.

Roxanne instructed the taxi driver to hightail it to the airport, and when we got there, we immediately went to the American Airlines counter to see when the next flight out was and if we could get on it. There were two options. We could head to Miami that evening and catch a connecting flight to Philadelphia in the morning, or we could stay the night in Grand Cayman and catch a flight out the next day. We were all in agreement to take the flight to Miami and find a hotel there for the night. I wanted desperately to be back on American soil.

Thank the Lord, the next, and final, flight to Miami for the day was leaving at five-thirty, which gave us just enough time to change our tickets and check our bags.

"Oh my God, look," Roxanne said, pointing to a television when we neared our boarding gate.

I looked. Saw the image of the cruise ship on the screen with the words "College student missing at sea" below.

"Shit," I uttered, surprised. Though I shouldn't have been. I should have expected there to be media coverage of Drake's disappearance. Especially after Ashley Hamilton's disappearance in Artula less than a year ago. Another student missing from the same college—there was bound to be extensive media attention.

The television set was perched high and the volume was low, but Roxanne, Jolene, and I crowded below it, looking up and straining to hear what the newsanchor was saying.

". . . massive search in the waters of the Caribbean have failed to find him. No one is sure how he fell off the SunSeeker *Glorious* cruise liner, and the FBI is currently investigating. Drake Shaw is the second student from Lancaster University to disappear in less than a year. You may remember the case of Ashley Hamilton, who vanished on the island of Artula while vacationing there for spring break last March. So far, the police are still investigating her disappearance, but say there are no viable leads."

Finished speaking, the male anchor turned to the woman beside him. Appearing remorseful, she said, "So sad. Let's hope there's a happy resolution to this case."

"The Coast Guard is still calling it a search and rescue, so there's hope," the male anchor responded.

The female newsanchor began to talk about a quadruple homicide in Oklahoma, and I lowered my gaze from the television set.

Roxanne linked arms with me. Jolene rubbed my back.

And then we continued on to the gate, where we would head back to the United States.

But I was returning as an incomplete person. Because half my heart was gone.

Lost at sea.

How the hell are they here already?

That was my thought the moment I saw them, because I knew they were here for me. Here because of Drake.

Having cleared Customs at Miami International Airport, Jolene, Roxanne, and I were heading toward baggage claim. And that's when I spotted the media, just past security. A whole team of them. Video cameras were rolling, and reporters stood at the ready armed with microphones.

When they saw me, they advanced as a single unit, moving with the swiftness of vultures.

Then came the pandemonium.

"Didi Randall, tell us what happened on the cruise."

"Did your boyfriend jump?"

"How did Drake Shaw end up in the ocean?"

"The second missing student in less than a year—do you think Lancaster University is cursed?"

I stood, frozen, as microphones were thrust into my face. Cameras flashed. Reporters vied for the best position around me. I had no clue what to say.

Roxanne was the one to speak. "We have no idea what happened. As you can imagine, Didi is devastated."

"Who are you?"

"Roxanne Miller. I'm one of her best friends. Please, all we want to do is head back home. The last couple of days have been a nightmare. Didi needs time to deal with everything that's happened. We all do."

There were more questions, but Roxanne and Jolene shielded me from the media, guided me past them. And then came a question that stopped me cold.

"How do you respond to the fact that Janine Shaw, Drake's mother, believes you might know something about his murder that you're not sharing?"

I whirled around. "*What?*"

"She says you haven't called her," a pretty blond reporter said, as though that in itself was some sort of crime. "That she hasn't heard from you since Drake's disappearance. She finds that odd."

"Because I just got back to the States." My retort held a tinge of anger, but I couldn't help it. I'd taken time to call my parents while in Grand Cayman, but wasn't yet ready to talk to Mrs. Shaw. As it was, I was barely holding it together. Speaking to Mrs. Shaw was something I wanted to do in the comfort of my dorm room when I got back to school. Because hearing her grief would trigger the emotions I was trying my best to keep in check.

"She believes it's unlike you not to call her, given your five-year relationship with her son," the blonde pressed on.

"And that makes me guilty of murder?" I asked disbelievingly. "I didn't call her yet because I was hoping . . . hoping there would be good news. That Drake would be found. Then I wouldn't have to give her the bad news I knew would devastate her."

"Didi has been through hell," Jolene added. "She only called her parents two hours ago when we got to the airport in Grand Cayman. Why are you looking for a scandal instead of reporting the truth?"

"We can't report the truth when you won't answer questions."

Who was this blond bitch, I wondered? Someone new on the job, trying to work her way up the ladder with a big story?

"You want the truth?" I said. "Fine, ask me questions. I'll tell you what you want to know."

"Maybe you shouldn't say anything without a lawyer," Roxanne whispered in my ear.

My eyes bulged at my friend. She thought I needed a lawyer? "I did nothing wrong," I said in a low tone. I knew how people who ran from cameras on the news looked: guilty. And I had nothing to hide.

So I faced the media, ready for their questions.

"Can you tell us what happened on the ship?" This from an African-American reporter whose microphone boasted the CNN logo.

"I wish I could," I said. "All I know is that I was supposed to meet Drake on the pool deck at midnight—late Monday night, early Tuesday morning—but he didn't show."

"Do you know if he was drinking?" another reporter asked, a man this time. "He wouldn't be the first college kid to drink too much and—"

"Drake wasn't a big drinker," I interjected. "There's no way he would have fallen overboard accidentally."

"So either he was murdered," another male reporter deduced, "or he committed suicide."

"Drake would *not* take his own life." I wanted that theory debunked immediately.

"But he must have been a little despondent, what with the rape allegation and all." Another woman, this time a brunette, asked that question.

My heart rate accelerated. So they knew about the allegation at Lan-U. It figured. All anyone had to do was a little investigation on the Internet to find the story on The Gossip Hour.

I reiterated, "He was never charged with any crime."

"But some of Drake's friends have said he wasn't quite himself after being publicly humiliated on the Web site The Gossip Hour," the brunette continued. "It exposed the rape, even if he wasn't charged."

"That whole story was a disgusting lie," I said adamantly. "And Drake would never kill himself over a lie. None of that matters." Frustrated, I sighed. "What *does* matter is that Drake's strong. He's an athlete. If anyone can survive in the ocean, he can. Please keep the pressure on the Coast Guard so they don't stop looking for him. I firmly believe that he's alive somewhere, perhaps floating on something. Please . . ." I knew I sounded desperate, but how could I give up on Drake?

"Yes," Jolene agreed. "The search *must* continue. Please pressure everyone you can to commit resources to help find him. Stop digging for dirt. There is none."

"Oh no?" It was a challenge, and it came from the blond bitch. One of her perfectly sculpted eyebrows shot up. "But isn't it true, Didi, that you and Drake were involved in a fatal accident back in Oakland, California? Four years ago?"

A cold chill passed through my entire body. An excited hum spread through the crowd of reporters and spectators that had gathered around us.

God help me . . .

The blond reporter referred to her notepad, as though she needed help remembering something. I knew it was an act. She knew exactly what she was going to say. She had simply been waiting for the right moment to drop her bombshell.

"He was driving, hit a pedestrian. A woman named Erin

Lowell." The reporter stared at me, and I could see the look of victory in her blue eyes. She felt she'd hit pay dirt, made the story of a missing student into something salacious enough to sell papers for days. "You were passed out in the passenger seat, too drunk to drive."

I said nothing. I was too paralyzed to speak.

"Didi, what's she talking about?" This from Roxanne.

"That . . . that was an accident," I said after a moment, ignoring Roxanne and speaking to the crowd. "An awful, awful accident."

"But he took a life nonetheless, didn't he? You say Drake didn't kill himself, but he's been carrying the guilt from that accident around with him for years. Maybe the guilt finally got to him."

"You bitch," I snapped. I wanted to hit this woman. Slap the smug look off her face. "Are you interested in saving Drake or destroying his reputation?"

"You're asserting that he didn't commit suicide," the woman said, gently now, as though talking to a small child. "I'm trying to look at all the factors in his life that could have led to him doing something like that."

Suddenly it was quiet, all the other reporters looking at the blonde—the only one who had found this dirty tidbit from Drake's past.

"According to reports from that night, you and Drake were at a party, and when you left, you were both fighting furiously. Some speculated that his anger caused him to lose control and strike the innocent woman."

"I was in the car with him. It was an accident."

"But you never could give an accurate account of what happened one way or another," the woman went on, as though on a personal mission to destroy me. "Because you were intoxicated."

"It was an *accident*!" I shouted, advancing. The reporter actually reeled backward, as though she thought I was going to hit her. Roxanne or Jolene gripped my arm, trying to control me. "That's why Drake was never charged! Accidents happen every day in this country. And what the hell does this have to do with Drake being missing?"

"This interview is over," Roxanne said, stepping in front of me to shield me from the vultures. "No more questions."

And then Roxanne ushered me out of the airport and to a taxi, where she put me in the backseat. The taxi driver was given instructions to stay put until Roxanne and Jolene returned with the luggage.

I sat, trembling. Terror was like a living, breathing entity sitting beside me in the back of that cab. Not just sitting next to me, but placing a hand over my mouth and smothering me.

My secret exposed. For all the world.

I thought my life had gone to hell after The Gossip Hour aired its dirty allegation against Drake. But this was worse.

Much worse.

Because now I was in the seventh level of hell.

Chapter Twenty-seven

THE TAXI DROVE TO a budget hotel near the airport, where we learned that, yes, there was a room available. Roxanne and Jolene waited until we were upstairs before they asked me any questions.

I settled on the bed and closed my eyes, hoping to avoid the inevitable. But Jolene's voice broke the silence.

"Dee, what was that reporter talking about? You and Drake were in a crash that killed someone?"

I opened my eyes. Inhaled deeply. "It was an accident."

"All this time, you never said anything," Roxanne said.

I knew what she was alluding to. The fact that we had all

shared the most painful of secrets with one another. But she didn't understand. This was something I couldn't share. It was far too devastating.

"It was the worst night of my life. Something I wanted to forget," I explained. "I don't like to talk about it."

"I don't like talking about my mother," Roxanne said. "The fact that she's in prison. But I told you about that. Told you both."

I sat upright. "Prison is not the same thing as killing someone. And since when are we required to share our most painful secrets? Some things a person wants to keep to herself."

"Why are you snapping at us?" Jolene asked. "Obviously we're curious."

I buried my face in my hands. I was unraveling at the seams, I could feel it. "I'm sorry. I'm not angry with you. I'm angry because Drake is missing and suddenly the media is out to make him look like some kind of monster. As if he deserved to die for a mistake. If they think he killed himself, they'll never keep looking for him."

Roxanne was pacing near the door, her arms crossed over her chest. Reading her body language, I judged her to be upset.

"Roxy, I'm sorry," I repeated. I squeezed the back of my neck, which still hurt from my fall down the stairs. "I'm stressed. We're all stressed."

Halting, she faced me. "What if that reporter is right?" she began. "What if Drake did jump?"

How could she ask me that? She knew Drake, knew he wasn't capable of suicide. "He didn't."

"I know it was an accident," she went on, "but if he was wracked with guilt because of running that pedestrian down . . . who knows?"

"He wouldn't kill himself," I reiterated.

"How can you be so sure? No one would have ever believed that Rachel Jepson would kill herself, and yet, if she took all those pills, isn't it obvious that she did?"

For a long moment, I was silent. I couldn't tell Roxanne what she wanted to hear. The reason I knew, without a doubt, that Drake wouldn't have killed himself over the accident.

So I said, "Because his father died last summer. His mother was having a hard enough time as it was. Drake wouldn't kill himself because doing so would destroy his mother." I groaned long and loud, beyond frustrated. "This is exactly the kind of tangent I don't want people going off on. If they think he wanted to kill himself, maybe they'll call off the search."

"Do you really think he's still alive?" Jolene asked, her voice barely above a whisper.

The question was the elephant in the room. The one I didn't want to see.

"It's been a long time," she went on. "I know he's strong, but—"

"Stop!" I shot up off the bed. "You two want to give up on Drake, fine. But I'm not going to. Until we know what happened to him, I'm going to believe he's alive. I have to."

And then I grabbed my purse and stormed out of the room.

I ran to the stairwell and charged down the stairs. But no matter how fast I ran, I couldn't escape my reality.

Do you really think he's still alive?

At the bottom of the stairwell, I sank onto the concrete floor and began to sob. I'm not sure how long I sat there, braced against the cool wall, crying my eyes out. I cried until there were no more tears.

My knee hurt from being pressed against the hard floor for too long, so I got up, sat on a nearby step, and then dug my cell phone out of my purse. It was time to call Drake's mother. There was no point putting it off any longer. I needed to make her understand that just because I hadn't called her already didn't mean I was hiding some sort of vital information.

She answered on the first ring. "Didi?"

"Yes, Mrs. Shaw. It's me."

"What on earth happened? No one will tell me anything. I need to find Drake. I need to find my son." Janine Shaw sounded hysterical, and my heart split in two. Despite what she believed, I didn't have any answers. There was nothing I could tell her that would make the situation better.

"I don't know, Mrs. Shaw."

"How can you not know?"

"All I can tell you is that Drake was supposed to meet me Monday night on the pool deck. I showed, he didn't. And that's all I know."

"You didn't look for him?"

"I did look for him. Of course I did. But I assumed . . ." My voice trailed off. I didn't want to finish my statement. I didn't want to tell Drake's mother that I had been worried he might have gotten involved with someone else on the ship.

"Assumed what?"

"That he wasn't ready to get back together with me."

"Why did you wait so long to report him missing?" Mrs. Shaw demanded. "Do you know what happened to him?"

"No, I don't."

"And yet you didn't call."

"Because I didn't want you to be worried."

"Worried?" Mrs. Shaw shrieked. "My son is missing at sea!"

"I didn't know that at the time. I thought . . . I thought we just kept missing each other."

Mrs. Shaw scoffed.

"Why did you tell the authorities—and the media—that you think I have information about what happened?" I asked her.

"Because I've known you for years. I couldn't believe you wouldn't call about something like this. It was out of character."

"Exactly, we've known each other for years. You should know how much I love your son."

"But did you still love him after he was accused of rape?"

A beat. "I did. Of course I did."

"Then explain to me why he said that if anything were to happen to him, it would be murder."

"I can't. All I can think is that maybe the woman who said he raped her was out for vengeance. She ended up on the cruise, too—with some relatives. They started a fight with Drake, by the way. Or . . ."

"Or what?"

I said nothing. How could I tell her my list of convoluted theories? They would sound ridiculous. Like a pack of lies.

"Or what?"

"Or he got into a fight with some other people. I don't know. Mrs. Shaw, when Drake told you he thought someone might murder him, what else did he say?"

"Nothing."

"Nothing?"

"I asked him to elaborate, and all he said was that he was

worried that someone maybe wanted to hurt him because of something they thought he'd done."

"He didn't say anything else?"

"No." Mrs. Shaw's voice cracked. "I didn't ask for any more. I thought . . . I thought he was being paranoid."

"He didn't mention anything about Seth?"

"His housemate? No."

We fell into silence. I tried to replay in my mind every conversation I'd had with Drake since Natalie's allegation had come to light. The one thing that stood out was the way he had stressed that I not push Seth, not piss him off with any accusations.

Did he suspect that Seth was dangerous?

He said he would tell me only when he got the proof.

"Do you really think he's gone?" Mrs. Shaw began to sob. "I keep thinking—hoping—that maybe he got off the ship in Jamaica. That he's hiding out because he's scared."

I couldn't help it. I felt a surge of hope. Was Mrs. Shaw right? Had Drake somehow managed to bypass the protocols and get off the ship?

"Anything's possible," I said, wanting to cling to that. "We just have to believe it."

The tone in the room was somber when I returned. There was no small talk. We were all physically and mentally exhausted and tried to get some rest.

My brain wouldn't shut down. Every time I closed my eyes, I imagined Drake falling over the ship's railing.

Do you really think he's still alive?

A fall from the top of the ship . . . had he even survived it? Or had he crashed into the water with the velocity of someone crashing into a brick wall?

Unable to sleep, I channel-surfed. Tried to follow every news story that had to do with Drake.

And that's when I discovered that the blond reporter who had dropped the bomb about the fatal accident four years ago worked for *The Inside Scoop,* a tabloid "news" show out of Miami—the kind of tabloid show that made *The National Enquirer* seem legit. Yes, they aired the footage of me yelling at the media. Exploited it, in fact.

I should have known my meltdown would make the news. Screw the search for Drake—meltdowns led to ratings.

But what pissed me off more than anything was the commentary accompanying the segment. "Does Didi Randall have something to hide? Does she know more about what happened to her boyfriend, Drake Shaw, that night on the ship? Some sources claim she was arguing with Drake only a short time before he disappeared. Did Didi, fueled by anger at Drake because of his alleged sexual assault of a fellow student, snap and kill him?"

Not to mention the reporter commenting on my lack of tears, as if that meant I was some sort of coldhearted serial killer. She didn't understand that I had to keep my emotions reined in. If I didn't, I would completely unravel.

It was after midnight when I turned the television off. Were people actually coming forward to say they'd seen me and Drake arguing, or was that simply slander on the part of *The Inside Scoop*?

Would it matter? Once allegations were leveled in the media, people started to believe them as true. And people would now think that I had something to hide where Drake's disappearance was concerned.

I wanted to scream.

I wanted to die.

But most of all, I wanted to turn back the hands of time and tell Drake never to step foot on this ill-fated cruise.

I closed my eyes, but the tears escaped, trickling down the sides of my face and onto my pillow.

Chapter Twenty-eight

SOMETHING CAME TO ME as I slept. Remembering the conversation I'd had with Natalie, something suddenly struck me as odd.

In part, it was the way she had so easily been convinced that Drake wasn't the one who'd raped her. I'd heard stories of people who'd been cleared of wrongdoing by DNA evidence, and still the victims believed that the acquitted person was guilty of the crime. All Natalie had was Drake's word—and how often did people lie to protect themselves?

All the time.

I believed Drake wasn't guilty, but why would Natalie so

easily change her tune? After how she had persecuted him at Lan-U, that simply didn't make sense to me.

But fueling my certainty that something was wrong was also something she said. Something I needed to question her about.

When we got back to Lan-U, I looked Natalie up on Facebook. We weren't friends on the social networking site, but I sent her a message.

I need to talk to you. Urgently.
If you're back, call me. 717-555-2218.
—Didi

I was glad when, two hours after I sent the message, I got a reply from Natalie. She told me that she was at the Pittsburgh airport, but could meet me at seven that evening. On the terrace outside of the Terrell dining hall, the college's main cafeteria.

There were, as expected, media on campus. I saw videographers filming shots of the various university buildings. I'd also driven by Seth's house and saw camera crews camped outside. Natalie had mentioned proof, and if Seth was still away, this would be the perfect time to search his room. The problem was bigger than the media outside. There was also the issue of not knowing what I was looking for.

Roxanne, Jolene, and I were surprised to get to our dorm building and find no media waiting outside. I had expected more questions. But perhaps the media had gotten all they wanted from me—sound bites that portrayed me as a vindictive bitch.

I counted it as a blessing.

I also counted it as a blessing when Jolene left the room to go see Scott. And despite her fling with Devon, Roxanne said she was going to head over to Rick's room.

At six fifty-five, I was outside of Terrell Hall. Some students were milling about, but most were inside, escaping the cold. There was a light dusting of snow on the ground, but the temperature wasn't below freezing. Still, bundled as I was in Drake's varsity jacket, a scarf, thick socks, and Uggs, the chill began to penetrate through my layers.

I took my cell phone out of my pocket. Seven after seven.

It was early enough that I didn't figure Natalie was blowing me off. But the fact that she hadn't called to tell me she was going to be late made me wonder if she was going to show.

Hugging my torso, I moved around on the spot, trying to keep myself as warm as possible. I began to turn in a counterclockwise motion, scanning the area. Still no Natalie.

Just as I completed a three-hundred-and-sixty-degree turn, I saw the shadow come to life. I started as it advanced from beyond a tree.

It took me a moment to realize it was Natalie.

"I almost thought you weren't coming," I said.

"This way." Without waiting, she turned sharply to the left and walked toward the side of the building. There, she slipped into the shadows, and I did the same.

"Why are we hiding?" I asked her.

"Because I meant what I told you on the ship. I don't trust anyone."

Was she being paranoid? Or did she plan to do me harm where no one would witness it?

I glanced around. Saw no one. When I faced her again, she said, "I guess you heard."

"Heard?" I asked.

"About Drake. They've called off the search."

A strange, tingling sensation spread through my body. And then a strangled cry slipped through my lips. "No . . ."

"The Coast Guard says it's been too long. That there's no way he could have survived."

My knees buckled, and I braced both hands against the brick well to steady myself. My breaths came in rapid succession, but it felt like I wasn't getting in any oxygen at all. After the way the media had vilified both me and Drake yesterday, I hadn't tuned in today. I couldn't stomach seeing any more twisted coverage.

"I'm sorry," Natalie said.

"Are you?" I challenged.

"Of course I am. I . . . I feel awful. And the way they're talking about him in the press . . ." Natalie's exhale was audible. "I want to make this right. Did you find the proof Drake talked about?"

"I didn't look yet."

"What? Why not?"

"Because I don't know if I believe you."

Even in the darkness, I could see the look of shock on Natalie's face. "I laid it all on the line for you, told you everything."

"That's the problem. I don't think you did." When Natalie didn't speak, I continued. "Why did you believe Drake so easily? You were convinced he'd raped you, and all he had to do was say, 'Nope, didn't do it,' and you believed him?"

"Because he said there was proof," Natalie replied.

I shook my head. "No, I don't think that's it." I paused, went on. "I've seen people believe that someone exonerated of a crime, with absolute proof of innocence, is still guilty. If you believed Drake was the one who raped you, I don't buy that you would be so easily swayed after one conversation with him."

"You can doubt me all you wan—"

"You said something," I pressed on. "Something that I kept thinking about all last night . . . and wondering."

Natalie narrowed her eyes.

"You said 'That wasn't my plan.' I thought nothing of it at the time, but now I can't help questioning if you meant that it wasn't *your* plan but *someone else's* plan. Is that what you meant?"

Natalie said nothing.

My neck prickled. I was onto something. "Someone planned to destroy Drake, didn't they? And you know who that person is. Because you lied to help set Drake up."

"I didn't lie," Natalie shot back. "I told you before: I told the truth as I knew it."

"Then why did you change your tune?" I couldn't help raising my voice. "Because the story you gave me, I don't buy it. Something else is going on. Did someone pay you to finger Drake?" That was an idea I'd also considered last night. Natalie hadn't just gone on the cruise—she'd gone on the cruise looking like a different person. "New hair, new clothes, new . . . cosmetic enhancements. Suddenly, you've got a whole new look. The kind of look that costs a lot. So, who wanted to set Drake up? Who wanted to discredit him? And why?"

"It wasn't like that."

"Oh really? Because I'm willing to bet that whoever set Drake up is the person behind what happened to him on the cruise."

"That's impossible."

"It isn't!" I was getting angry. "You know I'm right. And damn it, you better admit it—or I'll go to the FBI with what I know."

"It *is* impossible," Natalie stressed.

"You say that again, and I'm going to have to conclude that someone paid you and your family members to kill Drake. In fact, despite all the bullshit you've told me, it's the only thing that makes sense. I'm going to the cops with that." I turned and started off.

"It's impossible because it was Rachel!"

The urgent whisper made me stop. Whirl around. "What did you say?"

"I didn't get it at the time, but I've thought about it, too. Ever since Drake convinced me that he wasn't the one who . . . hurt me. I've thought about why Rachel was so insistent that I finger Drake as my rapist."

I closed the distance between us. "*Rachel Jepson?*"

"She was there, at the party that night. She saw me stumble down the steps from upstairs. I was half out of it, crying hysterically. Next thing I know, she was taking me back to my room, which was a godsend because I couldn't get back on my own. I was in bad shape. She asked me what happened. I told her that I was raped."

"And you told her Drake had raped you," I supplied. Natalie *must* have been the one to mention that.

"She was the one who said Drake raped me. Back at my room, I told her I thought it was Seth."

I said nothing, just waited for Natalie to go on.

"But then she said no, that it wasn't Seth. That it was Drake. That he'd raped other women. Including her."

"That's a lie!"

"Maybe it was. All I know is that Rachel told me that. She painted Drake out to be a sexual predator, and convinced me that I had to report him. She said she hadn't done so because she knew his family and had wanted to protect them at the time, but said that since Drake had struck again, he deserved no protection."

"What the hell?"

"I didn't want to go to the police. I . . . I just didn't."

"So you went to The Gossip Hour."

"I didn't want to. But after what happened to Rachel . . . I was scared. I mean, what if it wasn't an accident?"

"What do you mean?"

Natalie's shoulders shook. "I didn't know what to think. I just thought . . . what if Drake knew that Rachel had helped me, and wanted to hurt her?"

I felt a chill. And it had nothing to do with the temperature outside.

"You can't be serious," I said. "They were friends. In fact, why would Rachel want you to smear Drake's name?" None of what Natalie said was making sense. Rachel had been one of Drake's oldest friends. Even after their one-night stand, I'd seen her and Drake together, and Rachel had always been cordial and happy with him. She hadn't looked like a woman who saw Drake as some depraved sexual predator.

"That's what I asked her. She said that Drake needed to be stopped. I *had* been raped, and she was going on and on about how evil Drake was . . . so I figured she was right. And when people asked me about the rape, I didn't think I was lying when I said Drake had done it."

I turned away, thinking. It didn't make sense that Rachel would want to vilify Drake. She was one of his oldest friends.

The only thing I knew for sure was that Rachel couldn't be the one behind Drake's disappearance. Because she had died weeks before we'd gone on the cruise.

But had she been part of some plan to drag Drake through the mud . . . and then kill him? Had she been murdered so she could never talk about her part in someone's diabolical plan?

"Did Rachel pay you to name Drake as your rapist?" I asked.

"No. Rachel never gave me a penny."

"But someone did. Unless you're going to tell me that your family came into some money."

A beat passed. Then she said, "Inside the envelope with the note and the ticket for the cruise was also some money. Ten thousand dollars."

"Ten thousand dollars!" I shrieked.

"Shh." Natalie glanced around nervously. "I didn't tell you before because, well, because I felt stupid. It's so clear now, someone wanted me on the cruise as a scapegoat. But when I got the letter, it said Drake was giving me the money as a way to show how sorry he was, and because he didn't want me to sue him."

"And what? You thought you and he were going to literally sail off into the sunset together?" It was a hunch I had, that even though Natalie had claimed Drake had raped her, she'd been smitten with him. "Is that why you did the elaborate makeover, hoping you'd be pretty enough that he'd fall for you?"

Natalie said nothing, and I knew I'd hit the nail on the head.

Her motives didn't matter. What did matter was the fact that someone had given her ten grand. "Someone sends you a letter with a ton of cash, and you don't question it? You think that's perfectly normal?"

"I already told you, I feel really stupid now. Maybe I was just desperate for people to like me. To be pretty and popular." She shrugged. "I don't know."

Seth had money. He could have easily given Natalie that cash, paid her way to go on the cruise.

But still, I wasn't sure I could buy Natalie's alleged ignorance. "Someone gives you cash, no questions asked. That seems unlikely."

"I swear to you, I have no clue what's going on," Natalie said. "All I can think is that someone had a vendetta against Drake. Maybe it started with the rape. Maybe it started before. I don't know. Perhaps whatever proof Drake was talking about will hold the answers."

"And you don't know what that is?"

"No." She paused. "He didn't say."

I would have to go to Seth's place. Search Drake's room and see what I could find.

"I'm really freaked out," Natalie said, her voice barely a whisper. "I'm not sure what's going on, but I'm scared."

There was nothing to say, so I stayed silent.

"And maybe you should be scared, too."

"Excuse me?"

"If someone killed Drake, and you start snooping around . . ." Her voice trailed off, her statement remaining incomplete. But I got it. I understood. "I would help you, but they're not going to let me into that house. You have to do it. But just . . . just be careful."

"I will."

"And remember what I told you," she went on. "Don't trust anyone."

With that cryptic warning, Natalie turned and walked away, disappearing into the night.

Chapter Twenty-nine

TEN THOUSAND DOLLARS.

If Natalie was telling the truth and someone had given her that kind of cash, then it had to be Seth. He was the one person I could think of with the resources to do it.

According to her, Drake said there was some sort of proof regarding what had happened to her. Proof that cleared him and implicated someone else. Was it this proof that had gotten him killed?

Whatever it was, I was determined to find it. And with Seth likely still in St. Bart's, this was the perfect time to look.

Minutes after Natalie had left me, I was in my car and driving along Lem Morrison Drive, heading off campus. The house where Drake lived with Seth was a short distance away. When I'd driven by there earlier, I'd seen that the media had much of the street blocked, which meant I couldn't park in front of the house. Not that I wanted to. After yesterday's disastrous encounter with the press at the airport, I didn't want to give them any more access to me. If I parked my car in front of the house, they could easily box me in once they discovered I was inside.

But as I neared the residence, I didn't see any of the news vans or the crowd of people that had been there earlier. So I kept going, getting closer to the townhouse. Lo and behold, everyone from the media was gone. Not even one camera crew remained at the curb.

Thank the Lord for small blessings.

I put my Ford Focus into park. I wrapped my fingers around the door handle, prepared to exit the car. But I halted when I noticed the memorial at the base of the steps.

Flowers and cards. A few teddy bears. Also some candles, though if they'd been lit, the wind must have blown out their flames.

And as I stared at the memorial, it hit me again. Drake was gone. And with the search for him called off, I knew now that he wasn't coming back.

Funny how I could go along for a while, almost as if on autopilot, somehow compartmentalizing the devastating reality. And then something would bring it all back with the same crushing power the news had had the first time.

I raised my eyes past the memorial, staring instead at the townhouse's red door. Stared at it and remembered.

Drake standing at the top step with his hands shoved into the pockets of his jeans. Drake leaning against the railing and smoking a joint. Drake's eyes lighting up as he saw me approaching. Lord, how I'd loved him.

Would he really never step foot in this house again?

The thought made my throat swell with emotion. I swallowed, trying to bite it back. I had to hold myself together.

Because right now, I needed to focus on finding answers, not wallow in despair. I could only hope that finding whatever proof Natalie had spoken of would lead me to learn what had happened to Drake.

I exited my vehicle. A cold breeze swirled around me, and I hunched into my jacket, dipping my chin and mouth beneath the collar.

And then I started up the walkway. As I did, Natalie's parting words sounded in my brain. So I glanced left and right, checking to see if anyone was around me.

I saw no one.

Natalie had gone to the side of Terrell Hall when talking to me, hiding in the shadows, as if she was afraid of being seen with me. Why? And just how scared was she?

Rachel was dead. And Drake . . . oh God. Drake was likely dead, too. Maybe Natalie did have good reason to be scared.

But was Seth behind everything that had happened?

If he had done something to Drake, he had better pray to whatever god he worshipped for protection. Because I would go to the ends of the earth to make sure he paid for his crime. He might be able to get away with killing puppies and kittens, but murdering a human being was a whole other matter.

Seth was spoiled and acted entitled. I hated him. And I certainly had never understood the connection between him and Drake.

Sure, he drove fast cars and wore designer clothes. So what? Just went to show, money couldn't buy class.

But money could buy murder.

The lights were on in the house, which meant someone was home. I raised my hand to knock, but thought better of it. Instead, I tried the doorknob.

It turned.

I pushed the door open and stepped inside.

I don't know why, but my heart was pounding as I entered the house. Maybe I expected to see Seth standing in the living room pointing a gun at me. Or maybe it was because without Drake being here, I felt like I was trespassing.

At first, I saw no one. Then, from around a corner, Joe appeared.

He stopped dead in his tracks and stared at me with unmasked surprise. "Didi."

I stepped forward. "Hey, Joe."

"Shit, Didi. What the heck happened?"

A slow, shaky breath oozed out of me. "I don't know," I said, my voice a strangled sob. "God help me, I just don't know."

Joe had never been more to me than one of Drake's buddies, a guy I exchanged polite small talk with at most. But he walked toward me and wrapped me in a spontaneous bear hug as if we'd been friends for years. He held me for several seconds, and I let him, both of us needing this moment of comfort.

Tears fell down my cheeks, a quiet expression of my grief. Joe had earned the nickname The Bear on the football field because he was so big and muscular. But despite his ability to easily knock some of the toughest men around, his embrace was tender. To me, he was like a giant teddy bear.

After a long while had passed, I stepped backward.

Joe looked down at me and said, "Seriously, Didi. Drake fell overboard?"

"Apparently." I wiped at my tears, not bothering to correct him by saying that Drake was thrown. I wasn't going to debate semantics. Now wasn't the time.

"And no one knows what happened to him? No one saw anything?"

"Not that I've heard."

"You missed the media. They came by earlier, after it was announced that the search for Drake was called off. They asked all kinds of questions. And not just about the cruise, but that bullshit about Natalie, how she was supposedly raped. They also asked if we knew anything about that car accident from four years ago."

"*We?*"

"Kwame's here, too. Ryan hasn't come back from winter break yet, and Seth's still in St. Bart's."

Good. Seth wasn't here.

"I was like what the hell are they worrying about some accident for? Christ, Drake's missing."

"They're trying to make him out to be a monster," I said. "Crucify him in the press."

"I told them they could go to hell, I had nothing to say to them. Kwame, too. They hung around though, talking to people who were coming to the house to pay their respects." He paused, narrowed his eyes. "What are you doing here, by the way?"

"I . . . I guess I wanted to feel close to Drake," I lied. "I needed to be here and feel him, ya know? I can't believe he's gone. I . . . I just can't."

"Me neither." Joe shook his head solemnly.

"I'm gonna go to Drake's room. Hang out there for a while."

"No prob."

A wave of emotion hit me as I headed toward the steps. I could easily conjure up Drake's image, standing behind the sofa in the common room, yelling at the television as he watched a basketball game. Or that killer smile forming on his face as he came down the steps to meet me.

The happy memories morphed into a devastating one—the image of Drake being overpowered and thrown overboard the SunSeekers *Glorious.*

He said if anything ever happened to him, that it would be murder.

A moan escaped my lips, and I clamped down on my mouth to keep from making any noise. The time to cry would come again, but it would have to be later.

Right now I needed to find this proof that Natalie had spoken of.

Kwame, wearing a jacket, was leaving his bedroom when I reached the top step. He saw me and immediately opened his arms to me. I walked into his embrace.

"I'm so sorry, sweetie," he said.

"I know. Me, too." I eased back and told Kwame the same thing I'd told Joe. "I'm gonna hang out in Drake's room for a while. To be close to him."

Kwame nodded, letting me know he had no objection to my plan.

Moments later, I entered Drake's room. I stood at the doorway, scanning the area. The bed was unmade. Clothes were thrown haphazardly on a chair. It looked just as it always did, which struck me as intrinsically wrong. How could his room appear so normal, as if all was right with the world?

Don't think about it, I told myself. *Just search the room.* I didn't expect anyone to come to the door, but who knew if Joe or Kwame would want to check on me. I didn't want to be caught going through Drake's stuff.

I started with the drawers, sifting through them as quietly as possible. I took out notebooks and shook them, in case something helpful was hidden among the pages. At first I moved slowly, trying not to make any noise, but then I began to move more quickly. I needed to get through Drake's room and sneak into Seth's.

I went to the bed. Looked under it. Seeing a shoebox, I pulled it out and lifted off the lid.

My eyes widened. A gun lay inside.

A gun? Drake had a gun?

I covered the box with the lid and slipped it back under the bed. Then I continued my search. I lifted the mattress, not expecting to find anything there.

But something *was* there.

A large brown envelope.

I snagged the envelope and opened it.

Scanning the contents, I saw that the envelope held articles. Articles about the hit-and-run accident that had killed Drake's father. Each had been printed from various Web sites on sheets of white paper.

On the fourth page, beside a picture of his father's official city council photo, were words written in red ink: Accident? Or murder?

I felt a jolt of shock.

Murder? No . . . Drake couldn't truly have suspected that his father might have been *murdered*?

Last summer, as Moses Shaw was getting into his vehicle outside of a restaurant in Oakland after dinner, someone had run him down. It was suspected to be an accident, most likely at the hands of a drunk driver. But no one knew for sure, because the perpetrator had fled the scene and never been caught.

I flipped to the next page. This time, in the margin beside the article, Drake had written the question: Was this payback?

"Payb—" The word died on my lips as understanding came to me in a flash.

Oh dear God.

And then a tremor of fear shook my body from head to toe. The pieces of the puzzle were forming in my mind. Connecting.

"No." The word escaped my lips on a raspy breath.

Then I shook my head, frowning. No, my theory didn't make sense. There was one piece of the puzzle that didn't fit.

Rachel Jepson.

Yes, she was from Oakland. But she didn't fit in the big picture. She hadn't been involved in the accident that awful night four years ago.

Unless the killer didn't know that.

Lord have mercy.

The big picture was becoming clearer, and it terrified me.

Because if there truly was a connection between Rachel, Drake, and his father, then *I* had reason to fear.

Because the killer wasn't finished yet. There was one more person to make pay for what had happened.

Me.

Chapter Thirty

I SANK onto Drake's mattress, holding the articles in my hand. Thinking. Remembering. My brain was spinning so fast, trying to make sense of what was going on.

Four years ago, just before we had graduated from high school, Drake and I had been involved in a fatal accident. An innocent life had been lost because a vehicle took a corner too quickly. The woman, down on her luck and on the streets to score drugs, didn't have a chance. She was a daughter, a sister, a mother. There had been a public outcry for justice, with people suspecting that the son of the city councillor had been inebriated behind the wheel.

Moses Shaw had quickly gotten involved, instructing Drake and me to do exactly as he said. And before any charges could ever be made, Moses made some calls. Favors were called in and the problem went away.

Drake and I chose a college on the other side of the country, a place where no one knew us. Where the horror of one tragic night wouldn't haunt us forever. We had felt certain that the secret of what had happened that night would never come to light.

But if someone had murdered Drake, his father, and Rachel, well, someone knew where we were. And someone wanted us to pay.

My head throbbed. Something wasn't right. For more than one reason. Rachel Jepson hadn't been anywhere near the accident that night. She hadn't even been at the party. Surely a killer who had bided his time for revenge would know that.

And Rachel was the one who had put Natalie up to trashing Drake. If that was true, then she was part of a bigger conspiracy, one that had to be centered around Lancaster University. It simply didn't make sense that any of this had a connection to what had happened in Oakland.

So whatever had happened to Drake's father—accidental death or murder—it couldn't be related to what was going on now. It was simply a bizarre coincidence.

It had to be.

I felt sick as I placed the articles back in the envelope. Sick and confused. I had to talk to Joe or Kwame. Try to figure out Rachel's angle in wanting to smear Drake's name.

I went downstairs. Found Joe stretched out on a sofa in the living room. "Where's Kwame?" I asked him.

"Stepped out," Joe replied.

Of course. He'd been wearing a jacket. I walked into the living room and sat on the loveseat beside the sofa. "I have a question."

"Shoot."

"Tell me about Rachel Jepson."

"Rachel?"

I nodded. "Do you have any idea why she would want to trash Drake?"

"Trash him? No. They were friends."

"What about in the weeks before she died? Did she and Drake have some sort of falling out?"

Joe shook his head. But he didn't meet my eyes. "No."

"Are you sure?"

"She's dead, Didi. It doesn't matter anymore."

So there *was* something. "What if I told you that she's the one who put it in Natalie's head that Drake was her rapist."

"What?"

"Would that make any sense to you?"

"No." Joe sat up. "Hell, no. Natalie said that?"

"Yes."

"That's bullshit."

"But Drake and Rachel *did* have some sort of falling out, didn't they?"

Joe didn't answer right away. And then he said, "Let it go."

"Let it go?"

"Drake's dead. Rachel's dead. None of it matters any more."

"What's that supposed to mean?"

"Trust me, you don't want to know."

"Are you a part of the conspiracy?" I asked. "Did you want Drake dead?"

"What?" Joe couldn't have looked more shocked. "No. Jesus, what are you talking about?"

"Somebody killed him, Joe. And I think . . . I think somebody also killed Rachel."

Joe looked away.

Oh my God. He knew something. "Joe? What do you know? Was it Seth?"

He ran his fingers through his unruly brown hair. "Like I said, let it go."

I shot to my feet. "Damn it, I will *not* let it go."

"I don't know anything."

"You've already made it clear that you do," I said, steeling my jaw. "I'm not leaving here until you tell me what you know." When Joe said nothing, I started to walk out of the living room. "Fine. If you'd rather have the police question you . . ."

"Wait!" When I turned and faced Joe, he groaned. "Seriously, Didi, what I know . . . it's not going to help. In fact, you're going to wish I didn't tell you."

Despite my resolve to know the truth, a tingling sensation spread down my arms. I suddenly had a bad feeling about what he was going to say, and wasn't sure I should press the matter.

But I said, "Tell me anyway."

A few beats passed as Joe stared at me with intense green eyes. I looked back at him with resolve. Whatever it was, I wanted to know.

"It has to do with the night Rachel died."

"Okay," I said, sitting back down.

"After Seth showed those pictures of her at the party, she ran upstairs. With Drake."

"I thought she ran out of the house." I had been at the party, had watched Rachel flee from the living room in tears after Seth had shown the humiliating, X-rated photos of her.

"She did—after she went to Drake's room."

I looked at Joe in confusion. "What are you trying to say?"

"Haven't you heard? The autopsy showed that Rachel had a stomach full of sleeping pills. People wondered where she got them if she'd run out of the house and straight to her car. But she didn't. She went upstairs with Drake first." Joe stressed his last sentence. "Her roommate confirms that she never went back to their room that night. So where could she have gotten the pills?"

It was the expression on Joe's face more than anything. An expression that made it clear what he wasn't saying.

"You think . . . you think Drake killed her?"

"Maybe he did," Joe said softly. "And maybe the guilt got to him when he went on the cruise. Maybe he couldn't live with what he'd done."

So he jumped into the ocean, taking his own life as penance for his sins.

Could it possibly be true? I had been so sure of everything, but it was suddenly clear that I knew nothing.

Did Drake take his own life after all?

The minutes that passed seemed to stretch to eternity. The weight of what Joe had said, what he believed about a guy who was his friend, was hard to ignore.

"No." I shook my head. I wouldn't believe it.

I knew Drake. And he would never kill anyone, much less take his own life.

"Drake said she'd become a pest, always coming on to

him," Joe explained. "She had it in her head that they were meant to be together. But he loved you, Didi."

My eyes narrowed in puzzlement. "So you think he killed her because she wouldn't leave him alone?"

"Drake said she only started dating Seth so she could come by the house all the time, see him."

"But . . . but then what Natalie said doesn't make sense. If Rachel was in love with Drake, why would she want to drag his name through the mud?"

The next moment, the answer came to me. *Of course.* She wanted to break me and Drake up. With the story about Drake raping Natalie, Rachel thought I wouldn't stay with him. Especially after his indiscretion with her months earlier. I would dump Drake . . . and Rachel would be there to pick up the pieces.

Maybe she'd made one last play for Drake after Seth had shown those pictures of her. She'd gone to his room with him, hoping in her quest to be comforted to make one last effort to steal him away from me. But Drake had rejected her. And that's why she had run from the house, gotten into her car, and driven off in despair. Maybe she'd made a stop in the house bathroom to down a bottle of whatever pills had been available. Or perhaps she'd already had a bottle of sleeping pills in the car with her.

But Drake hadn't given her the pills. That I knew without a doubt.

"Drake didn't like to take Tylenol, or aspirin," I said to Joe. "There's no way he would have had a bottle of sleeping pills. Remember last year when he busted his toe on the court? He refused the prescription for Tylenol with codeine. He didn't believe in medicating himself. If he had a headache, or if he couldn't sleep, he smoked some pot." I paused briefly. "Drake wouldn't have given Rachel any pills. He didn't believe in using them and he wouldn't have had any. Which means he didn't kill her."

Joe pursed his lips, then nodded. "I forgot about that. You're right. He didn't like to take any kind of medication if it could be avoided."

"Do any of the guys in this house take sleeping pills?" I asked.

Joe pursed his lips. "Not that I know of."

"It sounds like Rachel made one last play for my man, and when he rejected her, she took off." Which meant that despite the various scenarios I'd contemplated, Rachel most likely *had* committed suicide. She wouldn't be the first woman to kill herself because of a broken heart.

And then I heard Drake's voice in my mind. *Rachel obviously killed herself. I didn't think she'd do it.*

Had she told him she would? Had she, in her attempt to secure Drake's love, threatened to take her own life before she left his room?

Hindsight being twenty-twenty, I was almost one hundred percent positive that Drake had been speaking with certainty about Rachel having killed herself. I had to conclude that, in desperation, she had told him she would. Perhaps that's why he had been so unhappy in the weeks after her death. He felt guilty that he had let her run off, not believing she would actually commit suicide. Once she had, regret that he could have stopped it consumed him.

But he hadn't wanted to share with me why he knew, because it would mean revealing to me that Rachel had been pursuing him. And after his one night with her, that was something I wouldn't have wanted to hear.

There was, however, still the issue of Natalie and what she had claimed. According to her, Drake had said there was proof about who had raped her. I needed more answers.

"Joe?" I began tentatively. "You were here the night Natalie said she was raped."

A beat. "Yeah."

"Was she? She now says she doesn't believe Drake violated her, but she's not changing her story. She maintains she was raped that night. Possibly even gang-raped."

"She's lying!"

But there was something about Joe's tone, about the way his eyes wouldn't quite settle, that told me he was lying.

"She *was* raped, wasn't she? Did you stand by and let it happen? Did you witness it and do nothing? My God, tell me you weren't one of the guys who assaulted her."

Joe chuckled nervously. "Come on, Didi. Why would you believe a word Natalie says?"

"Because there's proof," I said. "And Drake found it," I added. A bluff. "And that's why he was killed, wasn't it? Because Seth wanted to keep him quiet. Only he didn't know that Drake got the proof to a lawyer before the cruise."

The color drained from Joe's face, making it a chalky white. "Oh Jesus."

So there *was* proof. Proof of the rape. But what?

The answer came to me in an instant. A video. Or pictures. It had to be.

"Were you behind the plot to kill him?" I asked.

And then it hit me: I was alone in the house with Joe. If he *were* involved in what had happened to Drake, would he want to silence me?

I flicked my gaze toward the door. Tried to calculate if I could make it there without Joe tackling me.

It didn't matter. I had to try.

So I jumped up from the loveseat and bolted. But I didn't get far before I felt Joe's thick arms wrapped around my waist.

Chapter Thirty-one

I SCREAMED. Flailed my arms and legs. All a wasted effort, because Joe clamped a hand over my mouth and carried me back to the living room as if I weighed no more than a newborn baby.

He put me on the sofa, but sat beside me, keeping me blocked with his stocky arms and body.

"Let me up, Joe!" I punched at his arms, making no headway. "Please!"

"Damn it, Didi. Stop fighting me."

"Whose plan was it to kill Drake? Your's and Seth's? Kwame and Ryan, too?"

"Shut up!" Joe yelled, spittle flying from his mouth and landing on my face. "Shut up and calm down."

I was gasping in air, trying not to cry. But I stopped fighting him. I didn't stand a chance against him physically.

"I'm not going to hurt you," he went on in a softer tone.

"You pretended you had no clue what happened to Drake," I said. Tears streamed from my eyes and down my temples.

"I don't!"

"Then what's going on?"

Silence filled the air. It seemed like an agonizingly long time before Joe spoke. "I told Drake not to do it. To leave it alone."

"Not to do what?"

"Not to push the issue of exposing who raped Natalie."

"Is there a video?" When Joe didn't answer right away, I repeated my question, yelling it this time. "Is there a video?"

"Yes!"

"And you're on it," I surmised. And again, I felt a spate of panic.

"Are you gonna listen or what?"

"Will you let me sit up?"

Joe stared at me as though trying to judge whether he could trust me to stay put. After a moment, he released his hold on me and helped me to a sitting position.

"Well?" I said.

"You're right. Seth raped Natalie."

"My God."

"He's sick. I mean that literally. Seriously twisted. You know about the kitten. The puppy. Well, somewhere along the way, he decided a little rape would be fun. But it'd be even better if he taped it, a memento he could watch over and over again."

"And you knew. Drake knew. You . . . you guys let him get away with it?"

"We didn't *let* him."

"But you said nothing."

"Because Seth had us right where he wanted us."

"Meaning?"

"Meaning he had information that could get us arrested. And if not arrested, expelled from Lan-U. I couldn't afford to lose my scholarship. Don't you see?"

"Arrested?" I said, alarmed.

"Drake and I . . . we both sold a bit of dope for Seth. Just on campus . . . to people who asked. It wasn't like we went out searching for customers. Seth supplied the dope, we helped sell it. When Drake threatened to report him to the authorities about the rapes, Seth threw the drug stuff in his face. And I . . . I knew he'd do it. I mean, Seth was fun to hang out with at first, but like I said, he's twisted. It didn't take long to realize he was the type to take us all down with him."

"Wait a minute. You said 'rapes,' plural."

"He did it more than once. A couple other times. Those girls were so drugged, I don't even think they knew what happened."

"Oh my God. And Drake knew about this?"

"Like I told you, he wanted to report Seth, but Seth had the drug dealing over our heads. Once Drake was blamed for Natalie's rape, he knew he had to act. His reputation was ruined. People looked at him with disgust and hate. He was motivated to see that the truth come to light."

God, poor Drake. He had been killed because he wanted to clear his name. It wasn't fair at all.

"Where's the video?" I asked.

Joe narrowed his eyes. "I thought you said Drake found it."

I smiled sheepishly. "I lied. But I want to find it. If it's here, I need to get it. Give it to the police."

"The police?"

"Drake is dead," I said with difficulty. "And it's because of that video. Because Seth didn't trust him to stay quiet about the rape. So he had to silence him."

Joe shrugged. "I'm not so sure about that."

"How can you not be sure?" I asked, incredulous.

"It's just—and maybe you'll think this sounds crazy—but I don't see Seth killing Drake. After the first rape when Drake threatened to report Seth, Seth quickly made it clear to all of us that if any of us were stupid enough to finger him, we would all go down. So none of us spoke. But after Natalie was raped, Drake told me in confidence that he wanted to stop Seth. He knew the only way to do that was to get his hands on the video proof. And trust me, he didn't want to give Seth a heads-up that he was looking for it. The thing was, he searched Seth's room and couldn't find it."

"Seth didn't know what Drake was planning?"

"No."

It couldn't be. Seth *had* to have known.

"And even if he did, I don't see him as the type to kill anyone. He'd threaten to expose your dirty secrets first, take pleasure in your own humiliation. But murder? I don't see it."

"You said yourself that Seth is sick and twisted. Sick and twisted people can't be trusted because they're insane." Joe watched me carefully as I stood. "I have to find the video," I said. "Maybe Drake missed it in Seth's room."

"What does it matter now?"

"Other than clearing Drake's name? I'm pretty sure it's going to take a murderer down. All I want to know is if you plan to stop me."

Several seconds passed with Joe and me staring at each other. I couldn't gauge his mood by reading his eyes.

Finally, he shook his head. "No. I'm not going to stop you. You want to search Seth's room, have at it."

Joe said he needed to leave the house to clear his head. He was going to go for a long walk.

Maybe he just didn't want to be around should I find the video evidence. It didn't matter. I didn't plan to hand it over to him.

I went back upstairs to search Seth's room. But first, I went to Drake's room and retrieved his gun. I'm not sure why. But I suddenly wasn't sure what was going on, and if Drake had felt the need to have a gun, maybe I ought to have it in my possession.

The gun stuffed into my jacket pocket, I went to Seth's door. I feared it might be locked. But I placed my hand on the doorknob and it turned.

And though I expected to see the large boa constrictor, the sight of the albino creature in its large glass cage made me gasp. Or maybe it was more of a cry. I couldn't help thinking of that helpless kitten, how it had been sacrificed for sport.

I paused to listen for any sounds, and hearing none, closed the door behind me.

The room was neat. Surprisingly so. But then I remembered how Drake had said that Seth was a neat freak.

Which meant I couldn't search the room at ease the way I had searched Drake's. Seth would be able to tell that something was out of place.

I set about going through his drawers, and found even the insides were extremely neat. Notebooks stacked one on top of the other. Pens and pencils arranged neatly in a narrow tray.

I lifted one notebook. Flipped through it. Then another. I went through the entire drawer, searching for something I wasn't sure was even in the house.

But I couldn't give up. I went to Seth's bed the way I had gone to Drake's. Unlike Drake's bed, which had remained unmade, Seth's bed was made with military precision. I had a feeling that if I measured the creases at the corners, they would all be of equal length.

I lifted the top mattress and peered underneath. Nothing.

Though I let the mattress down carefully, the bedspread was no longer perfect. I did my best to straighten it, then I moved on to the closet.

Anticipation made my chest swell when I saw the silver box. I had one similar to it in my own dorm room.

It was the kind of box that held CDs and DVDs.

Dropping onto the floor, I quickly grabbed the metal box and pulled it onto my lap. I opened the lid and went through every DVD and CD it contained. All legal copies of movies and music.

"Damn," I uttered. Where was the video?

I replaced the box where I'd found it. Frowning, I stepped backward from the closet. And then my gaze wandered to the snake.

A sick energy instantly filled my stomach. The snake cage . . .

Oh my God. *That's* where the video was. Beneath the newsprint covering the bottom of the cage.

I was right. I knew it.

The sound of a door slamming got my attention.

Instantly, I hurried to the bedroom door. I stepped into the hallway and closed the door a millisecond before I heard the pounding of footsteps coming up the stairs.

Seth appeared.

My heart pounded so hard, I thought it would explode.

Seeing me, the change on Seth's face was instantaneous. The surprise. Then the suspicion.

"Hey, Seth." I forced a smile. "I was just . . . I was just in Drake's room . . ."

Seth's eyes flitted to my left, the side of the hall where Drake's room was, and then to my right, where his room was. I saw the question in his eyes. If I had been in Drake's room, what was I doing close to *his* door?

"I . . . I couldn't resist taking a look at your snake," I said. I had to say something that would explain my presence outside of his room.

"I thought you hated snakes."

"I do . . . but I was curious. Did you just get back from St. Bart's?"

Seth continued to eye me with suspicion, then he said, "Yeah."

"How was it?" I asked, trying to sound nonchalant.

"Why would you care about St. Bart's after what happened to Drake?"

Why indeed? "I'm just . . . I was trying to be polite."

"What the hell happened on the cruise ship?" Seth asked. He actually sounded angry.

"I know the same thing everyone else knows. Drake somehow fell overboard."

"And you know nothing else?" Seth asked accusingly.

"Why would I?"

"Because I saw Drake's mother on the news saying that she thought you knew more about what happened than you're letting on. Drake was my boy. If you know something about his death . . ."

"I don't," I said, my tone clipped. Did Seth truly have the gall to act as though he believed I had something to do with what had happened to Drake?

His face suddenly contorted in pain. "Drake's really gone?"

I swallowed. Then said softly, "Yeah."

"Jesus H. Christ. Oh fuck."

And to my utter surprise, Seth seemed genuinely upset. Had his conscience gotten to him?

Or was he just a good actor? Weren't all sociopaths excellent at playing whatever role they wanted?

"The Coast Guard called off the search," I said. "I keep hoping some fisherman found him. That in a few days, we'll get some good news."

"Maybe I can get my dad to fund a private search," Seth said.

Again, I was surprised. But it was easy for Seth to say that, especially if he knew a search wouldn't produce any results.

"Um, Seth, I've got to run. I'm meeting someone."

"Oh. Yeah, sure."

An uncomfortable moment ensued. Not once had Seth and I ever spoken for this long.

Nor this amicably.

"See ya," I said and quickly turned. I all but ran down the

front steps and out of the house, fearing that Seth would follow me. Once on the sidewalk, I reached for my car keys in my right pocket, while pushing my left hand into my other pocket to cover the gun I'd found in Drake's room.

I glanced over my shoulder. No Seth. But that didn't mean he wasn't coming.

My fingers were trembling so badly I couldn't press the button to release the car's locks.

Was that a sound behind me? I started to run, not bothering to stop at my car, fearing Seth could overpower me there. Turning left, I charged down the street, pumping my arms hard, panting furiously. About a hundred feet away, I dared to glance over my shoulder.

Seth wasn't coming.

Wary, I slowed, then positioned my body beyond a light pole. I stood there, glancing in the direction of the townhouse. One minute turned to two. Seth still hadn't appeared at the door.

I took a tentative step back in the direction of my car. Then another. But with every step, I was prepared to turn around and bolt if I had to.

Or use the gun.

I got back to my car without incident; once there, I quickly got inside and drove off. It wasn't until I reached my dorm room that I stopped to consider the gravity of what had happened.

I had failed. I didn't get the video.

And now I never would.

Because it wouldn't take Seth long to be onto me. He would realize that items in his room had been disturbed and attribute that to me.

Dropping down onto my bed, I buried my face in both hands. Seth would easily conclude that I'd been searching his room for evidence of his crime.

I had no doubt he would proceed to destroy it.

And thereby destroy the very thing that proved he had motive to want Drake dead.

Chapter Thirty-two

I BARELY SLEPT the entire night. Alone in my room, I was on edge, fearing that Seth might show up at my door at any moment.

Oh, he was good. He had acted truly devastated about Drake's death when he saw me, playing the loyal and hurt friend with the skill of an Academy Award–winning actor.

But I didn't believe it. Not for a second.

There was only one person who had the resources to drop ten grand without batting an eye, and to arrange for a hit on someone while he was thousands of miles away. And that person had a motive for wanting to keep Drake quiet.

It *had* to be Seth.

I was glad when the first rays of sunlight spilled into my room. True or not, daylight made me feel safe. People didn't try to shoot or strangle someone in the light of day.

I had avoided watching the news since the layover in Miami. But after last night, and learning from Natalie that the search for Drake had been called off, I tuned in to hear the latest updates.

Irrationally, a part of me expected to hear good news. To hear that despite all odds, a fishing boat or a pleasure craft had picked Drake up. Or that an unidentified man, perhaps suffering amnesia, had turned up on the shore in Jamaica.

But there was no talk of miracles. In fact, the news was downright depressing. This morning, Drake's mother was scheduled to appear on television to give a statement concerning her son.

I glanced at my clock. It was nine fifty-seven. Janine Shaw was due to speak at ten.

Three minutes later, the newscast began. Standing at a podium in front of reporters and beside her brother, Mrs. Shaw spoke solemnly to the nation.

"I want to thank everyone for their overwhelming support in my time of overwhelming despair," Mrs. Shaw said. She was wearing a brave face, one that showed determination to move forward in the face of adversity. A framed photo of Drake rested beside her on the podium. "As you all know, the search for my son has been called off." She paused briefly, and I saw her jaw flinch. "As much as I want to believe that my son is still alive, I feel . . . I feel . . ." Janine's voice cracked, and then her face crumbled. She began to sob uncontrollably, and my own tears started to fall. The camera closed in on her face, highlighting her crushing grief. She leaned into the brother at her side, and he held his sister, looking crestfallen as he comforted her. Then Mrs. Shaw sniffled, wiped at her nose and eyes with a Kleenex, and continued. "I feel that given the circumstances of my son's disappearance, he is no longer with us."

And after having sobbed uncontrollably only moments before, Mrs. Shaw's face suddenly contorted with anger. "But no matter what anyone says, my son did *not* commit suicide. With every fiber of my being, I believe that what happened to my wonderful son, Drake, was *not* an accident. The drops of blood on the railing prove that there was a struggle. Someone killed my son, and I want to know why."

"Mrs. Shaw," one reporter said, "do you believe that your son's girlfriend had something to do with what happened to him?"

I held my breath as I waited for Janine's response.

"Right now, I'd like to see investigators focus on finding answers that will lead to an arrest. As you know, it's been confirmed that a man who did not work for the cruise line was somehow able to impersonate a SunSeekers staff member. Mysteriously, he was not on board when the ship set sail from Grand Cayman. I'm hoping that the authorities can uncover his true identity, because I believe *he* holds the answer as to what happened to Drake. I don't believe this man was simply a con artist on board to rob passengers."

When I'd first heard the news of this mystery man in the wee hours of the morning, I'd been stunned—and then relieved. Special Agent Diaz and the ship's staff captain may have thought I was speaking gibberish at the time, but upon further investigation, they had learned I was telling the truth. Hopefully they would be able to find this "Greg," because if Seth had hired him, he could testify to that fact.

"And once and for all," Mrs. Shaw continued, "I'd like the authorities to drop the theory that my son may have committed suicide, because Drake would *not* have jumped overboard. He was afraid of heights, so it makes no sense that he would jump. He went as far as to book a room without a balcony, because he didn't want to risk any mishaps." A moment of silence, then Janine's face crumbled once more. "I love you, Drake. I love you with all my heart and I miss you."

As she cried, her brother helped her down from the podium. Reporters continued to ask questions, but she didn't answer any more.

I turned off the television and lay in my bed for several minutes, allowing my emotions to overwhelm me. I cried unashamedly, knowing others in the residence hall may hear me. Seeing Mrs. Shaw's grief at losing her only child was more than I could bear. We had both lost him.

And we hadn't just lost him. He'd been taken from us.

Murdered.

It was that thought that had my tears stopping. Had me sitting up on my bed. Like Mrs. Shaw, I had gone from despair to anger. Because Drake's murderer had to pay.

Would I ever be able to prove Seth's connection to Drake's death? I had stupidly shown him my hand, and he was smart enough to destroy any evidence of him raping Natalie. Greg would be smart enough—and well paid enough—to disappear.

But Natalie . . . She could speak about what had happened to her. Her rape, the money she had been paid, her going on the cruise . . . Surely that would be enough for the police to investigate Seth.

I got up and began to get dressed, determined to find Natalie. We would go to the police, both of us.

The door to my room rattled. I went still. Jolene?

Or someone else?

Slipping my shirt over my head, I quickly moved to the corner of the room behind the door. That way, once it opened, I would be out of view.

The lock turned. The door opened. I held my breath.

And then Jolene's head appeared.

Seeing me, she widened her eyes. "Dee, what are you doing behind the door?"

I shook my head, grinning slightly to indicate I was being silly. Instead of answering her question, I asked one of my own. "How's Scott?"

"He's good," Jolene said, a smile touching her lips.

My pulse still racing, I crossed the room and sat on my bed. "Did you talk to him about . . . about The Gossip Hour?"

"I did. He said he had nothing to do with it. And I believe him."

"You're sure?"

"He wants to work things out. He still loves me. And I know Scott. He would never hurt me like this."

I frowned. "Was there anyone else you told, then? Someone else who knew about your abortion?"

"Nobody. Only you."

Damn. By process of elimination, Jolene had to think that I'd revealed her secret. But there must have been someone who'd overheard us that night in the bar.

"And you told Roxanne," Jolene said, matter-of-fact.

"You don't think . . . Roxanne wouldn't do that."

"She's the *only* other person who knew."

"Someone must have seen you at the abortion clinic," I countered.

"You really think there was someone from Lan-U lurking around the clinic?" Jolene asked, then shook her head.

A moment of silence followed. Jolene was adamant, and there was nothing I could say.

"I think Roxanne leaked my story to The Gossip Hour. In fact, I think she's running the show."

"What do you mean 'running the show'?"

"Just what I said. I think she's the one running The Gossip Hour."

Now I was the one to shake my head. "No. She . . . she can't be."

"I suspected it before, but I wasn't sure."

"No," I said, more insistent this time. The story about Drake, all those vicious comments about me on the blog . . . "There's no way Roxanne would hurt me like that."

Jolene came to the bed and sat beside me. "I'm going to tell you something. And I want you to reserve judgment, because I'm not saying what I did was right. But . . . I had to know."

"You're speaking in riddles."

"I went to The Gossip Hour Web site and submitted something. When we were on the cruise. I went to the Internet café and submitted some gossip about Roxanne."

My mouth fell open. I couldn't believe what I was hearing.

But I suddenly remembered Roxanne's comment that had baffled me at the time. *I think she's sneaky. The kind of person you can't really trust.*

"It was about how she pays people to write her papers for her. How she would have failed most of her courses if not for hiring others. Lo and behold, that bit of gossip never made it onto the site."

"You . . . you did that?"

Jolene nodded. "And the next thing I know, the story about my abortion surfaced. I almost think she *knew* I was the one who sent the story about her. So she leaked the story about my abortion as payback."

I was beyond confused. Roxanne had warned me that Jolene was sneaky. What if *she* was coming up with this story about Roxanne when she was really the person behind The Gossip Hour?

I had always felt that the person behind the Web site was someone who knew me personally, someone who wanted to hurt me. Suddenly, I wasn't sure I should trust what Jolene was saying.

"What were you and Natalie really talking about on the cruise?" I asked without preamble, remembering that she and Natalie had been walking and talking, but quickly parted when they saw me.

"What?"

"She told me that someone paid her way to go on the cruise. That someone wanted her there as a scapegoat. And she left a note under our cabin door saying not to trust my friends. She acted like she didn't know who had paid her way, but maybe she knew all along and wanted to warn me."

"I wrote that note."

The confession stunned me into silence.

"You think you can trust your friends," Jolene quoted. "But I've got news for you. You can't."

"What the hell?" I asked. Anger shot through me. "What the fuck is going on?"

"Like I told you, I had started to suspect that Roxanne had something to do with The Gossip Hour. Which meant she had deliberately wanted to hurt you and Drake."

"But why?"

Before Jolene could answer the question, my cell phone rang. I reached for it on the night table—and saw Roxanne's number flashing on the screen.

I hesitated before answering, almost not sure I should. But before the phone rang a third time, I pressed the talk button and placed it to my ear.

"Roxanne, hi."

Wounded sobs sounded in my ear.

"Roxanne," I said, alarmed. "What is it? What's wrong?"

"It's Natalie," Roxanne said. "She committed suicide. Oh my God. She's dead."

Chapter Thirty-three

I FROZE. Natalie was dead?

"You . . . you're sure?" I asked, even though I knew the question was ridiculous. It was the kind of question someone in shock asked.

"Yes, I'm sure. I was at Terrell Hall and just heard. Everyone was talking about it."

Natalie had committed suicide? It didn't make sense. Why would she kill herself after giving me that warning about watching my back?

"How?" I asked. "How did she do it?"

"She slit her wrists," Roxanne said, and I heard her voice

catch. "Her roommate found her on the bed . . . I hear it was awful. I mean, she was on the bed, blood was everywhere . . ."

"Oh God." I gasped at the image. At the horrible reality. "I can't believe it."

"I know," Roxanne said. "I feel so bad."

"Why? You didn't do it."

"I know, but . . . I feel like I should have tried to reach out to her instead of mocking her. And now she's gone."

Natalie was dead. Her wrists slit. Suicide?

Or murder?

"Was there a note?" I asked. "Did she say why?"

"That's the kicker," Roxanne said. "Jane was too distraught to even look for a note. She left the room screaming and ran for help. The paramedics came, and the police. And they did find a note, Didi. And you're not going to believe it."

"What?" I asked, not sure I could handle another surprise.

"In the note, she apologized. She said she couldn't live with herself for what she'd done. That she was sorry for killing Drake."

A shock hit me hard. "What?"

"She killed him, Didi. She killed Drake."

"That's what she said?"

"The whole story is on The Gossip Hour site."

I caught Jolene's curious gaze as I went to my desk and sat in front of my netbook. I didn't answer the question in her eyes, just typed in the url for The Gossip Hour Web site.

Moments later, the site popped up. And there it was—confirmation.

Some sad news today, folks. Something that is fact, not rumor. Lan-U student Natalie Laymon has committed suicide. It's the latest twist in a mystery that is baffling our college.

You'll remember that just about two months ago, Natalie accused popular Lan-U student Drake Shaw of sexual assault. Just last week, Drake disappeared while on a cruise in the Caribbean, most likely while en route to Jamaica from the Bahamas. It is believed that he either fell overboard accidentally or by misadventure—or was deliberately murdered.

Natalie, who hated Drake for what he had allegedly done to her, was widely suspected by most as having something to do with Drake's death. (Although some speculated that the dearly departed's ex- girlfriend could possibly have been involved.)

Me? I thought, reading that last sentence again. Who the hell was doing all this "speculating"—or was this premeditated sabotage? If Jolene was to be believed, this was Roxanne's doing. And yet Jolene was the one I had seen talking with Natalie, and hurriedly parting when she realized I had seen them together.

Natalie's wrists were slit. Clearly a suicide. She even left a note, apologizing for killing Drake on the cruise. She said she couldn't live with herself for what she'd done. But despite that note, I can't help but wonder if it *was* really suicide. Or if it was murder. Is there a killer on the loose here at Lancaster University? And is it possible that the killer is Didi Randall? She hated Natalie for crying rape, and she hated Drake for screwing around on her.

My stomach sinking, I did a double take. This couldn't be happening. The person behind this blog couldn't truly be naming me as a possible suspect in Natalie's death!

"Who is doing this?" I asked into the phone. "Who wants to make people think I'm a killer?"

But Roxanne didn't respond, and I realized that she was no longer on the line.

"Dead," Jolene whispered above me. She had been reading the blog along with me. "Natalie's dead."

I whirled around. "You expect me to believe that Roxanne would want to make the world think I'm a killer? Because if you're to be believed, she's the one running this Web site."

"I'm only telling you what I know. I submitted gossip about her and it was never posted. How likely is that?"

"This doesn't make sense," I said, turning to look at the computer screen again. This was the first time the blog had named names, perhaps because the story about Drake and Natalie's death was fact, not rumor. And I had already been vilified in the press, my possible involvement in what had happened to Drake publicly questioned. But still.

"This isn't just speculation. It's a personal attack."

"From someone close to you. Someone who wants to hurt you."

"Roxy and I have been friends for years. She joined SCTA and fought alongside me against injustice."

"I don't know her motives," Jolene said.

"This *is* personal. But it's Seth behind it." I quickly filled Jolene in on what had happened last night at Seth's place. "He's pissed that I was in his room, knows I was searching for evidence, and wants to discredit me in case I try to go to the police with my theory. He's good. I'll give him that."

"If you say so."

"Why should I believe you?" I snapped. "You come in here

with this theory . . . it could just as easily be you behind The Gossip Hour."

"Why would I leak that story about my abortion?"

"I don't know!" I couldn't hold in my anger. "Maybe so you would look like a victim."

"Wow." Jolene slowly shook her head. "I came here to warn you, and you turn on me."

"I don't have time for this bullshit," I snapped. "I need to prove Seth is a killer."

Her jaw tightening, Jolene spun around and left the room, slamming the door behind her.

I cringed, then inhaled deeply. Let her be mad. She came in spinning a wild theory with no real proof. If she would submit something about Roxanne to The Gossip Hour, how far a stretch would it be to think she had submitted the gossip about me?

And even if Jolene hadn't been the one to sabotage my name, she was merely speculating. She and Roxanne had only become friends through me. Who knew if Jolene was jealous of my close friendship with Roxanne? It would be stupid, but not implausible.

I called Roxanne's cell phone. It rang four times and then went to voice mail.

Frowning, I sent her a text.

Roxy, where r u? Call me back!

There was no call from Roxanne. No text message. I called her again, and her cell phone went straight to voice mail. I sent her a message on Facebook, but a couple of hours later, there was still no reply from her.

When five o'clock rolled around, I was starting to get worried. Roxanne had called to drop the bombshell about Natalie. Why wouldn't she have called me back?

I was walking toward Terrell Hall when my cell phone rang. I quickly dug it out of my pocket and looked at the Caller ID. An Oakland area code was flashing on my screen.

Wondering who it could be, I clicked to answer. "Hello?"

"Hey."

It took me a moment to place the voice. "Chris?"

"Yeah. It's me."

I stopped walking. "What's up?"

"I heard about Drake on the news. I wanted to see how you're doing."

"Right." I sighed softly. "Of course." Chris would have had to be vacationing on Mars to have missed the news about Drake.

"How are you?"

"A mess," I admitted. "Somehow I'm keeping it together, but it's been tough. The not knowing what happened. Nor why."

"I'm sorry," Chris said. "Drake and I weren't friends, but I know how painful this must be for you."

"Thank you," I said softly, meaning it. I especially appreciated the sentiment because he could have easily said nothing. Saying he and Drake weren't friends was putting it mildly. There was a time the two had hated each other.

And it all went back to that night four years ago. A night when Chris, a guy who had always been my good friend, made a play for me. I'd been drunk and pissed with Drake for his inattention, so I'd reciprocated Chris's flirting. And the truth was, there had always been a part of me that wondered. Wondered what it would be like to kiss Chris.

Chris thought his crush on me was a secret, but I had known about it. Known and played dumb. But that night, once Drake got mad at me for something stupid and pretended I didn't exist, I flirted back.

And the next thing I knew, Chris and I were in the closet by the front door, making out, and then the door was flying open, and an irate Drake was grabbing me out and cussing something awful at Chris. Drake dragged me out of the party, both of us pissed at each other.

I was hazy on the details after that. All I knew was that I'd gotten behind the wheel of the car. It was my car, and I'd wanted to drive it.

I never should have been driving, and I would always live to regret it . . . because I hit a pedestrian.

Drake had acted quickly, calling his father, who advised him to put me in the passenger seat and get behind the wheel. Drake hadn't been drinking. If he said *he'd* been driving, the fatality would be an unfortunate accident, not a crime.

Drake's quick actions had saved me from a DUI charge.

Which was why I owed him everything.

I stifled a sob. Then realized that Chris was calling my name.

"Sorry," I said. "What did you say?"

"I asked if you've heard any updates from the police."

"No. Nothing. And I . . . I'm confused."

"What does that mean?"

"I don't know what to think. One minute I was sure that someone from Lan-U was behind what happened to Drake. But . . ."

"But what?" Chris asked gently.

I could tell him. He knew all about that night. "You know that Drake's father was killed last summer, right?"

"Yeah."

"Well, Drake had articles about his father's death in his room. Apparently, he thought it might have been murder."

"It was a hit-and-run," Chris said.

"Yes, it was. But Drake apparently thought it might have been murder. That it was payback because of . . . because of what happened four years ago. The accident." I could speak freely because Chris knew what had happened that night.

"Payback?"

"If Drake is right, then someone was mad because they thought Drake's father was able to influence his friends in high places to not pursue any charges." The cold getting to me, I began to walk again. "And this same person would have been mad with Drake because he was the one behind the wheel. But the person doesn't know . . ." My voice cracked, but Chris already knew the worst of it. "If that's the reason Drake was killed, then I'm not sure I can live with myself."

"Didi, whatever happened to Drake, you can't blame yourself."

"Easy for you to say."

"I'm serious. You can't be responsible for the mind of a sick individual. Even if this is about four years ago. And truthf—"

"I've got to go," I said abruptly, cutting him off. And then I ended the call.

Tears were streaming down my cheeks. Having given voice to the theory of revenge—and knowing it could be true—was suddenly more burden than my shoulders could support.

No longer hungry, I pivoted on my heel and turned back in the direction of my residence building instead of the cafeteria. Emotion was getting to me, and I wanted to get back to my room before I fell apart.

Back inside my dorm room minutes later, I hugged my pillow and cried. Cried over the fact that I would never see Drake again. And cried even harder because he may have died over something I had done.

My phone beeped, indicating I had a text message. Taking my phone from my pocket, I clicked a button to read what I'd been sent.

I'm here, Didi. At Lan-U. Wanted to tell u that,
but u hung up. Let me know where u r.
I don't want u 2 b alone at a time like this.
Chris

I held my breath as I read the message, not sure what to make of it. Chris was here? He had gotten on a plane and come to Lan-U?

To comfort me?

Or for another reason?

I didn't respond. I lay on my bed in the dark, numb. And when my phone rang, I almost didn't answer it, because I was certain it was Chris. But when it rang a third time, curiosity got the better of me and I looked at the caller ID screen.

Roxanne.

I quickly pressed the talk button and put the phone to my ear, hoping voice mail hadn't kicked in yet. Before I could speak, I heard her crying. Just like when she'd called me earlier today.

"Hello? Roxanne?"

"Didi . . ." Roxanne barely managed my name before breaking down in a fit of tears. "Oh God. I need you, Didi. Please."

"What's going on?" I asked. My pulse was racing. Something was seriously wrong. I knew it. "I called you back all day, you never answered your phone."

"Listen to me," Roxanne said, her voice filled with desperation. "Listen to me good. Because this isn't a joke. He says . . . he says he's gonna kill me."

My world tilted off its axis. Surely I hadn't heard Roxanne correctly.

"Are you there?" she cried.

"Yes." The word escaped with difficulty.

"He's serious, Dee. He said if you don't come now, he's gonna kill me." She began to sob. "If you don't do what he says, I'm as good as dead!"

Chapter Thirty-four

MY BRAIN WAS SCRAMBLING to make sense of what I was hearing. Scrambling to fit Roxanne into the puzzle. I couldn't.

But solving the puzzle right now was not the issue. Saving Roxanne was.

"What does he want me to do?" I asked, trying to keep calm despite the throbbing in my head. "My God, how did this happen?"

Roxanne didn't speak for several seconds, not until she was able to get her sobbing under control. "I was walking on campus, and the next thing I knew someone was grabbing me.

Saying he was going to kill me if I didn't lead him to you. I . . . I had to call you. I'm sorry, Didi. I . . . I'm sorry. But . . . but I don't want to die."

Oh God. This was real. Someone had Roxanne.

I should have known something was wrong. Roxanne never took this long to get back to me.

"What does he want?" I asked. My heart was pumping as if it was on speed. I had no clue how to solve this situation, if I could even give this person what he wanted.

"I don't know," Roxanne replied. She had calmed down somewhat, but fear still permeated her voice. "Wait, he wants to talk to you."

There was some shuffling, and then a man came on the line. "Come to the church. The one on campus. Do it now or your friend dies. And if you think of calling the cops, you may as well be the one slicing your friend's throat. Because that's what's going to happen to her. I'm going to slice her throat from ear to ear. I'll give you ten minutes to get here."

There was something about his voice. Something familiar. But I couldn't place it.

"What's this about?" I asked. "What do you want with me?"

"Your sins will find you out, young lady. No matter how long it takes, the past catches up to you."

"The accident," I said, certain now.

"It was no accident!" the man yelled. "Get here in ten minutes or you'll have the death of another on your conscience!"

In the background, Roxanne began to wail again, and my heart nearly imploded. My mind immediately conjured the gruesome threat, the blood seeping from a wound in Roxanne's neck so deep she wouldn't stand a chance of survival.

I whimpered. Why was this happening?

More shuffling. Then I heard Roxanne's tear-filled voice. "Didi, please come now."

"I'm coming, Roxy. I'm coming."

And then, in a whisper, "It's Greg."

"Greg?"

"Yes." Roxanne's voice was even more faint.

Greg? I was confused.

But in an instant, it hit me.

And then a chill slithered down my spine. "You mean Greg from the ship?"

"Yes," Roxanne managed. "Didi, I don't want to die."

Those were her last words before the phone line went dead.

For several seconds, all I could do was sit on my bed and stare into space.

Greg had tracked me down. How had this happened?

And why? Why was this happening?

Unrequited love? Was this guy a stalker of the first order?

I stood. It didn't really matter what he was, only that he had Roxanne. And he was going to kill her unless I showed up at the church.

I glanced at the digital clock on my night table. It was 6:19 P.M. No one would be at the church now.

No one except Greg and Roxanne.

I stared at the clock until the digital display changed to 6:20 P.M. The time was ticking away. If I didn't get to the church in ten minutes, Greg would kill Roxanne.

But if I did, he would kill me.

And I'll admit, for about another twenty seconds, I selfishly debated what I should do. Should I keep myself safe? Or should I save my friend?

But I had already lived with the death of one person on my conscience.

I couldn't live with another.

I couldn't call the police. If I did, and they went charging into the church to rescue Roxanne, she would die. It was possible she wouldn't, that the cops would execute some sort of elaborate plan where they were able to take Greg down before he could slit Roxanne's throat. But was I willing to take that chance?

I had no clue what the scenario was inside the church. Where Greg had Roxanne. If they were even inside the church or waiting outside somewhere to make sure I came alone.

One wrong move, and Roxanne was dead.

No matter how much I wanted to call the police, I couldn't.

I slipped into Drake's varsity jacket, zipped it up, slipped into my Uggs, then wrapped a scarf around my neck. Every fiber of my being was saying don't go. Don't do this. This is stupid. Just call the police.

And yet I understood suddenly why other people who were warned not to call the police didn't. Because no one wanted to chance the life of a friend. No one wanted to live with that on their conscience. I knew more than anyone exactly what that felt like.

So I ignored that inner voice trying to warn me. And I slipped out of my dorm room, went downstairs, and then walked out into the night.

Chapter Thirty-five

INSTINCTS.

We all have them. They're meant to protect us. To serve as a warning that we are about to enter into danger.

As I opened the door of the church, I had the overwhelming sense that I should have listened to mine. Because even as I was heading here, a small voice in my mind had told me not to go.

It was nothing I could put my finger on, just a premonition that things were not as they seemed. A sort of nervous energy had spread through my body after the thought, *Don't go.*

I had gone. And suddenly I knew, without a doubt, that I

should have listened to my gut and stayed away. My brain was screaming that everything about this situation was wrong.

It was the car. And the fact that it was *here*. That's what didn't make sense to me. So I almost didn't get out of mine. I almost drove back to my dorm building.

But Greg had said one thing that rang true. *No matter how long it takes, the past catches up to you.*

I could run, but I would never escape this confrontation. They would come for me in my room. Or at some other time. I had to deal with this now.

That's why I entered the church.

An immediate sweep of the area told me it was empty. The campus church was illuminated only by candles on a table at the front. The flames cast an eerie glow on the ceiling, and shadows danced over the walls and stain-glass windows. People came here for peace and comfort, but those were the last emotions I was feeling right now.

Moving my eyes from left to right, I surveyed the rows of seating ahead of me. Anyone could be hiding in the pews. Or even behind the altar. I was exposed, and I knew it.

Clutching my purse at my side, I slowly started down the aisle. Maybe I should have just turned and left. That would have been the smart thing to do.

But I was here now, and determined to put an end to this one way or another.

The sound of shuffling caught my attention when I was about halfway down the aisle. The back of my neck prickled, sensing danger.

This was it.

Slowly, I turned.

Surprisingly, I wasn't startled. Maybe because it was just as

I had expected. The silver barrel of a fairly large gun was aimed at me.

I had tried to run from my sins for four years, but now there was nowhere left to run.

It all came down to this. This moment.

The gun was between us. And I was on the wrong side of it.

Instincts.

They can save you if you heed them.

Or kill you if you don't.

I slipped my hand ever so cautiously into the purse I had made sure to bring, hoping the shadows would shield my actions.

Because as much as I had thought that coming here would lead me to danger, I had been smart enough not to come unprepared.

I had my own gun. And I was ready to use it.

Before I'd even crossed the threshold into the church, instinct had told me to make a call. So I had taken my cell phone from my pocket. Searched my recent incoming numbers. Found the Oakland digits that belonged to Chris.

"Hi, Di—"

"Chris, listen to me," I said, cutting him off. "If you're here at Lan-U, I need you to do something. I need you to call the police."

"What?"

I prayed he wasn't inside the church, that he wasn't a part of this. I was counting on the fact that he wasn't. "Tell them I'm at the campus church. I'm about to head inside. Someone wants to kill me. Call the police and tell them what's going on. Call them now."

"Are you serious, Didi?"

"Yes," I said. I was keeping my voice low.

"Then don't—"

"Call them *now*," I instructed him.

Then I had hung up and turned my phone to silent.

I was glad I had made that call. Because as I stared at Roxanne standing thirty feet away from me, pointing a gun at me, I knew my instincts had not led me astray.

"Ladies and gentlemen," Roxanne began as she walked toward the aisle from the pew where she'd been hiding. "I have a juicy bit of gossip for you today. Didi Randall, one of the most popular girls on campus until recently, has taken her own life. Consumed with guilt because of her part in the death of innocent civilian, Erin Lowell. Didi's dirty secret has finally caught up to her. She even killed her boyfriend, Drake Shaw, because he was going to expose her as the true driver of the car."

"I . . . I didn't kill Drake."

"Oh, I know that," Roxanne said, walking closer. "I know you didn't kill him, because I did. Well, I admit I had some help."

I sensed him before I heard him, and I slowly turned. Greg, or whatever his name was, was walking down the aisle behind me. In his right hand was a fairly large butcher knife. Swallowing my terror, I turned, enabling me to face both of them, and took a few steps backward.

"Imagine my surprise when before Drake went overboard, he told me something." My eyes went to Roxanne. Her expression had morphed into something truly evil. "He said that *you* were driving the car, Didi. Not him."

Drake had said that? After years of protecting me, he had finally betrayed me . . .

"You've pretended all this time to be so perfect. But I guess I should have known. You were always trying to overcompensate with your I'm-so-wonderful-I'm-going-to-right-all-the-wrongs-in-the-world bullshit."

"I know I'm not perfect. And you'll never know how much I wish I could turn back the clock, and rewrite that night."

"It wasn't an accident!" Roxanne yelled at the top of her lungs. She advanced quickly now, and I thought for sure she was going to pull the trigger. "It wasn't a fucking accident!"

I said nothing, just stared at the woman I'd considered my friend. But she had never seen me as that. Had she befriended me only as a way to get close to Drake?

"Do you know who Erin Lowell was?" Roxanne asked.

"I only know what the media said. That Erin was a drug addict—"

"Don't you dare! Don't you dare use the media spin to describe her."

"I'm sorry." I cringed at Roxanne's anger.

"If you were sorry, you would have spent some time learning about the woman you killed. You wouldn't have let Drake's father smear her in the press. Paint her out to be some depraved drug addict. You would have learned that she was a beloved family member." Roxanne paused, walked to within ten feet of me. "You would have known that she was my mother."

"Moth—" The word died on my lips. Then, confusion. "Mother?"

"My mother was white," Roxanne said, answering my question. And then her eyes flitted toward Greg.

Just like that, I got it. Greg, a black man, was Roxanne's father. Her mother had been white. She had never once said she was biracial, though it was obvious her heritage was mixed.

"But you said . . . you said your mother was in jail."

"I lied," Roxanne snapped. "My mother was never in an accident that killed someone. She's not in jail in Pennsylvania. Why would I tell you a story so similar to the one you had experienced? To see if you had a conscience. To see if you had any remorse over a woman losing her life. But not once did you tell me what Drake had done, even though I'd just confessed my ugliest secret. Now I know why. Because you weren't protecting Drake. You were protecting yourself."

My hand fell from my purse. The fight had gone out of me. Regret replaced my fear. All I could think was that maybe I deserved this. That it was time I paid for what I'd done.

"I know that nothing I say can bring your mother back, but I'm very, very sorry. If I could take back what happened, I would in an instant. If I could exchange my life for hers, I would."

"Well, you can't," Roxanne quipped.

"But you can pay for your sins with your blood. And you will."

At Greg's comment, my eyes flew to his. "If you want, I'll come clean now. I'll go to the cops and confess the truth."

"And how long will it take the authorities to tie your confession to what happened to Drake, to Moses Shaw?" Greg asked. "We bided our time, waited long enough so that no one would ever see a connection."

"And you think they'll see no connection now?" I asked doubtfully.

"If anything, they'll believe that Drake killed himself. Or that Natalie and her brother exacted revenge. We were very, very careful. There's nothing to tie us to him."

"They're already onto you," I said to Greg. "They know you were on the ship pretending to be one of the staff."

"But they'll never learn my true identity."

His answer pissed me off. Carefully, I placed my hand along the opening of my purse. Adrenaline pumped through my veins. The fight was back—the fight to stay alive.

Maybe if they had only come after me, I could accept that. But they had killed Drake. And Natalie.

"Why did you kill Natalie?" I asked.

"Because sooner or later she might have figured it out," Roxanne replied without any emotion. How had I missed this utterly cold, evil side to her?

"I doubt it. She thought Seth was the one who paid her way on the cruise. And why did you even involve her? Why bring her on the cruise at all?"

"Because she was the perfect scapegoat," Roxanne explained. "She hated Drake. Hated him for raping her. But offer people a bit of money and an apology, and they're ready to forgive. It was pitiful how easily she played into our hands."

As Roxanne gloated, I slipped my hand into my purse. Quickly grabbed the gun.

Her eyes widened with surprise when she realized that I now had a gun pointed at her.

"Drop the gun," Greg instructed. "The time it takes you to kill her, I'll be on you so fast. And I'll slit your throat."

Cocking the gun's hammer, I began to slowly back away. "At least I'll kill one of you."

And then I fired. Because if I didn't, I knew Roxanne would.

She screamed, and her gun went flying. Greg growled like an enraged beast and lunged at me. I dove into a pew, but he was right there, making angry slashing motions with his knife but not connecting.

"Dad!" Roxanne cried. "Daddy!"

Only then did Greg halt, asking without turning his head. "Are you hit?"

"My arm. God, Daddy, it hurts!"

I scrambled to tighten my jittery fingers around the trigger again. I squeezed, but nothing happened.

The hammer. I hadn't cocked it.

In a nanosecond, Greg realized my error. As a smile of pure evil spread across his face, he raised the knife.

"Drop your weapon!" someone screamed.

I whipped my head toward the back of the church. Two policemen stood there, legs askance, guns raised.

Greg looked at them, too. His eyes became jittery and I knew what he was thinking.

That he had enough time to finish me off.

He slashed. I raised my arms to block the blow. The knife sliced my palm.

A gunshot filled the church.

And this I will never forget as long as I live. The way Greg's eyes went vacant a millisecond before the left side of his head exploded. His brain had died the moment the bullet had entered his right temple.

Then his body was crumbling, falling forward. And I was jumping backward before Greg could fall on me.

And for one moment, there was stillness.

But Roxanne's wounded scream broke the silence the instant before Greg's body hit the floor.

It probably took no more than a few seconds, but those seconds seemed to stretch into hours.

The next thing I knew, police officers were rushing down the aisle. One went to tend to Roxanne. The other quickly came to my pew.

He stopped at Greg, verified that he was dead, and then approached me. "Are you okay, miss?" he asked.

"Yes, I'm okay."

"Let me see your hand."

Only then did I realize that it was oozing blood. "Oh God."

"This one's shot," the officer with Roxanne announced.

"This one's got a knife wound," the officer returned, then examined my hand. Assessing the damage quickly, he wasted no time unraveling my scarf from around my neck and making a tourniquet. I watched him, fascinated, almost as if he were working on somebody else.

I could hear the officer with Roxanne calling for backup and paramedics on his walkie-talkie. "She's a part of this," I said. "She's his daughter. They both lured me here because they wanted to kill me."

"The paramedics are on their way," the officer said. "Once you've been taken care of, you'll give a statement."

Perhaps Roxanne had overheard me, because between her sobs she started yelling. "She shot me! She tried to kill me."

"It was self-defense," I said quickly. "Please, don't let her get away with this. I was the one who had my friend call 9-1-1."

"We'll get to the bottom of this, miss."

I glanced to my left then. Saw Chris standing at the back of the church. Emotion slammed into me like a Mac truck. Tears filled my eyes as my lips curled into a smile.

He smiled back.

"Sir," the officer with me said, placing a warning hand on his gun as he looked at Chris.

"He's okay," I said. "He's my friend."

And then Chris ran down the aisle and cut through the pew behind me. I was already climbing over the church bench to meet him.

He pulled me into his arms as he reached me, hugging me long and hard. As if he never wanted to let me go.

Chapter Thirty-six

AT THE HOSPITAL, my palm was stitched and bandaged. The wound was deep but would heal without any complications. Had my wrist been slashed, and a radial artery, the situation could have been dire.

From the hospital, police escorted me directly to the station where they questioned me about the night's events. I told them everything, including my part in the death of Erin Lowell. I supposed they would pass that information along to Oakland authorities, and time would tell if I would face justice for my act of stupidity that night four years ago.

Chris, God bless him, was with me every step of the way, even though he had to stay in waiting rooms in both the hospital and the police station. But once the police were done with me and told me I could leave, Chris was able to take me back to Lan-U.

I was in his rental car with him now, a large Buick.

"Thank you," I said for the umpteeth time. "I appreciate you being here for me . . . through everything."

"I wouldn't be anywhere else."

Which brought me to the question I hadn't yet asked. "Why did you come out here? I'm grateful—don't get me wrong—but why did you get on a plane and head to Lancaster from southern California?"

"I guess . . . I just wanted to be here for you."

"And you thought nothing of traveling across the country to be there for a friend?"

Chris gazed at me a long moment before turning back to the road. "I think you can figure out why."

My pulse accelerated. And though he was right, I still said, "I can?"

"Don't people travel to the ends of the earth for people they love?"

Now my heart pounded. But I said nothing.

"Ever since I saw you again, well, I couldn't stop thinking about you. My feelings are still there, Didi. That's why I came. Because I still love you, and I wanted to be here for you."

His words touched me. Lord knew they did. But I said, "Chris, it's too soon."

"I'm not asking for anything," he said. "I have no expectations."

And for some reason, I wanted to cry. Maybe because I had let Drake come between me and Chris and the solid friendship we'd once had.

I settled my head against the headrest and expelled a sigh. "I know I shouldn't blame myself," I said. "But I can't help it. I was the one driving the car that night, yet Drake was the one to pay with his life. This . . . this is all because of me."

Suddenly, Chris was veering sharply to the right, pulling the car into the empty parking lot of an office building. I took in my surroundings before staring at him in confusion.

"Chris—"

"It's time you knew something," he said. "It's about that night." He paused, then went on. "You weren't the one driving the car."

In the seconds that followed, you could have heard a feather drop. That's how quiet the car was.

Finally I stammered, "Yes, I . . . I was. You . . . we . . . I told you."

"Yeah, you told me. And you were so hysterical at the time, even I didn't doubt it. But your story never sat right with me. I should have realized before it couldn't be true."

He was making no sense. "I don't understand."

"Why do you think you were driving the car?" Chris asked. "Every time in the past that I've tried to bring up the accident, you shut me down. But you need to tell me, Didi."

"Because Drake said—"

"Ahh. Drake said."

I made a face. "Of course. He's the one who had to tell me what happened. I was drunk."

"That's just it, Dee. You were *way* too drunk. When Drake dragged you out of the closet, he was *livid.* I've never seen anyone angrier. He practically had to carry you out of the house—that's how out of it you were."

"And then I demanded to drive the car," I said, the story I had known for the past four years.

"You remember that?" Chris asked me.

I hesitated a beat. "Well, not really, no."

"That's because it didn't happen. I watched from the window. I watched because I was scared for you. Drake put you in the passenger seat, then got behind the wheel and drove off like a bat out of hell."

Seconds ticked by. Chris's gaze never wavered. He didn't even blink.

"It can't . . . it can't . . ."

"It can't be true? Why not? Because Drake would never lie about that?"

"Why would he? He lied to protect me."

"That's what he wanted you to think."

I opened my mouth to speak, but said nothing. And then I tried to think. Think hard back to that night.

I did remember being in the closet with Chris, if not with total clarity. But I didn't really remember being in the car. The only memories of being in the car I had were the ones Drake had told me.

"I saw him put you into the passenger seat," Chris said. "But the only reason I didn't challenge what you told me was because I figured you could have stopped along the way and somehow he let you get behind the wheel. The thing is, that never really felt right to me, because I knew you were about to pass out. I'm not proud of that, by the way. How I took advantage of you when you were falling-down drunk. It's just . . . I always loved you. If all I could get of you were a few drunken minutes in a closet, then I'd take it."

"Why are you telling me this now?"

"Because you deserve to know," he said. He looked at me, a sad smile touching his lips. "It was bad enough that you thought you'd killed one woman. I didn't want you to live with Drake's death on your conscience. *He* was the one driving the car. And the way he sped off, I think he was driving like a demon when he hit Erin Lowell."

"Then why—" I couldn't even ask the question. I couldn't begin to fathom why Drake would lie to me about something like that for all these years. Make me believe I had done something I hadn't done.

"I bet you can guess why," he said. "Think back to that night and what happened, and you'll understand why Drake did what he did."

I shook my head. I was at a loss. Not only had I drank too much and blacked out, the only real memory I had of significance was flirting with Chris at the party. Then I remembered the chaos after the accident, and Drake telling me he would protect me.

And then an idea began to take root in my mind. I wanted to dismiss it as ridiculous, but hadn't I learned firsthand that revenge was a powerful motivator?

"He wanted to make me suffer because I'd been with you," I said, and I almost choked on the words. I didn't want them to be true. Didn't want to think Drake capable of that kind of devastating deception.

But Chris was nodding, his eyes filled with sadness and regret. "That's the only thing that makes sense, Dee."

He was right. It was the only thing that made sense.

"I should have told you before," Chris said. "Made you listen. But I also feared you would think I was trying to break you and Drake up because of my feelings for you. I feared you wouldn't believe me."

Drake had lied to me. I had never been behind the wheel of the car. And yet for years he had let me live with the guilt of killing someone. Someone *he* had killed while driving like a man angry enough to commit murder.

"I don't understand," I said, and choked back a sob. "All this time—"

Chris pulled me into his arms, and that's when I really let go. I cried and cried. Cried for Drake. For what had happened to him and to us. For Roxanne, who had once been my friend, because I understood that pain had led her to do what she'd done.

And I cried for the awful truth I had just learned.

"Did he ever love me?" I managed, each breath a painful gasp. This truth hurt. Perhaps more than anything else that had happened.

"I'm sure he did," Chris said. "But he felt he had to control you to make sure you would never leave him. What better way to control you than to have you owe him your life?"

Perhaps Chris was right. Perhaps Drake had loved me in his own way. But it was suddenly clear that my relationship with Drake had been a total illusion.

Nothing was as it had seemed. It hadn't been real.

Pulling away from Chris, I said, "Thank you. Thank you for telling me this now."

Taking my hand in his, he squeezed it. "I'm here for you," he said. "I always will be."

As I looked at Chris, a smile touching my lips, it was instantly clear why my mother had always liked him. He was one of the good guys. Decent. Honest. Loyal.

I never thought it was possible to fall in love with someone instantly, but as I looked at Chris, I knew that I loved him. Perhaps a part of me always had. And perhaps Drake had known that, which was why he'd done what he'd done.

Oh, we couldn't immediately jump into a relationship. I knew that. But in time, when this nightmare was behind us . . .

I let Chris hold my hand as he continued to drive back to Lan-U. I didn't know what tomorrow would bring, but I was ready to embrace it.